Chrysalis: A Race to Death

Book 4 of
The
Family Secret Series

Mary Coley

Mary Coley
2019

Chrysalis: A Race to Death

Published by Moonglow Books through Create Space
P.O. Box 2517, Tulsa, OK 74101 USA
https://www.marycoley.com

ISBN: 1723034509
ISBN-13: 978-1723034503

What Others Have to Say About Mary Coley's Books (from Amazon reviews)

Cobwebs: A Suspense Novel (Book 1)

"*Cobwebs* made me delightfully uneasy and kept me in suspense. I highly recommend it to suspense lovers." – Jackie D.

"*Cobwebs* takes an intriguing journey into dark places, family secrets, and into the forgotten history of the Osage oil boom. Mary Coley has written a fine novel of suspense and mystery that will keep you up into the late hours of the night."–Jackson Burnett

"The mystery was well plotted, the characters well drawn and compelling."–Sherrill Nilson

"*Cobwebs* is a beautiful suspense novel on so many levels. Once I started reading the story I was captured in the lovely silken web of words that this writer weaves so well."–J. Rhine

Ant Dens: A Suspense Novel (Book 2)

"*Ant Dens*" will make you fall in love with New Mexico (if you haven't already) and keep you guessing, page to page."–Tracy Robert

"If you are looking for a fast-paced mystery look no further. This is your book. Once I started this book I couldn't set it down. I just had to find out what happened to Becca."–Brittany

"A riveting, suspenseful mystery. This is a story of love ... secrets ... lies ... and the more you read, the deeper into the story you are drawn. *Ant Dens* is outstanding!"–Linda Strong

Beehives: A Suspense Novel (Book 3)

"With her potent spell of Oklahoma's natural beauty and human nature's sticky depths, Mary Coley lures her readers into a tale as intricate and agitated as the Beehives of her title."–Sara K. Rupnik

"In Jamie Aldrich, Nancy Drew meets Anna Pigeon and becomes more cerebral and stronger than them both. In *Beehives*, Jamie's sedate getaway in a state park in the Crosstimbers turns into a red- hot burn."–Jackson Burnett

"*Beehives* begins with a bang, and nothing is what it appears to be when a mysterious hermit's death detours Jamie Aldrich's romantic holiday with fiancé Sam Mazie into a dangerous discovery of long-ago secrets and modern-day treachery."–LouLou Harrington

"In *Beehives*, Mary Coley has put together an engaging story rich with Oklahoma history, immersing the reader in the natural beauty of Green Country and keeping the mystery going until the end."
–Joshua Danker-Dake

Other books by Mary Coley

The *Black Dog Series*:
The Ravine (Published 2016 by Wild Rose Press)

The *Oklahoma Series*:
Blood on the Cimarron: No Motive for Murder (Published 2017 by Moonglow Books)

Dedication

I dedicate this book to my readers! I've heard from so many of you who love Jamie, and wanted another adventure. Here it is. I appreciate your support and your encouragement.

Acknowledgments

A big shout out to my friends and neighbors in Ponca City, where I lived with my family for 16 years. Special memories drew me to create this current mystery around some special events and places in that town.

It is a unique little city, and during the time I lived there I was lucky enough to be involved in the Ponca Playhouse and the Arts and Humanities Council, partially because of my work as a journalist with the Ponca City News. Then, as the public relations director at the hospital (formerly St. Joseph Regional Medical Center) I was selected as a member of the Ponca City Leadership Class in the early 1990s. During that special year, I met many of the community's influential and longtime residents and learned more about the history and inner workings of that city.

Ponca City is rich in history and culture. The monetary contributions of oilmen like E.W. Marland and Lew Wentz allowed the city to thrive in the arts, making it possible for the community to offer cultural activities for its citizens usually not found in a place of its size.

The beautiful landscape and ranching history of the area, including the presence of the 101 Ranch and the Miller family, have created a place unlike any other in my home state.

I have appreciated the continued friendships and support that my Ponca City friends have given me as a writer. The stories and memories I have of this town will feed my creativity for years to come.

Cast of Characters

<u>Family</u>
Jamie Aldrich Mazie – high school science teacher
Sam Mazie – Osage, attorney, Jamie's husband
Lucas Mazie – Osage, Sam's brother
Theresa Mazie – Osage, Sam's mother
Reba Mazie (deceased) – Sam's first wife
Sharon – Reba's sister

Mary Jamison – Jamie's mother
Randy – Jamie's brother
Ellen – Jamie's sister
Aunt Elizabeth (deceased) – Jamie's great aunt
Trudy – Elizabeth's granddaughter
Vera – family member (cousin) and close friend of Trudy

<u>The Law</u>
Chase Longhorn – OSBI cold case detective
Det. Roland Blaise – Ponca City detective
Toby Green – Osage County Sheriff (Pawhuska)

<u>At the High School</u>
Caleb Miller – high school student
Davis Harwell (deceased) – a shop teacher at the high school
Romy Vaughn – drama teacher, director of the dinner theater
Gail Strickland – a vice principal at the high school

<u>At the Playhouse</u>
Rusty Clement – playwright of A Race to Death
Belina – a cast member

<u>At Lake Ponca/Wentz Camp</u>
Pamela Monroney – the executive director of Wentz Camp
Howard DeKalb – assistant director of Wentz Camp

i

Prologue

September 2008 - Sunday

The Watcher, wearing a black hoodie and surrounded by candy bar wrappers and empty potato chip bags, slumps in the front seat of a parked Honda. Crumbs litter the carpet and a musty smell fills the car.

Two houses away, Jamie Aldrich Mazie and her husband, attorney Sam Mazie, supervise two burly men in t-shirts unloading boxes from a moving van in the driveway.

Eyes narrowed, the Watcher taps the steering wheel and glares toward an unknown and unexpected third person who is pacing the porch of the Mazie home. The thin, gray-haired woman wrings her hands and frowns into the bright nearly-autumn day.

The Watcher's fingers beat a staccato rhythm in the shadow-filled car.

He's hardly aged, he's as good looking as ever. And his wife ... Thick dark hair. Not thin, not fat. Normal. So, why did Sam marry her?

The watcher studies the couple as they move beside the workmen. Both dressed in jeans and long-sleeved t-shirts, both in their late 40s.

They probably work out. The Watcher sneers and sips diet cola from a convenience store cup.

Revenge will be sweet. The Watcher sets the cup in the holder and grins. *He's got to pay, one way or another, for the rest of his life. Sam and his family. They've all got to pay.*

A vehicle approaches from the opposite direction. The Watcher slumps lower, pulls the edge of the hoodie down, and turns the ignition key of the ubiquitous white Honda.

Keep it together. Don't tempt fate. Only a few more days. A week?

The Watcher turns the steering wheel, makes a U-turn and drives slowly down the street, away from Jamie and Sam's new home. Anticipation races up the Watcher's spine.

Chapter 1

I glanced at my mother, slipped the creamy silk pillowcase over the bed pillow and tossed it onto the double bed. "Your window has a great view of these beautiful old trees. They must be a hundred years old. Mostly oaks, don't you think?" I spoke in my cheeriest voice, trying to pretend I wasn't exhausted, wasn't done in from packing and now unpacking hundreds of boxes full of the household things Sam and I had gathered during the seven years of our marriage.

Mother's face was stoic, as usual. "Don't ask me, Jamie. You're the science guru. Don't you know?" She ran her fingers through her short, gray hair and straightened her glasses before she pursed her lips and squinted at me. "Never thought I'd come back to live in Oklahoma, or have to move in with you and Sam. I've lost my privacy." She sniffed, but I didn't see any tears glittering in her eyes.

"It's the best solution. You might fall again." It was luck that my younger sister Ellen had found Mother on the floor not long after she fell, and that her only injury had been a twisted knee.

"You're making a mountain out of a molehill, as usual," she groused. "You shouldn't have made me come here. All my friends are in Albuquerque, and your sister."

I smoothed the bedspread and swallowed the words I wanted to say. Our new house had plenty of room. Ellen wasn't going to take Mother in, and no one wanted her to live in a nursing home. At seventy-five, she could live with minimal assistance for many years, I hoped.

Mother moved over to the window and surveyed the still-green trees. A frisky autumn breeze chased a few skipping brown leaves down the street. "Cottonwoods would be turning yellow if we were in New Mexico. And then the aspens," she whispered.

I tucked my shoulder-length hair behind my ears and glanced out the window. Sun reflected off the sides of the moving van as it backed down the driveway.

"You think they got everything out of that van?" Mother chewed one fingernail.

"Sam was arranging the boxes in the garage. I'll go find your lamp." I plugged the air freshener into the electric outlet next to the closet and adjusted the intensity bar so that the warm fragrance of vanilla poured into the room. "Why don't you rest for a minute? I'll be right back."

Stacks of boxes, divided by uneven aisles, filled both bays of the garage. I rolled my shoulders, aware that my tense muscles were from more than carrying and unpacking boxes. Had we made the right decision to move my mother in with us? She wasn't the only one losing privacy.

"Sam?" I called. "Any idea where the lamps are? The one for Mother's room?" I glanced around the garage at boxes and more boxes. I'd packed every one of them, and now I had to unpack them and find places to put everything.

"I stuck it in with the others." His voice, with its usual calm and almost melodic cadence, came from behind a tower of boxes. "I've piled the boxes according to room labels. Look for the living room section."

I inched along the rows of boxes, studying the labels.

Sam came up beside me. "I could use a break. How about you?" He rubbed the back of his neck and stretched.

"I'm okay for now," I lied. My muscles ached and the pain in my head throbbed. We had hours of work to do. I couldn't stop yet.

Sam slid his arms around me. His brown eyes twinkled. "A new beginning here, in a new place. Are you happy?"

I brushed a glob of dirt from his hair, rubbed at a streak on his cheek, and nodded. "Yes. It feels good. I'm hoping for the best."

"You mean, because your mother is living with us?"

I nodded again.

"It's an adjustment for both of you," Sam said. "But it's the right thing to do."

"I know it is. But I've loved having you all to myself." I gazed up at him, full of amazement that this man was my husband, and that we'd found each other in mid-life.

Dimples drilled into his cheeks as he smiled. "Hey, you've still got me all to yourself. No change there." He pecked my lips. "I need to take these books to the office." He grabbed the handle of the nearby dolly and scooped up two boxes labeled *law books.*

"Want me to come with you?" I savored the salty taste he'd left on my lips. I wanted him to say yes. I wanted to have a few minutes alone with him, away from any prying ears.

"No need."

I hid my disappointment by turning back to the boxes to search, but at the sound of the squeaky dolly, I stopped to watch him roll the books down the driveway to his truck. He stopped halfway and patted his pockets. "Hey, you've got my keys, don't you?"

I nodded, reached into my pocket for the keys and then tossed them to where Sam waited ten yards away.

He grinned. "Good throw. You still got that good arm," he yelled. "I'll be back soon." He pushed the dolly to the truck and unloaded the boxes into the back.

In the garage, I found the boxes labeled *lamps,* grabbed a box knife and slit the first one open. Inside, Mother's bedroom lamp, swaddled in bubble wrap, rested beneath two small table lamps. The lamp had been a fixture in her bedroom for as long as I could remember. I hoped its familiarity would help her feel comfortable in her new surroundings.

As I carried the lamp into the house, Mother called from her room. "Jamie? A man is coming to the front door. I saw Sam leave. Should you answer it?"

I smiled. Our two dogs had just lost their status as chief watchers. Mother would beat them to the punch, sounding the alarm if we had company at the

front door. She would love having a window that faced the street. We'd get a blow-by-blow description of everything that happened outside.

I glanced at the clock I'd already placed on a nail in the kitchen. The furry members of our family were due here in another hour. Their presence would turn this place from a house into a home.

The doorbell rang out a two-note call. I squinted through the peek hole at the man on the porch. He was tall, and most likely Native American, like Sam, judging from his black hair, high cheekbones and brown complexion. Dressed in khaki slacks and a white Oxford shirt, he didn't look like a thief or a potential home invader. A friend of Sam's? I shook off the uneasy feeling and opened the front door.

"Hello," I said through the locked glass storm door.

"Is Sam Mazie here? I was told this is his new residence." The man studied me with dark eyes.

"As of today, it is. I'm Jamie, his wife."

The man glanced around me and into the house. "Is he here?"

"Not at the moment." As soon as I spoke the words, I regretted them. Even though he looked professional, he could still be a criminal. "I expect him back any second," I hurriedly added.

"I'd like to talk to him today, if that's possible." The man reached into the pocket of his shirt. He pulled out his ID badge, with the letters OSBI printed in bold black, and a business card. I unlocked the door and took the card he offered. "I'm Detective Chase Longhorn, with the Cold Case Division of the Oklahoma State Bureau of Investigation," he explained.

My mind raced. Why would a cold case detective want to talk with Sam? My family was the one with an 80-year-old cold case, not Sam's. "What's this about?"

Detective Longhorn's forehead creased, and his eyes narrowed. "I need to talk to him, Mrs. Mazie."

"Is this about one of his cases?" Sam was very careful not to tell me much about his work, other than the bare basics. I quickly skimmed my knowledge of the current cases he'd mentioned.

Longhorn cleared his throat. "No."

If not about one of those, what else was there? "His family?"

"It's about the death of his first wife. When will he be back?"

The room dipped, and my fingers tightened on the door frame. This was about *Reba*? His first wife, and someone I knew little about. I wasn't even certain how she'd died. "Less than an hour," I finally said.

"I'll wait in my car, Mrs. Mazie." The cold case detective stepped off the porch.

I closed the front door as Chase Longhorn strolled out to his car, and then I took a deep breath. Just because this cold case detective wanted to talk to Sam didn't mean anything was wrong. *Don't jump to conclusions.* My heart was beating too fast to hear the advice my brain sent.

In the kitchen, I opened another box labeled *glasses,* unwrapped one, rinsed it in the kitchen sink, and dried it with a paper towel before filling it from the tap. I took a long drink. The cool, metallic-tasting water would take some getting used to.

Sam's first wife, Reba, had died two years before Sam and I reunited in Pawhuska nearly nine years ago. Decades had passed since we'd been childhood playmates. He'd still been grieving for her at the time, and I had been grieving over my recently-deceased husband, Ben. Those first few months, as our relationship deepened, I sometimes caught Sam staring into space, his dark brown eyes distant, his forehead creased. I respected his privacy and said nothing.

On the other hand, we'd often talked about my husband Ben's cancer battle and eventual death. I'd even told him about the local sheriff's suspicion that Ben's death had been an assisted suicide. I'd shared my anguish over the horrible months both before and after his death. But, during all those discussions, Sam didn't speak about Reba's death. There hadn't seemed to be any reason to delve into it. Wouldn't Sam have told me if he had wanted to talk about it? Was there a reason he had *not* wanted to talk about it?

Cold cases. Unsolved crimes. What had happened to Reba?

Chapter 2

In my purse on the kitchen island, my cell phone buzzed. I pulled myself away from thoughts about Reba and reached for it. The caller ID read *Gail Strickland,* the vice principal at the local high school where I now taught general science and biology. I punched on the speaker function and grabbed another glass to unwrap.

"Hey, Jamie. Is this a good time to talk?" Gail asked in a hurried voice.

"I'm unpacking. We moved this weekend, remember?" *Hadn't I told her about the move after Thursday night's drama club meeting?*

"Oh, yeah. That commute from Pawhuska must've been getting old. Nice you won't have to worry about driving at night once rehearsals start."

Gail had requested heavy involvement from both parents and teachers in the drama students' upcoming production, a dinner theater fundraiser. I'd already committed to helping with props in addition to serving as co-sponsor for the drama club.

"Living here will make things a lot easier for both Sam and me. Like I've often said the commute has been difficult. Having to grade papers late into the night after an hour commute doesn't give Sam and I much time together." I shifted from one foot to the other as I straightened the crinkled wrapping paper and folded it in half. Gail and I had taught together years ago in New Mexico, and she'd recommended me for this new job in Ponca City.

"You haven't heard the news."

"I haven't had time for news. We've spent the past few days packing up the house in Pawhuska, and now we're unpacking a million boxes the movers unloaded today." I reached for another glass. My nose tickled.

"If you checked your voice mail, you'd see that you probably have a dozen phone messages from me," she said in a flat voice.

I sneezed, grabbed a paper towel and blew my nose. "Has something happened?"

"Davis Harwell has been murdered."

Davis. I pulled in a quick breath, then mentally ran through the names of the teachers and parents I'd met since beginning my new job at the high school six weeks ago.

"The shop teacher," she explained. "He plays the gardener in the play, and he's Rusty's co-writer."

My memory clicked. *Tall with a mustache and beard. Smiled a lot.* "What happened?" The glass clinked as I placed it on the counter.

"He was stabbed at the Conoco station on Grand."

I sank onto a bar stool. "A robbery?"

"The police haven't said."

I visualized the gas station I had visited yesterday to fill up my gas tank after driving in from Pawhuska. "Did anyone see what happened? That's a busy corner."

11

"Not so busy at midnight. No witnesses, and the security camera wasn't working. It's horrible. But that leads to one of the reasons I called. We need an adult to fill the gardener role in the play. Any suggestions?"

"I'm the newbie, remember?" My thoughts whirred. Had Davis interrupted a crime, or had he been the intended victim? My mind wouldn't move on to the topic of the dinner theater.

"You've jumped into everything here with both feet. Teaching, tutoring, co-sponsoring the drama club. You've made a lot of contacts. Or maybe ... would Sam be interested? You're already involved, and you don't have kids at home. It's something you could do together."

I tried to focus on her request. No way my quiet man would set foot on stage if he could help it. A courtroom, yes, but ... "I don't think Sam's had any acting experience."

"For this small part, I'm not sure that matters. And besides, he'd add a certain intrigue to the production. Being new to the community and Native American."

"Not new, Gail. Born and raised near Pawhuska. He's had many clients from around here over the years. Lots of people already know Sam."

"Ever better. He'd be a draw. Talk to him about it, okay?"

A dinner theater production would be the last thing in the world Sam would want to do with what little spare time he had. "I'm not promising anything."

"Jamie, call me back as soon as you've talked with Sam. Despite the death, I'm sure Romy will push ahead with rehearsals, starting this Tuesday."

From what little I'd already experienced of the drama teacher, I knew Gail was right. Romy Vaughn was passionate and driven about theater. Older, with years of experience in drama and speech, she had a high level of energy matching the excitable teenagers.

"I'm sure there will be details in the Ponca City news. Maybe even the TV news out of Tulsa," I said.

"It's so awful. Surely they'll catch whoever did this."

"I hope so. See you tomorrow at school, Gail. And thanks for the heads up." I punched off my phone. My first weekend in Ponca City, and someone I knew had been murdered. Not good. Gail had few details, and I didn't want to know more. I wasn't going to get drawn into this investigation. It had nothing to do with me. And I didn't plan to ask Sam about playing the gardener. I was certain what his answer would be.

"Jamie? What was that all about? Who died?" Mother crossed the kitchen and leaned against the island. She smelled of antiseptic hand cleaner.

My habit of using my phone speaker was going to have to be nipped unless I wanted Mother to know everything about my life.

"One of the cast members of the dinner theater production I'm helping with was murdered last night," I said.

She covered her mouth with one hand. "Well, thank God you didn't find *this* body."

I was thankful, too. Years ago, I'd had a run of finding dead bodies and getting involved in police investigations. Luckily, for the past seven years, I'd steered clear of bodies and criminal investigations. I wanted to keep it that way.

"Did you know the murdered person?" Mother asked.

"He was a teacher. I saw him at school occasionally and at meetings about the play. He had a small role. The police will probably interview everyone in the production in the next few days."

"You're involved in a play? You're a science teacher." She frowned.

"I signed up to be the drama club co-sponsor. They needed someone to help and the play intrigued me. It's called 'Race to Death.' A local playwright wrote it, based on the Ponca City Grand Prix, a nationally-sanctioned natural road race held out at Lake Ponca years ago. I guess everyone thinks the locals will flock to see it. But after this murder, I'm not sure the play will see the light of day."

Mother crossed her arms and narrowed her eyes. "I've been in this town for two days and there's already been a murder. Are you sure it's safe here?"

"There's crime everywhere and always has been. We hear about it more now with all the cable news stations trying to fill 24 hours with news." I folded another piece of packing paper.

"Humph." Mother marched out of the kitchen.

I unwrapped the last glass in the box and thought about Davis Harwell. If it was a gas station robbery, why had Davis been killed? He didn't seem the type to get heroic and confront criminals during a crime. In addition to playing the role of the gardener, he'd been helping the playwright write the play. Would his death delay or even halt the production?

I turned on the water in the sink and lathered my hands with lavender-scented soap. I closed my eyes, pulled in the aroma and tried to relax. I would have to work at suppressing my building irritation. Mother had every reason to be irritable, she'd been uprooted against her will. I, on the other hand, should be grateful to have my mother here. I should not be irritated by whatever she said, no matter how annoying.

Mother charged through the kitchen toward the garage. Seconds later, her voice, loud and fast, carried to me from the back door. Sam had come home, and Mother was giving him an earful.

My stomach clenched. I hadn't forgotten about the detective who lingered outside. Why did he want to talk with Sam about his first wife, after all these years?

Chapter 3

"...total stranger. And she opened the door. Could have been a murderer. Someone was killed last night at the Conoco station. Talk to her, Sam. You're not living in Pawhuska anymore. This town is dangerous." Mother led Sam into the kitchen. He navigated the obstacle course of boxes as he crossed the room.

"What's this about someone coming to the door?" He rubbed the back of his neck. He was as tired as I was.

I handed him the detective's business card. "Chase Longhorn. OSBI. Ever heard of him?"

He tapped the card with one finger. "I know this family. Maybe I know him. It's been twenty-five years since high school. He might have been a year or two ahead of me. What did he want?" He leaned against the kitchen island.

I glared at Mother. "Didn't she tell you?"

She glared back. "I was in my room. I wasn't listening to what he said. I'm not a snoop."

Sam gave us both a stern look.

"He wanted to talk to you," I explained. "He said he'd wait in his car. I assume he saw you drive up."

The doorbell rang. Sam scrutinized the business card as he moved out of the kitchen toward the front door. I followed, and Mother trailed behind us.

Sam pulled the front door open. A puff of autumn breeze blew into the hallway, carrying a faint musky scent. "Can I help you? I'm Sam Mazie."

"Chase Longhorn. OSBI," the detective stated.

Sam studied the detective as the two men shook hands. "Do we know each other?"

"I grew up in Pawhuska. I remember you, but it's been years since I lived there." He took a step back and folded his hands.

Sam shoulders relaxed. "How can I help you, Chase?"

"I'm with the OSBI's cold case squad out of Oklahoma City." The detective looked at me and then back at Sam. "Can we talk privately?"

"I don't have any secrets from my wife." Sam slipped his arm around my shoulders. His warm fingers caressed my upper arm.

"This concerns your wife, Reba."

I glanced at Sam and saw the color drain from his face. His arm dropped from my shoulders. "Let's speak out on the porch."

As Sam stepped away, I reached for him, but he brushed past and out the door.

"Give us a minute, Jamie." Sam pulled the door closed.

My face stung as if he'd slapped me. What did Sam not want me to know about Reba's death?

"Well, how do you like that? Sam's kept secrets, Jamie," Mother said in a low voice from behind me.

In the kitchen, I unpacked another box. My curiosity buzzed, and I tried to check my rising anxiety. Sam would have a good explanation, I told myself. He always did.

Sam and Chase Longhorn had spent nearly ten minutes on the porch before Sam came into the house and down the hall to the kitchen.

"Let's have a glass of tea," he suggested. He reached for two of the glasses I'd just removed from the dishwasher, loaded the glasses with ice, then filled them from the refrigerator tea jug.

I stood stiffly near the kitchen island. "That was humiliating, Sam. First, you tell him we have no secrets from one another, and then, you take your discussion outside and exclude me completely."

Sam put the tea jug back into the frig, and collapsed onto a bar stool beside the island. "I'm sorry if I humiliated you. That wasn't my intent."

My heart pounded. "Why did he want to talk with you about Reba?" I took a small sip of the tea, letting the liquid cool my mouth.

Sam leaned forward, elbows on the granite countertop, and rested his head in his hands. "He investigates cold cases."

"What is he investigating? How did Reba die?"

He rubbed his jaw line with one finger and pushed away from the counter.

"Sam?"

"The last thing I want to do is upset you." He looked out the window and into the back yard. On the back patio, the wind chime tinkled in the breeze. "This should be a happy day. A new start. Together."

"Upset me? This isn't about me. Why was the detective here? What happened to Reba?"

"My wife wasn't well. She was ... mentally ill." Sam's voice cracked.

I leaned toward him across the island, watching his ashy face, taking in the distress that registered around his eyes. Breathless, I waited for him to explain.

"She was diagnosed as bipolar. Manic-depressive." He closed his eyes. "There are varying degrees of the illness. When she told me she was pregnant, she seemed happy, but her mental condition quickly worsened."

I sucked in a quick breath. I could imagine how upsetting it would have been to have a pregnant–and unstable–wife.

"She had so many ups and downs," Sam continued. "She'd rage about her family and rant at me about anything and everything. The medicine the doctor gave her didn't help. It might have made it worse–if she was taking it. I never knew for sure."

I laid one hand on top of his. "I'm sorry, Sam."

His smile was lopsided. "I love you Jamie."

My heart pounded. I remembered the first time he said those words to me, all those years ago in Pawhuska. It had been hard to believe them then, when we hadn't seen each other since we were pre-teens, but, after the years we'd spent together since, I knew it was true. "And I love you. Nothing's changed. But, I need to know what happened. What is Chase Longhorn investigating? Did something happen during the delivery, Sam?"

"When Reba died ... there were questions. Eventually, the coroner ruled it suicide. And she wasn't pregnant, she never had been." He took a long drink of tea and swiped one hand across his mouth. "There was no baby. Ever."

My face tingled. Suicide. And no baby? With my whole being, I felt the sadness evident on Sam's face. My heart ached. All these years later, he was still devastated. The look in his eyes was the same look I'd seen off and on over the years. Reba's death haunted him.

My heart ached. He'd been excited to be a father, I was certain. Only to find out it had all been in his wife's mind.

"I'm confused. She committed suicide? Why is Chase investigating her suicide?"

"Someone was convinced they should review the case. Her death was re-filed as 'suspicious.'" Sam straightened. "Her body is being exhumed."

Chapter 4

My throat closed. I'd been through the exhumation process before, knew how it felt to have your loved one's casket dug up after months of interment. How much worse would it be to have it done after more than ten years? But the burning question was, why the exhumation?

"What are they looking for?"

"They suspect she might have been murdered."

A chill slipped down my spine.

I contemplated the horror of that suspicion for Sam. But, the scenario wasn't clear in my mind. How could a suicide be reclassified as murder? "How did she kill herself, Sam?" I wanted to know, and yet I didn't. My relationship with Sam was close to perfect; I didn't need this knowledge. My curiosity needed it; my heart didn't. I wanted to withdraw my question.

He stared into space for several seconds, and then said, "You've been through the death of a spouse, you know what it's like. You were suspected of assisting with Ben's suicide. When it happens, all eyes are on you. With suicide, people think you should've known it was going to happen. Should have been able to stop it."

"But now they don't think it was a suicide." I clamped my jaw shut. I wasn't going to ask any more questions. If Sam told me, okay. If he didn't, that was okay, too.

Sam stared at the floor. One lock of his long shiny hair hung over his face. "A few years before her death, an Osage named Bosque came to see me." Sam tossed his head to get his hair out of his eyes, but it promptly fell back into his face. He rubbed his hands on his thighs. "Longhorn asked me about him."

"Who was he? And why would he connect this person with Reba's death?"

"He wasn't a good Indian," Sam commented, shaking his head. "He sold drugs, worked as a thug getting paid to assault people, robbed homes. You name it, he did it. He wanted me to defend him when he was arrested for breaking and entering, but that's not the kind of law I practice. Family law doesn't usually pull me into criminal court. Bosque ended up with a court-appointed attorney. He was sent to jail for several years on a burglary conviction but got out early on good behavior." Sam rubbed his forehead with one finger. He pulled in several deep breaths.

"Go on," I urged.

"I had no idea what happened to Bosque until Chase Longhorn came here this afternoon. He told me Bosque was recently arrested in Tulsa for a drive-by shooting. He wanted a plea deal, offered to turn over evidence in another case." Sam lifted his head and stared at me, his brown eyes deep and unreadable.

A bad taste settled in my mouth.

"He offered to tell them how Reba really died." His mouth shifted but no words came out.

"What does he say happened?" I breathed out the question, standing motionless, fearful of the answer.

Sam pinched his eyes shut. "He says that Reba's death was not a suicide. She hung herself, in our garage. He 'helped' and I paid him to do it."

I closed my eyes and sipped my tea, hoping to dilute the acidic taste in my mouth. My body went cold and I seemed to be looking down at my kitchen from somewhere up above. I heard myself ask: "What evidence did he provide?"

"Only his word. And the word of other smalltime criminals who are willing to swear Bosque told them this years ago."

I crashed back down to earth as anger replaced fear and disbelief. "It's his word against yours, and you're an upstanding citizen. Surely that carries more weight." I leaned toward him across the island.

"Chase Longhorn disagrees."

Something about the way he spoke the man's name told me that during the few minutes they'd spent on the porch, Sam's memory of Longhorn had come back. They had a history, and it wasn't good. "What does this detective have against you?"

"In high school, he was the jock. I was the smart kid. But he was competitive off the field, too. With girls," Sam smirked.

Competition between young men, and not sports related. "Was he in love with Reba?"

Sam gazed out the window at our backyard. The leaves in the trees danced to the tinkling wind chimes. "He thought he was."

I ran my fingers through my hair. A helpless, overwhelmed feeling pressed down on me, as it had years ago when I was suspected of assisting my husband Ben's death. Nowhere to turn, no idea what to do, no way to disprove the allegations.

"Did you tell Longhorn why Bosque might want to frame you?"

"I told him Bosque was angry at me for not representing him. I can think of no other reason."

I pulled in a deep breath and tried to relax my tense shoulders. My frustration, even as overwhelming as it seemed, was probably minimal compared to Sam's. "How can I help?"

"You're helping now, by listening, by believing in me. We are beginning a long journey. I know how these things go. Every bit of dirt will be laid out in the open. Dirt about her. Dirt about me. Dirt about my family. And in the end, they may well decide that I am guilty of murder-for-hire."

"They have nothing on you," I cried. "We'll fight it. I'll be behind you every step of the way." My heart raced. I couldn't believe this was happening.

"It's going to be brutal."

I pulled Sam up off the stool, wrapped my arms around him and buried my face in his neck, tears choking my throat. His masculine scent filled my head. I kissed his chin and then his lips. He responded against me.

Mother barged through the doorway into the kitchen. "Sam? What's going on with that detective? Tell me everything now."

Sam and I pulled apart like teenagers caught doing something we shouldn't. We were in our own home, but things had changed. Mother was with us, and she would be in the middle of our business no matter how hard we tried to prevent it.

"You better sit down," I said, swiping at the tears filling my eyes. "Sam has something to tell you."

Chapter 5

Mother perched on the edge of a kitchen chair, her face stoic, her eyes staring alternatively at the wall or at Sam's face, as Sam explained what cold case detective Chase Longhorn had said. The story progressed, and her backbone straightened like she had a flagpole stuck down her blouse. When he finished, she didn't look at him or speak.

"If you have any questions, please ask," Sam stated. "I'm going over to the retirement village to tell Mom what's happened."

Mother's look followed him as he left the room. She lifted her chin and pointed it my way. "Sam should have told you about this before you were married," Mother spewed. "A false pregnancy! And suicide! Maybe murder!"

I willed myself to stay calm. I knew my husband. I was certain he had nothing to do with Reba's death. This man–Bosque–was framing him. Why?

"Imagined pregnancy, Mother. And not murder. Neither of those are Sam's fault."

I turned away from her to stare out the window. Red brushed the edges of the maple tree's dark green leaves. The wind stirred the leaves and my emotions whirled. I loved my husband. I trusted him. But still, I wondered, why had he never told me any of this? Why had I naively accepted his silence–and his obvious pain–about the death of his first wife?

"He's hiding something, Jamie," Mother blurted.

I shook my head. Sam was a private person. He kept parts of himself closed off to me. Closed off to everyone. It had never bothered me that he didn't talk about Reba's death. But, we'd been together eight years. Shouldn't we have talked about Reba at some point? I hadn't wanted to probe into something that obviously pained him.

Now I knew why it pained him.

"What are you going to do?" Mother asked.

"Support Sam. Refuse to believe he had anything to do with Reba's death. Apparently, there's a possibility that she was murdered. The initial verdict on her death was suicide because she hung herself, but the new statement from a convicted felon offers a different scenario. They are going to exhume the body. I've been through that experience, Mother, with Ben. Sam will need our support."

"They'll look for new DNA evidence. I've watched those TV programs. All they have to do is find a stray hair and they can convict." She grabbed a bottle of spray cleaner from a box on the floor and squirted a stream of it onto the granite countertop, then swiped the counter with a paper towel.

"There's more to it than that, Mother." A reflection of light on the wall drew my attention back to the window. Outside, a familiar car turned into the driveway. My cousin Trudy was here to bring our furry family members home to their new house.

"More company?" Mom stepped up to stand beside me and watch as the driver's door opened and our sixty-something year-old relative lumbered out. Immediately behind her, three basset hounds spilled from the car.

"What in the world?" Mother groaned.

"Queenie and the pups. Earlier than expected, but I bet Trudy wanted to see the house. She couldn't wait another minute." Relieved to have a diversion from the topic of Reba's murder, I headed for the front door, nauseated by the scent of the lemon-scented cleanser.

I loved Trudy's down-to-earth personality, and even though she was sometimes mixed up in her perceptions, there was a grain of truth in her observations. We'd met years ago, during my long-overdue return to Pawhuska. Since then, she'd been living with her grandmother—my great aunt Elizabeth—only a mile from where Sam and I eventually lived in Pawhuska. Elizabeth had died this past summer, and Trudy still needed a lot of comforting. It was going to be an adjustment for her to have Sam and me an hour away. Even though I'd seen her the day before, the sight of her walking up to my house lifted my spirits.

After I pulled the front door open, our dog, Queenie, charged into the house, her low-slung frame nearly dragging the floor and her toenails clacking. Immediately behind her, two slightly smaller, younger bassets raced across the porch and into the house, their long ears swinging nearly to the ground. "Hey, Queenie, Augie, and Zeus. Welcome to our new home, Trudy."

"This is your new place? Can you show me around?" Trudy stepped in. She gawked at the high ceiling of the entryway as she set an animal carrier on the floor. The gray and white cat inside the cage mewed.

I hugged her, then bent to waggle a finger inside the cage. "Hi, Princess. How are you, sweet thing?" The cat meowed and batted at the wire side of the cage. I waved Trudy on into the house. "As you can see, we've barely started unpacking."

"Yes, things are a mess." She regarded the stacked boxes and piles of items covering the floor. "I couldn't wait any longer. Queenie misses you and Sam. Augie and Zeus do, too. And then, there's Princess. I bet you've missed all these furries."

I knelt to pet the dogs. All three pushed close, long pink tongues lolling from their mouths. Doggy scent enveloped me. In the carrier, Princess yowled.

"I'm sure I didn't." Mother backed down the hall toward the living room, frowning.

"Cousin Mary, you don't like animals?" Trudy stepped closer to Mother and lifted her arms for a hug, but dropped them when Mother crossed her arms, discouraging contact.

"I keep a clean house," Mother stated. "Don't like pet hair, or the dirt animals drag in. Never saw any reason to have creatures in the house."

"She'll get used to it." I smiled at Trudy. "That's part of living with Sam and me, Mother. You knew that when you signed on."

"Doesn't mean I have to like it," Mother grumbled.

I grinned. "They'll be sleeping on her bed before the end of the month."

"I - don't - think - so." Mother watched the three dogs trot into the living room, noses to the floor, sniffing.

"I'm so sad," Trudy wailed. "I don't want you to be all the way over here. I want you across town, like before. We have to drive a whole hour to see you. My Liz won't be able to make the trip very often."

My Liz. Her reference to her deceased grandmother startled me. "Trudy? You know your grandmother isn't with us anymore."

She hung her head and shifted her weight from one foot to the other. "Yes, she is. Not her body, but we talk all the time." Tears rolled from Trudy's eyes. She brushed her hair off her forehead with one hand and smeared the wet on her cheeks with the other.

"That's nonsense," Mother huffed.

I touched Trudy's shoulder. "I'm sure you feel her presence in your house, Trudy. She lived there for so many years. I have no doubt her spirit is still lingering."

"She's there all right." Trudy's lower lip trembled.

"Let me show you our new home." I put one hand on her shoulder and nudged her toward the living room.

Trudy raised her head and stepped forward. Inside her cage, Princess yowled again.

"For heaven's sake," Mother complained.

"Let the cat out of the cage, please," I requested, hiding a grin as Trudy and I walked away.

Behind us, Princess yowled even louder.

Chapter 6

"I miss you, Sam," Trudy said as she threw her arms around Sam's neck. She kissed his cheek and squeezed him in a bear hug.

"It's only been a day since we saw you, Trudy." Sam smiled patiently. Princess jumped onto a nearby lamp table and flicked her tail at Sam. He stroked the cat, who purred and arched her back.

"I miss you anyway. When will you be back to Pawhuska?" Trudy gazed up at him. He was a full head taller than she was.

"My practice is here now. But my office in Pawhuska will be open Thursdays and Fridays, every other week." Sam stroked the cat and scratched her white face.

"That's not very often. You have people who need you, like me. And our friend, Vera." She pouted.

"Trudy, most of my clients are from ranches and small farms around here. They won't mind driving to Ponca rather than Pawhuska. For some of them, it's closer."

Trudy frowned. "Some of them will mind." Her lower lip jutted out.

"How is Vera?" I changed the subject. "I saw her last week at the grocery. She still looked pale from her long summer cold. I'm surprised she didn't come with you today."

"She's been staying over at my house. She had to work today." Princess dashed to Trudy and arched her back as she leaned against Trudy's legs. Trudy bent over and massaged the cat's ears.

"I'm glad she's staying with you. Elizabeth would want her there. That house is too big for you alone," I said. An uneasy feeling filled me.

"Me and Augie Doggie like it when Vera's there."

Hearing his name, one of the basset pups lifted his big head and looked at Trudy from where he lay on the rug in front of the stone fireplace. Queenie and Zeus opened their eyes, too.

Mother stalked into the room, her hands on her hips. "What are we doing for supper? I'd best get something started in the kitchen if you aren't going to cook, Jamie," she grumbled.

"I thought we'd order some pizza. Trudy, do you want to stay to eat?" Mother was a meal planner, and I wasn't. This was going to be another bone of contention between us.

"Augie and I need to be home by dark. When should I leave?" She gazed out the windows, where the golden light of late afternoon shimmered on the bushes and leaves.

Sam glanced at the wall clock. "Best be gone in about 15 minutes, then. It's getting dark earlier these days."

"And colder. I don't like it when the nights get cold and I have to close the windows when I go to sleep," Trudy whined.

"I thought we talked about not leaving your windows open. That can be dangerous," Sam scolded.

"Just the upstairs. I keep the downstairs windows locked up tight like you told me."

"Good. Even in Pawhuska, there can be bad people looking for a way to get in a house."

"Augie Doggie would let me know if someone tried to get in."

The dog's tail pounded the floor.

Fifteen minutes later, I walked Trudy and Augie to her car. Zeus wanted to tag along, but I shoved him back inside the house and closed the door. The two young dogs had raced around the house for the last half hour, playing tug-a-war with a rope and wrestling while Mother watched with narrowed eyes and arms crossed. Zeus would calm down when his brother was gone.

On the driveway, Trudy wrapped her arm around me in a fierce hug. Frowning, she glanced at the front windows of our house, and then focused on me. "Do you think My Liz is still in my house?"

"The two of you were so close, it could be true." Although I had never seen a ghost, if it was possible for a spirit to linger anywhere, my great aunt Elizabeth would linger in her old Pawhuska home.

"Sometimes there are other people there, too."

"What do you mean?"

"Other people. G..ghosts, I think."

"Like who? Elizabeth's babies? Her husbands?" I knew all there was to know about Elizabeth's life. She'd kept diaries, and I'd read them all. I could imagine that a half-dozen old ghosts–stillborn babies and dead spouses as well as two murder victims whose deaths I had witnessed–might haunt the place. Thankfully, I rarely dreamed about that terrifying afternoon in Elizabeth's house. Trudy, with her sensitive, simpler nature, was much more likely than I to experience something out of the ordinary, or even paranormal, in that place.

Trudy shook her head "A new ghost came around this week and I hardly knew her. I should have told Sam."

"I'll share it with him if you want me to."

"Not tonight. He's so tired. Moving houses is hard on him."

"What should you have told Sam?" The unease I had felt earlier was back, full force.

"That new ghost I've been seeing this week? It's Sam's first wife, Reba."

My cell phone rang only a few minutes after Trudy drove away, pulling me out of deep thought. I had sat down on the front porch steps, thinking about what Trudy had said. I'd questioned her more about the ghost that looked like Reba, but she'd had little to add. The dress looked like a wedding, she said, and the bride wore a veil. Her face was blurred through the veil and her hair was shoulder-length and dark. Had Trudy really seen this ghost? I could think of no reason for her to make it up.

"But why would Reba's ghost come to your house?" I'd asked.

She had shrugged. "Sam is our friend. And Queenie was staying with me. Did you know that Reba gave Queenie to Sam as a puppy? Queenie didn't bark when the ghost came down the stairs."

I'd been stunned at this revelation. Trudy said goodbye and hugged me before she drove away minutes later.

Queenie had been a gift to Sam from Reba.

When my cell phone rang, I pulled it out of my pocket and answered.

"Mrs. Mazie? This is Caleb Miller. I'm calling about my tutoring session this week. Can I come a little early? I've got plans for later." The teenager spoke hurriedly, and then waited for my response.

I rubbed my forehead and thought ahead to Wednesday. What lessons had I planned for the week? Genetics and Mendel, as well as how genes influence the life cycle of the monarch butterfly, which would soon be making its annual migration south through Oklahoma. For some students, the concept of DNA and genetic traits was easy to grasp. For Caleb, it was not.

"That's fine, Caleb. I'll be in my class after school. Come when you can."

I was reaching to punch the phone off when he blurted: "Um, I need to leave by 6. My date is at 7. Okay?"

"No problem. Thanks for calling ahead of time. That's very responsible of you. Will I see you at rehearsal on Tuesday?"

"I think so. Thanks, Mrs. Mazie." He disconnected the call.

I stood up and stretched, bracing myself to go inside the house. A white Honda drove past, and then a red Chevy truck. Music blared from both, disrupting the quiet neighborhood. Inside the house, Queenie and Zeus barked. I climbed the porch steps and went in, my brain focused on Reba's ghost. I didn't believe in ghosts. But, according to Trudy, Queenie hadn't barked. Did Queenie recognize the ghost?

I reminded myself that ghosts didn't exist.

Two short stacks of boxes remained in the kitchen. There was still much to do. Unpacking in this room also meant dishwashing before putting things away. I was exhausted. The remaining things would have to wait until tomorrow.

A package of chocolate chip cookies had been left on the counter. I ate three of them one after another while my thoughts remained on Reba's ghost.

I punched in my daughter Allison's phone number. I'd promised to call her in Springfield, Missouri to let her know how things were going between me and her grandmother. The conversation would be short. I didn't want to tell her anything about Reba's disinterment or the problems her step-father Sam might be facing. A similar call would take place between my son and me in a few more days.

"Mom! I was wondering about you. Are you in the house?" Even at the end of what had probably been a busy weekend, Allison sounded upbeat and excited about life.

I gave her the rundown on the move, letting her know that we were 'all in' and that her grandmother was adjusting as best she could. Then, the conversation lagged.

"I know you need to get to bed, Mom, but I have to tell you one more thing. The monarchs are flying through! They've made our milkweed patch a regular butterfly motel. I've seen three chrysalises. Have any flown through Ponca City yet?"

"I've seen a few, but we don't have the right plants in the yard. I'll plant some milkweed and butterfly bushes next spring. The butterfly unit is next in my syllabus, I'll teach about that this week or next. I hope we have butterflies when it's time for the students to learn the facts."

I hung up a few minutes later with butterflies on my mind. Each year, the number of butterflies dwindled. People in cities often cleared away weedy-looking plants like milkweed that the butterflies ate and laid their eggs on. Huge migrations had become a thing of the past. With more education programs about the monarch, scientists hoped numbers of the beautiful insect might increase again. I hoped so, too. I looked forward to the fall migration every year.

I pulled out my planner and looked at the lesson plans I'd created for the week in the three different subjects I taught, then I reviewed the experiments the students would be completing in both the general science class and biology. I'd planned only lectures this week in Anatomy and Physiology. But that meant I'd have to give quizzes to be sure the students paid attention. I drafted a few quiz questions over the information we'd be reviewing before Reba's ghost filled my mind again.

A few hours later, I crawled into bed next to Sam, wondering if I should tell him what Trudy had said about the ghost. I didn't believe ghosts were real, but there were many things we can't even begin to understand. All those years ago when I met Sam, something had guided me, led me back to my own history in Aunt Elizabeth's house and at the old homestead. Had it been my great grandmother's spirit? That one explanation was the only one I had.

I was certain Trudy had not seen Reba's ghost. Sam had been Elizabeth's attorney as well as a lifelong friend, and maybe Queenie had been her dog, too, but those weren't reasons for the ghost of Reba to be at Trudy's. It was an odd coincidence that 'Reba' had 'appeared' to Trudy the same week that her suicide had been reclassified as 'suspicious.' Someone was playing ghost. Why? And more important, who? Was the man Sam called Bosque involved? It didn't seem logical. Someone else had to be behind both the disinterment and the ghost. My mind couldn't make sense of it.

Sam's snores interrupted my thoughts. My mind replayed Chase Longhorn's visit and considered the murder of fellow teacher Davis Harwell before my thoughts circled back to Reba's disinterment, and her ghost.

It would be hours before my mind let me sleep.

Outside the house, the Watcher lingers as the lights go off. Hands tremble with excitement.

It's started. Another week, two at the most, and my revenge will be complete. Good-bye Sam, and good-bye Jamie.

The Watcher waits a few more seconds, to be sure the house is asleep, then startles when a ray of light peeps around the shade of another room at the front of the house.

The Mother's room?

Her presence requires more planning. At the worst, I'll kill her with Jamie. At the best, she'll be left behind to mourn, and to wonder if there was anything she could have done to stop what happens.

The answer is: Nope! My time has come for sweet revenge.

The little light gleams. The Watcher yawns. A few more minutes pass before the Watcher fades into the moon shadows of the huge trees.

Chapter 7

Monday

On the drive to school early Monday morning, my heart thudded in my chest and thoughts spun in my head. Sam and I had spent a restless night. About 3 a.m., he'd left our bed for the guest room; I'd learned at breakfast that sleep had continued to elude him, too.

The final buzzing thought that I remembered having in the wee hours of the morning was the totally unimportant need to find someone to play the gardener in the high school fundraiser.

A part in a dinner theater production was the last thing Sam wanted or needed right now. I had to get Sam out of this, and that meant I needed to find someone else to play the role of the gardener. Of all the things in my life that I had no control over, at least I could do something about that.

Two hours later, my classroom phone beeped at the start of my second-hour class.

"Ms. Mazie?" The school secretary's voice quivered. "There's a police officer here to speak with you."

I sucked in my breath. Why did a police officer need to talk to me, especially when I was at work? "Okay. Let me give the students an assignment, then I'll be right there."

I glanced at the roomful of teenagers. They were hurrying to their desks, except for a cluster of students at the back of the room. The air in the room circulated, driven by the ceiling fan, and the scents of shampoos, body wash and anti-perspirants melded together in a soup of smells.

"Class? Take your seats, please." I waited until everyone was seated. "I'm needed in the office for a few minutes. Please review your notes from last Friday's experiment. I'll be giving a brief 10-point quiz when I get back. We'll start today's experiment after the quiz."

Students muttered and backpacks dropped to the floor, echoing throughout the room as I stepped to the door and out into the hallway.

In the office, a man in gray slacks and a blue shirt waited at the receptionist desk. He looked up. "Mrs. Mazie?"

"Yes."

"Detective Roland Blaise. I'm investigating the murder of Davis Harwell. I'd like to ask you a few questions." Blaise motioned me over to a corner of the office, away from traffic at the main reception area. "Aren't you the drama club co-sponsor? And you're working with the group to put on the dinner play at Wentz Camp?"

"Yes." I turned my back to the reception desk, where the student assistants looked on curiously.

"Davis Harwell was both an actor and a co-writer of that production, wasn't he?" He pulled a small yellow pad from the pocket of his jacket with one hand. The other held a still-steaming paper cup of coffee. The aroma reminded me that I'd not yet had my morning cup of caffeine, and I needed it badly.

"Yes. I have never worked directly with him. This is my first semester here."

"I've been told the two of you were ... friendly."

"I barely knew him." I frowned. This was an unexpected line of questioning. I straightened and took a step back from the detective, feeling wary.

"Where were you Friday evening?"

"I was packing boxes in Pawhuska," I stated in a low voice. "The moving van loaded us late Saturday and delivered our things here Sunday afternoon. Last weekend." A student bumped into me on his way to the front desk.

"Can anyone verify your whereabouts?"

"My husband. And several other people who stopped by as we were loading boxes." The two students were still watching. "He was murdered during a robbery, right?"

"So, your husband is your alibi, and I suppose you are his."

Someone dropped a book and I jumped. "We were in Ponca City Friday afternoon for the real estate closing, and then we drove back to Pawhuska to finish packing. The moving truck came at 2 p.m. Saturday." I crossed my arms. I needed that cup of coffee.

"So, you *were* here in Ponca City Friday night."

42

"No. We were here for the closing, and then went back to Pawhuska for supper and to spend the night."

"You and Harwell were friends?"

I glanced again at the watching students, wishing I'd insisted that this conversation take place elsewhere. "I hardly knew him. We met when the cast was announced at the first production meeting during the second week of school. I haven't seen him since. Rehearsals start tomorrow night."

"Is your husband a jealous man, Mrs. Mazie?"

"What?" My temper and my voice rose. My face burned.

"Did he care that you were active with the drama club and the local theater group and forming other liaisons?"

"Liaisons?" I leaned toward him and whispered harshly. "I am only involved with the theater group because of my new assignment as the drama club co-sponsor. Several high school drama students are participating in this dinner theater play. It's a fundraiser."

"Where is Mr. Mazie from?"

Blaise's questions were having the desired effect, to catch me off guard. I swallowed and took a deep breath before canvassing the office again. A knot of students stood talking by the copy machine. One girl's look met mine as she pushed the start button. Paper spewed into the output tray.

"He was born and raised in Pawhuska. He is a practicing attorney and has clients throughout Osage, Pawnee and Kay counties. You can look him up in the Bar Review. He publishes articles frequently."

Detective Blaise's head jerked as he looked up from the small notepad. "I had a conversation this morning about your husband with an OSBI detective. Interesting." The detective squinted at me, and then scribbled on his pad.

I crossed my arms and chewed at my lip. "I need to get back to my classroom."

"You may go. You'll hear from me again." Blaise snapped the notebook shut.

I barreled out of the office and down the hall, leaving the detective behind. I didn't like what he'd implied about Davis Harwell or his reaction to my husband's name. Longhorn must have told him about his current cold case.

And it was likely that word of my interview with the detective would spread throughout the school long before the class day was over.

Chapter 8

Immediately after school, I gathered the quizzes I'd given the second hour class. Tonight; after supper, I'd grade them. I stuffed the papers into my bag and headed to the car, thoughts of upcoming lessons and the week's 'To Do' list circling like gnats in my head.

"Jamie? Got a minute?" Gail Strickland broke into my thoughts as she stepped up beside me.

"Gail. I was in the office earlier, but I didn't see you." Actually, I hadn't even looked into her office.

"I heard. I'm guessing the detective was talking to you about Davis. I'm still in shock about it." She shook her head and peered at me. "I have to ask you something. Off the record. And you know, I don't place any credence whatsoever on this comment. It's about Davis Harwell. An insinuation has been made that the two of you had a 'thing.' Is that true?"

My mouth dropped open. "Absolutely not. Who said that?" First the detective, and now Gail?

"It doesn't matter who said it. I believe you. But you need to know some people are trying to damage your reputation." Gail nodded in sympathy as she spoke in her typical matter-of-fact tone.

I swallowed the ball of spit rolling around in my upper throat. "Thanks for telling me."

"The rumors will subside. People will see you with Sam, and realize the rumors are untrue. Take Sam with you to the funeral and act normal. Other than that, not much you can do. I'm glad you made the move to Ponca City. Maybe we can meet for coffee outside of school. Or go to a movie," she said. "Did you have a chance to talk to Sam about the role in the play?"

I shook my head. "Not last night. And I don't think he'll want to–"

"Ask anyway, okay? I've got a meeting at the library. We'll talk more later." With a quick wave, Gail walked away; I started my car. I wasn't ready to pass judgment yet as to whether the move to Ponca City was an improvement in my life. Right now, I wanted to get through the next few days and put the investigation into Reba's death behind us. Hopefully, Trudy's 'hauntings' would end with the investigation.

I also wanted to know who was spreading this rumor about me and Davis Harwell. The man had been murdered. The focus should be on finding the murderer, not on some ridiculous insinuation of a romantic liaison.

Mentally, I skipped through the list of teachers I had connected with personally at school; Maggie Dent, the English lit teacher; Sarah Mayes, another biology teacher; and Mark Zahler, the orchestra teacher. I had met most of the other faculty, or seen them at weekly school meetings, but those three had been friendly and helpful, especially Sarah. I couldn't imagine any of them participating in passing rumors about me. Who else would even care?

My workday was far from finished. As the drama club co-sponsor and prop chairman for the play, I was overdue for a visit to the site of the dinner theater production, and then, there were papers to grade and lessons to review. I drove northeast out of town.

I'd been told little about Wentz Camp, a camp for youth built by bachelor oilman Lew Wentz in the late 1920s. The rolling grounds were located on the far northern end of the local reservoir, Ponca Lake.

Native trees and grasses crowded the straight country road. I relaxed and rolled down my window, taking in the warm afternoon and the earthy scents.

I thought about Gail Strickland, and about the years we'd worked together in Las Vegas, New Mexico. She'd moved here five years ago and it was her recommendation that had gotten me this new teaching job. Seeing her friendly face daily on the high school campus had made the transition much easier for me. Because of her and Sarah, who constantly asked my opinion on the biology experiments she was planning for her classes, the transition into teaching in Ponca City had been easy. I was grateful to have her on my side, standing up for me against the ridiculous rumors.

A sign announced Wentz Camp. I drove further on an asphalt road, across a bridge and up the blacktop to a fork in the road and another sign, where I turned right and quickly arrived at the camp's entrance.

A dozen or more small stone structures–almost like tiny castles–dotted the neatly mown lawn, spread out among native trees. Wrought-iron gates opened to a small parking area and a sign that noted the entrance to the dressing rooms and the camp's swimming pool.

Curious about what I might find beyond the bordering fence, I got out of the car, walked to the nearest gate, stepped through, and then followed a sidewalk to a nearby building. Once inside, I passed the men's and women's locker rooms. Beyond an open door at the end of the hallway, water shimmered. I stepped into the doorway. Below me, wide tiled steps, with room to lounge on each one, overlooked the Olympic-sized swimming pool and provided a view of the nearby lake and the surrounding forests. The last of the summer cicadas droned in the distance, competing with speed boat motors to break the quiet of the tranquil countryside.

My body relaxed. I'd been doing all I could the last 24 hours to deny that I was overwhelmed by the double whammy of a fellow teacher's murder and the upcoming disinterment of Reba's body, not to mention the appearance of Reba's ghost. Sam had been preoccupied since Detective Longhorn's visit yesterday and Mother had been subdued. I had been alone with a head full of thoughts, but here, they all seemed to float away and into the clouds.

Over the past eight years I had grown used to Sam's silences, but his moods were new to Mother. I usually left him alone when he was that way. It didn't help to badger or coddle him. Eventually, he would seek out my companionship.

"Can I help you?" Someone asked. The man standing beside me on the wide steps wore a name badge: Howard DeKalb. He smelled like mint-flavored toothpaste and, with a full head of white hair and a thick mustache, he looked a little like the actor, Sam Elliot.

"I'm Jamie Mazie. I have an appointment with the director to talk about the high school dinner theater production scheduled for late next month." A light moisture-laden breeze scented with grass fingered my hair.

"This will be a perfect place for your murder mystery. But didn't I hear that one of the actors was killed?" The sixty-something man smoothed his mustache with his fingers.

"A cast member was murdered at the Conoco on Grand last weekend."

"Will that hold up your production? I have to say, our calendar is full in December if you have to postpone the fundraiser. You won't be able to stage it here." He spoke with a slight drawl.

"I don't think we'll have to delay. We're looking for a new cast member. I think the director will try to meet the original schedule." Twittering swallows swooped down over the steps and made a wide circle over the nearby lake.

DeKalb pursed his lips and tilted his head. "What was the man's role in the play?"

"The character is a gardener. He walks onto a couple of scenes, has a few lines. It's a small part." I focused on the older man's face. Strong chin, piercing blue eyes, bushy eyebrows.

"Would they be open to a civilian taking on the role?"

Was he talking about himself? Relief surged through me. I might not have to ask Sam to play the gardener after all.

A middle-aged woman dressed in a gray business suit made her way to where Howard DeKalb and I stood on the stair-stepped seating. She smiled and smoothed her highlighted short brown hair.

"Mrs. Monroney, this young lady is waiting to talk with you," DeKalb said. "She's with the high school theater group."

The woman extended her hand formally. "Hello. I'm Pamela. And you are Mrs. Mazie. Nice to have you here. Have you been to Wentz Camp before?"

"No. My husband and I recently moved to Ponca. It's my first semester at the high school." I studied her face, willing to bet she was older than she appeared; her face had been 'tucked.'

"And you've already volunteered to sponsor the drama club?"

"I'm a science teacher, but I like working with the theater students. They're quirky and smart."

"What can I help you with today?" Her glance moved across the pool area and the lake.

"My primary assignment is props, but I'll be helping with stage sets as well. I need to see the basic layout for the staging."

"I'll show you the area and how we'll arrange for the production." She turned toward the stairway at the end of the bleacher-like steps which led down to poolside.

"I'm serious about taking on the role of the gardener," Howard called as I followed the director away from him. "Will you get back to me if the director will take me on?"

"Give me your contact information and I'll pass it to her."

"I'll jot it down and bring it to you," he called.

Pamela Monroney had already started down the stairs. I grasped the banister as I followed, my eyes on the amazing tile work of the pool area. The facility was beautiful, an unexpected thing to see out here in the country in far north Oklahoma.

"We sometimes add a stage right here to serve as a dais for weddings, ceremonies and so forth. It can be placed to meet your needs."

"Did Gail or Romy talk with you about the location?" I couldn't imagine they would leave it up to me, with my minimal experience in theater production, to make this crucial decision.

"Yes. We agree the stage should be placed on that end of the pool. We'll arrange tables along both sides and use long draperies as walls. Then we'll create alleyways using panels for the actors to access the stage, and to make scene changes."

"How many tables and chairs can you accommodate for the audience?"

"We've done functions of 100 people before. 10 round tables of eight to ten people. This is a fundraiser, right? Not attended by the entire school."

"That's right. A separate committee is working on ticket sales, and at $50 a plate, we would be thrilled to sell a hundred tickets. That price puts it out of reach of many families."

Pamela nodded. "Perhaps the drama club can perform the play again for a general audience. And with the notoriety building about the production, I'm sure you will sell lots of tickets."

"Notoriety?" I doubted that most people would immediately associate Davis Harwell with the production.

"This morning I heard a rumor that the production has been cursed. You lost one cast member last weekend, didn't you? And before we met, I heard a news report that a second cast member is missing."

I was clueless as to what she was talking about. She didn't offer any more information but continued to tell me about the Camp's layout, and the productions they had previously staged on the property.

Thirty minutes later, after a brief tour of the rest of the Wentz Camp complex, Pamela Monroney handed me her business card. As I headed for the parking area, Howard DeKalb rushed up and slipped me his contact info.

"I'll expect a call back soon. Rehearsals are coming up, I bet."

"Actually, tomorrow night is the first one."

"I'll see you there." He grinned.

In the car, I checked my phone for local news updates, and there it was:

Ponca City high school senior, Caleb Miller, has been reported missing by his parents. Last seen Sunday evening, Miller was reported missing before school hours this morning.

'If you have seen Caleb, or have information about his whereabouts, please contact the Ponca City police department, or call 9-1-1.'

Caleb. Not only was he one of the students working on the play, he was one of the students I was mentoring in science, and I'd talked to him just last night.

Chapter 9

Mother stood in the kitchen doorway, hands on her hips, as I came though the garage door into the mudroom. "Jamie? Did you want me to fix supper? You didn't set anything out to prepare. What time will Sam be home?"

I squeezed my eyes shut and willed myself not to snap at her. In the years since Sam and I had married, I had become accustomed to entering a quiet house and enjoying an hour or more of time to myself before Sam got home. I needed that time to decompress from a busy day at the high school. And today, I needed that time to get my head on straight about Sam and the looming questions about Reba's death. Not to mention Davis Harwell's murder and Caleb's disappearance.

Should I notify the police that I had spoken to Caleb last night?

"Jamie. Answer me."

Mother's tone of voice was all too reminiscent of my teenage years. I dropped my satchel onto the mud bench in the back hallway and tried to focus on the here and now with Mother.

"If you'd like to make something for supper, have at it, Mother. I'm not a meal planner." I pulled a glass from the cabinet and filled it with water from the frig.

"I don't understand how you can't be. How do you know what to buy at the grocery store? Doesn't the uncertainty drive you crazy?" She placed her hands on her hips and glared at me.

I could think of something that was driving me crazy a lot faster than my lack of meal planning. "There's ground beef in the frig for spaghetti or make a meat lasagna if you feel up to it. I think I have the noodles in the pantry, and cheeses are also in the frig."

"Okay. I was hungry for chicken, but if that's what you'd like to have ..."

"Fix whatever you want, Mother. Either one is fine with me. I'm going to change my clothes and walk the dogs before Sam gets home. Then, we've got boxes to unpack and I've got quizzes to grade, as well as homework papers."

"I'll fix your supper. I suppose it's the least I can do since you've given me a roof over my head."

"Thanks." I kissed her cheek as I scooted past her in the doorway. My mom was the queen of 'guilting,' but I couldn't let it get to me already or this first week of cohabitation would be our last. With everything else that was buzzing in my brain, she could become the irritation that sent me over the edge.

I stepped off the front porch in shorts and a t-shirt with both Queenie and Zeus on their leashes, ready for a brisk hike down the sidewalks of my neighborhood. Ranch-style homes built in the Fifties and Sixties stood on large treed lots with wide lawns. A warm breeze stirred the leaves and the afternoon sun tingled on my arms.

During that walk, I expected my brain to circle around the current issues of my life, but I hoped that when I got back to the house I would feel relaxed and in control.

A black and white police cruiser pulled up to the curb beside me; Detective Roland Blaise climbed out. I pulled on the dogs' leashes, and they sat at my heels, obediently. Zeus growled.

"Mrs. Mazie. I'd like to talk to you," the detective said.

"I was going for a walk. What can I help you with now?"

"Do you know Caleb Miller?"

Obviously, he knew that I did. Why else would he be here? "Yes. He's in the drama club, and I tutor him in science once a week."

"When was the last time you spoke to Caleb?"

"Last night. He called to confirm our regular tutoring session on Wednesday. I heard on the radio this afternoon that he's missing."

"His mother is certain you were among the last–if not *the* last–person to have spoken to him before his disappearance."

"I don't know where Caleb is."

"Did he indicate he planned to run away?"

"No. Why would he confirm our Wednesday tutoring session if he planned to run away?"

"Maybe to divert attention from the fact he was leaving."

I shook my head. "That doesn't seem like Caleb. He is conscientious. He cares about his studies."

"Was Caleb popular with the kids at school?"

"I've only been at the school six weeks, Detective. I can't say for sure about kids in general, but he had friends in the drama club."

"Any conflicts with other students that you were aware of?"

I thought back to science class last week, and then to Thursday night's drama club meeting after school. "No."

"What about interactions with any of the adults participating in the dinner theater?"

"It's a joint fundraiser of the local Playhouse group and the drama club. Most of the high school students are building the sets, planning the lighting and other stagecraft jobs. The adults have the roles in the production."

"And have the groups interacted?"

"Our first joint rehearsal is tomorrow."

"If you think of anything else, either about the murder or Caleb, please contact me."

Blaise climbed back into his car and drove away.

The late summer air was thick with the dusty scent of sycamore. The huge trees lined my street, their white splotched trunks standing in regular intervals in the front yards of the ranch-style homes, interspersed with an occasional sweet gum, oak or maple. I started off at a fast pace, the events of the last two days filling my thoughts.

Two blocks away, I stepped off the curb to cross the street at an intersection. A car horn blasted.

Chapter 10

I leapt backward, jerking the dogs' leashes and jamming a heel into the cement curb. I lost my balance, stumbled and fell to my knees in the street.

A car sped through the intersection.

I glared after the white Honda. The license tag was spotted with mud, so were the side and rear panels of the vehicle.

Queenie and Zeus licked my face.

Gingerly, I stood and put weight on my foot. Sharp pains shot up my leg.

I had barely escaped serious injury. And one of the dogs could have been hit or even killed by the speeding car. What an idiot!

Gingerly, I put weight on my foot again. No way could I continue the walk with the dogs. Instead, I limped toward home, fuming. The dogs trotted on their short legs to either side of me.

I'd be on the lookout for the Honda. Children rode their bikes in this neighborhood, and people walked or jogged. I should notify the police about the speeding car. Maybe they could add some speed bumps, or 'slow' signs, or assign policemen to monitor the street with their radar guns.

"What happened to you?" Mother asked as I limped into the kitchen.

I shrugged. "Twisted my ankle avoiding a speeder on the street."

She turned toward the refrigerator. "Let's get some ice on that. I've seen cars zooming by. Dangerous. What if it had been a child, or an elderly person who couldn't get out of the way?"

I'd already thought about those possibilities, but now, a new, even more chilling one struck me. What if the driver had been trying to run *me* down on purpose?

"Here's an ice pack. Sit down in the living room with this. I'll get you some ice tea," Mother said as she wrapped the bagged ice in a kitchen towel.

Two hours later, Sam found me in the living room, watching the news, my foot propped on an ottoman with the second bag of ice Mother had prepared wrapped in a towel around my ankle.

"What happened?" The hang-dog look he'd had when he entered the room faded into one of concern. He squatted beside my chair.

"I stepped off the curb without looking when I was walking the dogs. Almost got hit by a car."

"Jamie! Please be careful." He bent to kiss me.

I slid my arms around his neck and rested my cheek on his collarbone. "Tough day?"

He straightened. "It was good to be busy at work, but I can't stop thinking about Reba. And now I'm going to worry about you. I won't be very good company tonight."

"You don't have to be good company. It's enough to be together."

"You're so right. Thank you, my love."

He leaned in for another kiss, and right on cue — how would I ever get used to the lack of privacy?— Mother stomped in from the kitchen. Back straight and chin up, she looked ready to give orders to an army.

"Sam. I'm glad you're home. I guess Jamie filled you in on what happened to her. I was going to have to try to keep supper warm for you, but now I can serve it right up. Wash your hands."

Sam and I exchanged a look. "Yup, I need to wash up. Lawyers hands are always dirty, according to some people." A small grin lightened his eyes.

A wonderful aroma–garlic, onions and tomatoes–swirled through the air. Lasagna. My mouth watered. There were advantages to my mother's presence in our house, and supper-time was one of them.

At the supper table, I took another sip of the wine Sam had poured for me, letting the liquid roll around in my mouth and enjoying the slightly bitter taste of my favorite pinot noir. I willed my mind to drift, if it would. An uncomfortable, unidentifiable thought hung with all the other tumultuous images in my head. I didn't want to run it down now. Time enough for that, later.

The white Honda sits at the curb two houses down. Inside the car, the Watcher stares at the house, sees the shapes moving behind the dining room curtains. Fingers tap on the steering wheel.

Mary Coley

Stomach churning, the person in the black hoodie sighs.

Patience is a virtue, right? If I'd accelerated just a little more, Jamie would already be dead.

Chapter 11

Tuesday

The students rambled in and out of my classes without sideways glances at me. I heard Caleb's name spoken quietly.

During my lunch break, I sat alone at a table in the teachers' area of the cafeteria. Clanging trays, chairs screeching against the cement floor and loud conversations echoed in the large room. The aroma of something fried hung in the air.

I wasn't on monitor duty, but, like teachers and students alike, I ate quickly during the short lunch time. Maggie Dent plopped down next to me for a few minutes, ate quickly and then left. Sarah Mayes sat with her sack lunch and asked about my move as she ate a peanut butter sandwich. Mark Zahler passed my table and wondered if I was settling into the new house. He listened to my answer and moved on.

No one else stopped at my table. I felt sure that the rumor of my liaison with Davis was running rampant in the school, and that I was being ostracized, even though there was no truth to the rumor.

Afternoon classes passed as usual. I lectured, explained procedures and answered questions. When classes ended, I spent the obligatory time in my room for office hours, and then escaped from the school with a bag full of assignments to grade. I wasn't ready to go home. I drove to Lake Ponca, and the small park area on the western side of the lake.

I entered the picnic shelter area through narrow gates and drove the short winding road around two small duck ponds. Several families had parked nearby, and the kids were throwing bits of bread or crackers to the resident ducks. They squealed when the big birds lunged to grab the bread from their hands. I drove into the parking area near a large picnic shelter similar in construction to those at Osage Hills State park, where Sam and I had spent an interesting week before our wedding seven years ago. Because of the materials used and the architecture of the shelter, I had no doubt this park was also constructed in the late 1930s by the CCC program of the Works Progress Administration under Franklin D. Roosevelt.

Golden leaves rained from huge ashes and elms as I climbed out of the car. They swirled around my feet, rattled and skipped across the asphalt parking lot and onto the spacious park grounds. Children were swinging in tall swing sets and a couple of teenagers were playing badminton using a net strung in a wide space over sand. Rows of picnic tables filled the shelter houses, and the huge stone fireplaces were clean and ready for the first fires of fall. Piles of wood had been stacked neatly nearby.

Lost in the moment, I limped across the recently-mown lawn to a stream bubbling over rocks, then followed it uphill to its source, a wide cement spillway. Steps led up to the top of the structure. From there, I could see the lake and the far shore, as well as the lush green of the forested park next to the spillway. I imagined my children, as they'd been two decades ago, racing with their friends across the grass, lounging under the trees, searching for Easter eggs and playing in piles of autumn leaves. I relaxed.

The current events–including Reba and Davis and Caleb–were far removed from my mind. I didn't want to go there; I wanted to stay in this daydream about the past and pretend those things weren't happening in my world.

An engine roared in the parking lot. I descended carefully from the top of the spillway onto a pathway that meandered down into the park. Clouds swirled in the sky. On the park road, the engine raced, and I thought about the Ponca City Grand Prix and the play Rusty Clement had written for our fundraiser.

The race had been held little more than a mile away. Now, Davis had been killed and Caleb was missing. As far as I knew, the only thing they had in common was the play. Like the re-investigation into Reba's death and the appearance of her ghost in Trudy's house, it was an odd coincidence.

"*Are you sure* you don't mind washing the dishes, Mother? If I don't leave now, I'll be late for rehearsal."

"Go ahead, dear. I can take care of cleanup. Have a good time."

Her words duplicated what she had always said to me as a teenager when I went out for the evening on a study date or to a basketball or football game.

"I'm expecting chaos. Maybe I'll be surprised." I couldn't help but feel apprehensive about the upcoming rehearsal. Two members of a small cast and crew would be absent. One of them was dead. I didn't want to be 'borrowing trouble' but I wondered if somehow this fundraiser/dinner play was not meant to be.

"I've found that low expectations garner exceptional results. Be prepared for chaos and you can avert it," Mother said as she scraped food scraps into the sink disposal.

Did she speak from experience? "If I didn't have to be there in ten minutes, I'd ask for examples from your life."

Her expression flattened into a mask; she pressed her lips together.

Mother had always kept her life's secrets close to her heart. I knew relatively little about her early life. It was only by chance that during a September stay at Osage Hills State Park seven years ago, I learned the story of my mother's first love, and about the estrangement of her best friend. Since then, her demeanor had softened a little, but Mother kept secrets. I was probably better off not knowing all of them. On the flip side, she certainly didn't need to know all the secrets I kept.

She flicked her hand at me and turned to the sink. "See you after a bit."

I'd been dismissed. No secret revelation was coming tonight.

Chapter 12

The sun dropped close to the horizon as I drove the few miles to the Poncan Theater, circa 1920s, and home of the Ponca Playhouse Community Theater on downtown Main Street. The sunset sky glowed, touching the colorful leaves of the maples and sweet gums, adding a red shimmer of enchantment to the well-maintained streets. The drive was too short; I wanted to draw out the experience and savor the sunset, but I was a poor drama club co-sponsor if I was the last to get to rehearsal. I parked around the corner from the theater and walked slowly to the front of the Mission-style building.

"Hey, Mrs. Mazie." One of the drama students, a girl wearing black jeans, a zipped black hoodie and wide blue eyeliner, lounged on the steps at the front entrance.

"Brooklyn. Am I late?"

"No. I'm waiting for Zeke."

The pair were friends, but I didn't think it was more than that. They wore similar clothes and makeup, but I had never witnessed any public displays of affection between them. Proud of their individuality, they appeared to care little about the sneers and comments other students sometimes made. Bullying was an issue in this high school, like most schools. I called out the bullies privately when I heard the verbal abuse and made a point of encouraging the victims to stand up for themselves and ignore the comments as best they could.

Inside the old theater, I followed the sound of voices through the lobby, past the concession stand and into the auditorium. Buttery-popcorn scent lingered in the air, even though the industrial-sized poppers were currently empty. Two side aisles led to the stage, where several adults and students sat in the front row of seats or lounged half-on, half-off, the edge of the stage.

"... we have found a substitute. Howard DeKalb, on staff at Wentz Camp, will play the role of gardener. His familiarity with the Camp will be helpful when we move our final rehearsals there and prepare for our performance." Romy Vaughn, the speech and drama teacher, leaned over the back of a folding chair positioned exactly in center stage. "Has anyone heard anything about Caleb?" She pushed her long graying hair off her face and cleared her throat. Her voice sounded raspy and rough.

The small group of students shook their heads, and the adults regarded one another.

"I'll keep hoping for the best. And I know you all will, too."

I tested my memory, trying to put a name to each face as I looked around the auditorium. It was an easy task with the students I saw weekly in drama, but harder with the adults who had auditioned through the Ponca Playhouse. I remembered Howard, but there were other men and women I had not seen before. A tall slender blond woman about my age caught my look and smiled. She tilted her head and widened her eyes with some familiarity. Had we met before? I didn't think so. She opened her lips as if she was going to mouth some message from across the room, but then closed them and smiled.

"Several of you have already talked with the police about Caleb, and I expect Detective Blaise to come to rehearsal tonight," Romy said. "Please answer his questions. Caleb has been gone nearly 48 hours, and time is of the essence."

"Hi," a voice whispered in my ear. The woman from across the room stood at my elbow now. "We haven't met. I'm Belina. I'm the vixen. In the play." Her straight white teeth gleamed.

"Belina. That's an unusual name."

"She's a Catholic saint. My mother liked it. Belle, for short, but I prefer Belina."

I introduced myself, adding, "I'm the drama club co-sponsor, but I teach science at the high school."

On stage, Romy introduced the playwright, Rusty Clement. He cleared his throat and spoke. "I have great memories of the Ponca City Grand Prix, held the weekend closest to July 4. So, I wrote this play. Mystery cloaks the final races in 1992, adding additional drama. Many people are convinced that the death of a driver was not an accident. I'm still investigating, even though my friend and race enthusiast Davis Harwell is gone. We were working on the ending ... It may still be rewritten." He regarded the cast members, a grim look on his face.

"Lived here long?" Belina whispered in my ear. "I'd remember you if I'd seen you before. You have such nice, long, thick hair. Pretty color, too."

"Thank you. My husband and I have been living in Pawhuska. He's from there." I kept my eyes on the stage, where Romy was patting the playwright's shoulder. He disappeared behind the side curtain.

"I know Pawhuska well," Belinda whispered once more. "My family is from Fairfax."

"You probably know my husband's family. The Mazie's."

"Of course." She nodded, then turned back toward the stage.

"I think everyone's here," Romy Vaughn said. "Let's do a read-through and block the scenes. For those who don't know him, Marshall is our student stage manager. And Jamie Mazie, the drama club co-sponsor, is helping with props." Romy Vaughn nodded toward me and motioned for me to come up to the stage.

"Nice to meet you," Belina said softly as I moved away.

Halfway through the blocking session, Detective Blaise entered the theater from the rear. It had been a slow go, with a couple of Playhouse newbies unable to remember whether 'Stage Right' and 'Stage Left' referred to the actors' viewpoint or the audience's.

Romy stopped rehearsal and asked that everyone be available to the detective and stay either backstage or in the green room during a thirty-minute break. I reviewed my prop notes and suggestions about the staging while the detective spoke with one cast member after another. When he approached me, I wondered what possible question he could have. We'd already talked twice this week.

"Mrs. Mazie. Have you heard anything from Caleb today?"

"No. I don't expect him to come to his tutoring session tomorrow."

"Do you always meet at school? Have you ever met anywhere else? At your home, maybe?"

"No, Detective. I'm tutoring him. We always meet at school, at the end of the class day." I kept my voice even, and low. Anger wouldn't help my case.

"How many times have you met so far this semester? At school, or anywhere?"

"Tutoring began the third week of class, when it was obvious he needed extra help. I'd have to look at my class record to be certain, but we've probably met three times."

"And Drama Club? How many times has he attended?" He peered at me, reminding me of a bird of prey, a vulture studying a mouse. I didn't like the analogy.

"The club started meeting the second week of school. Students signed up the first week. So, we've met five times. Again, I'd have to check my records to be sure."

"And Caleb Miller attended each one?"

"Yes."

The detective made notations in his notebook, then closed it and tucked his pencil and the pad into the pocket of his jacket. "That's all for now. I have a few more people to talk to. Which person is Belina?"

I looked around the stage and into the auditorium but didn't see her. "You might check the green room, around the corner, back stage." I pointed the way and then watched as he stalked off.

A moment later, as I finished my review of the script with prop considerations in mind, Rusty Clement walked up.

"Jamie, can we talk?" The slender man smiled before glancing around the stage. No one stood close to us. "You seem like a no-nonsense type. Serious and not prone to exaggeration," he said softly.

I smiled and waited for him to say more. Where was he going with this?

"This play is a serious piece, it's not just for entertainment. I'm afraid it may have gotten Davis killed."

I focused on the man. "Why?"

"I hope I can trust you. I may need your advice. And some special last-minute props if I take this where it needs to go." His look darted across the stage as he leaned closer.

"I'll do what I can, but you've lost me. What do you mean, where it needs to go?"

Footsteps clomped on the wood stage. Rusty stepped back and cleared his throat as Romy Vaughn hurried up to us.

"Did you talk to the detective?" Romy asked. "We've given him enough time, I think. We have so much to cover tonight. Let's get back on track." Romy glanced at me, and then whirled to face the auditorium and the groups of students clustered in the theater seats. "Your attention, please. Let's pick up where we left off."

Rusty crossed the stage and ducked behind the curtain.

Chapter 13

Three hours later, I pulled the car into the garage and trudged into a silent house. Queenie and Zeus trotted across the empty kitchen to greet me. I offered dual ear scratches.

"Crazy busy day, dogs. One of my students has gone missing. The detective came to rehearsal and talked to everyone, including me. For the third time this week. That, one top of everything else." They looked up at me with droopy brown eyes full of sympathy.

It wasn't strange for Mother to have gone to bed, but it was a little odd for Sam to have already called it a day. I tiptoed to our bedroom and peeked in to see his sleeping form beneath the sheets. Today had been a commuting day for him, which meant early up and out of bed to drive to Pawhuska. I'd been doing the reverse commute for the past six weeks. It would take him some time to get used to.

I closed the door and returned to the kitchen island, where I spread the papers and lists of needed props I'd gathered during the rehearsal. We'd managed to work through the scenes, and I had a much better idea of not only what the scenes required in the way of props but what items might enhance the staging. Now, I had to figure out where to find the things I needed. Beg, borrow or pay garage sale prices, whatever it took. It sounded like Rusty might alter the play, and there might be more props to find. Since he hadn't given me a list, or told me what he had in mind, his additions would have to wait. He'd acted suspiciously. What was he planning? Was Romy aware of it, too?

Princess strolled in and rubbed against my legs, purring loudly. I lifted her onto my lap and petted her soft, thick fur. She accepted my touch only for a moment before she leapt away.

I barely heard my cell phone buzzing from my purse–I remembered silencing it at the beginning of rehearsal. I laid down my pen, reached for my purse and pulled out my phone.

The caller ID screen read: *Trudy*. For most people, it was too late to make a phone call, but Trudy didn't sleep well, and sometimes spent her nights doing chores or watching TV.

"Hi. Everything okay?" I asked, still sorting out the various lists I'd written during the rehearsal.

"Jamie," Trudy wailed. "You've got to come home. These ghosts scare me. I can't sleep, and they pop up ever'where, even in my bedroom. I don't know how to make them go away!"

I sank down onto a bar stool's cushioned seat and laid down the pen I'd grabbed up to make notes on the lists. "What do you mean, they're everywhere? How many? What are they doing?"

"Elizabeth don't scare me. I'm glad to see her. But the man in the kitchen I don't like. Without Sam here, I don't want a man in this house." Trudy sniffed.

Aunt Elizabeth had lost several husband's during the decades she had lived in the house. Could this ghost be Trudy's construct of one of them? But she also knew about the two men who'd been murdered in front of me in the kitchen nearly ten years ago. Her anguish about those memories could have conjured them up.

"The other one—Reba—she goes up and down the stairs. Tonight, she was in my bedroom. I'm scared, Jamie. Can you come?"

"I thought Vera was staying with you. Is she seeing these ghosts, too?"

"Vera went to Barnsdall today. Her cousin's sick. I been alone, except for Augie Doggie. And he's a puppy, you know."

Augie was far from a puppy, but his playful nature made him seem so. Of all the pups in the three litters Queenie had mothered, he was the most likely to chase a ball. If there was someone in the house, though, the dog would sound an alarm.

"Does he react to the ghosts? Growl, bark?"

"He howls. Except at Elizabeth. And he won't go into the kitchen. I had to move his bowls to the hallway tonight when they showed up."

I imagined the scene in that old house, with Augie Doggie howling and Trudy fretting and the ghosts flitting about. Would a dog howl at ghosts?

"Trudy, tell me what happened tonight." I frowned. My stomach twisted. I didn't like this situation. I was afraid for Trudy. Real people could harm her, and whoever was in the house was most likely very real.

"That man was in the kitchen. I went to fix some soup, and I felt him in there. The hairs on the back of my neck stood straight up, and I got them goosebumps on my arms."

"Did he talk to you?"

"No. He hangs around the pantry. And Augie Doggie goes to howlin' out in the hallway. I zapped my soup in the microwave and got out of there. I don't know what to do, Jamie. Can't you come?"

Now I had goosebumps on my arms. My only experience with ghosts was the frequent feeling I'd had that my deceased husband Ben remained close to me for a time after his death. Despite my education in science, I knew that unexplained things existed that defied any logical explanation. There was a possibility– however small– that Trudy was experiencing a psychic event.

More likely, she was experiencing human intruders. And it had something to do with Reba.

From the alleyway behind the house, the kitchen window is unobstructed. The Watcher chews a fingernail and stares.

A fitful wind blows from the north, shaking the leaves of the trees.

"Soon. Soon," the Watcher repeats, muttering, eyes closed. The Watcher's cell phone rings.

"What? She locked herself in her room? Push her harder. I want her to run out of the house, screaming. Push her down the stairs if you have to."

The Watcher punches the phone off. Angry. **"This is taking too long."**

The car's engine turns over and the White Honda rolls slowly down the street.

Chapter 14

Wednesday

I woke to discover Sam's side of the bed empty. I pulled on my robe and hobbled toward the kitchen. My ankle was still sore early in the day. Before Sam left for work, I needed to tell him about Trudy's call and the quick trip to Pawhuska I planned for after school this afternoon.

I stepped into the kitchen as he called, "Thanks, Mary! Breakfast was great." The back door into the garage closed.

The scent of frying bacon filled the kitchen; my mouth watered.

Mother wore a self-satisfied smile as I settled onto a stool. A plate of scrambled eggs, bacon and toast sat in front of me on the island.

"You don't cook much for your husband," Mother observed as she placed the skillet in the sink for washing.

"We're both very busy. Cooking isn't the big deal it was years ago." This was true, but her observation made me wonder if I was neglecting a wifely duty.

"It should be. Your health is important. And men appreciate a woman who cooks." She nodded smugly.

My father had been appreciative, certainly, but that was only one man. What 'men'? Was there another secret in her life? Considering what I'd uncovered about her before, I wouldn't be surprised.

She caught my look, and a curtain seemed to drop over her face. I had no time to pursue the question of 'other men' this morning. It would have to wait.

"I guess you'll both be home for supper? I'll have to go grocery shopping." She dried the frying pan and slid it into the cabinet, poured a cup of coffee and gazed out the window at the backyard. Outside, Queenie and Zeus barked.

"Let me give you some money. And thank you for doing the shopping." I dug through my purse for my wallet, pulled out several crisp $20s and laid them on the counter. After gobbling down the breakfast, I returned to the bedroom to dress and put on my makeup.

Twenty minutes later, I grabbed my work satchel, which was jammed with the homework assignments I'd graded last night after Trudy's call, said goodbye to Mother and hurried out the door, my ankle carefully wrapped with an Ace bandage for the second day in a row. I should have told her about my quick trip to Pawhuska, but I didn't. I hoped to be home for supper in plenty of time.

At the start of my planning period, I walked to the teachers' lounge for a cup of coffee. Maggie Dent sat at a table, fingering a steaming mug. She nodded a greeting and then stared down into her drink.

I sat down across from her after filling a coffee mug. "Morning, Maggie. Everything okay?"

She peered at me. "Sure. And you?"

Something in her look told me that what she said was not exactly true. I knew better than to think it was all about me, but there was something in her look. "I've been better. Kind of a rough week."

"I'm so worried about Caleb. He is one of my top students. It's not like him to do something like this on purpose." Maggie fingered the rim of her coffee mug.

"No, it's not. I tutor him on Wednesday's after school. Science is not his best subject."

"I think English lit is. His essays are stellar. He's a writer in the making." She shook her head, blew on her coffee and took a tentative sip.

"I'm hoping he turns up soon, and that he's unharmed," I said.

"We all hope that. Another interesting rumor is starting to run the halls." She peered at me.

"Oh? Guess I haven't heard it yet."

"You will, soon enough. These kids. They are so focused on the negative these days. Not that I really blame them."

I waited for her to tell me the rumor.

She sipped her coffee before continuing. "They're saying he was involved with a teacher. Anyone who had anything to do with him is under the microscope." She smiled sadly. "Guess that includes me. And you."

I sat up straighter. "Me? I was his tutor. Nothing more."

"Just saying. That's the word in the halls. Student missing. Teacher to blame."

Two more teachers pushed into the lounge, chatting about the latest episode of "Biggest Loser" on television the night before.

Maggie drained her coffee and stood. "Gotta get back to class. Let's talk later."

I finished my coffee. Another rumor to deal with. First, Davis, now Caleb. This school was a hotbed of speculation.

The line of high schoolers leaving campus moved slowly. Students rambled nonchalantly in between cars to get to their own, unconcerned about horns honking and car stereos blaring. They stared at their phones and sashayed without looking up.

I'd posted a sign on my classroom door, asking any student who was looking for me to send an email and I would contact them tonight, after 9 p.m. I hoped I wouldn't have to spend too many hours in Pawhuska calming Trudy, and that traffic would move smoothly on Highway 60.

Eventually, I made it out of the parking lot and onto the city street; within five minutes, I was on Lake Road, headed toward Lake Ponca, Kaw Lake and eventually Pawhuska. The road was familiar because of my daily commute; houses next to the road, many of them traditional ranch-style homes surrounded by centuries-old oaks or pecan trees.

I rolled down my window as I sped across the dam of the big Kaw reservoir. Below me, on the smooth blue-brown water, a speed boat cut through the mirrored surface, creating a wake; the motor roared. Behind it, a skier held onto the ski rope and flew over the wake, bouncing on the glassy water, then pulling himself back behind the boat before zipping to the other side.

In the distance, a party barge floated near a cove with a white beach. A few low-decked bass boats zoomed to their next fishing spot at high throttle. White gulls lifted into the air, and a great blue heron flapped across an inlet.

After crossing the dam, the highway connected with Oklahoma 60, the road to Pawhuska. Miles separated ranch houses and the grass-covered horizon was the gently undulating hills of Osage County.

When I'd made this drive to and from Pawhuska daily, it had become rote. I'd hardly noticed the pastures flashing by, or the cattle and horses grazing peacefully. The area known as The Osage was a rancher's heaven.

My mind dwelt on Davis' murder, and then on Caleb's disappearance before it skipped back to Trudy's phone call last night. She had wanted me to jump in the car right then and drive to her. I'd assured her that Augie Doggie would protect her if there was real danger. Put a dog in a situation that demanded they protect their owner, and I was certain Augie would.

But, she still insisted that I come after school today. I did not want to disappoint her.

No doubt, whatever Mother had decided to cook for supper was in the early preparation stages now, at 3:30 p.m. After a glance at the digital dashboard clock, I increased my speed. Supper would be on the table by 6, about the time Sam usually got home, and I was going to have to hurry to make it back by then. A visit with Trudy was usually not a short event, especially if she had something on her mind.

In Pawhuska, I turned off the main street to drive past the cemetery. It was a short cut of sorts, the back way to Elizabeth's-Trudy's-house. It would always be Elizabeth's house to me, even though she no longer lived there. Physically, anyway. According to Trudy, my great aunt was a spiritual resident.

The gravestones of the big cemetery stretched over the little valley, rows climbing up the hillside on the north and west sides. Cars and people indicated that a burial must be in progress. Twenty or more people, as well as a back hoe and other equipment, clustered around the spot in the cemetery where I knew Reba's grave to be.

One figure stood out, a Native American man in a leather jacket, heavier than Sam, but with the same straight, shiny black hair, not quite as long. *Chase Longhorn.* Startled, I wondered if Sam knew the disinterment was happening today–right now.

Chapter 15

Trudy met me on the porch of the house, swinging the walnut front door wide before I had even climbed the steps.

"Jamie, thank goodness you came. I'm at my wit's end with these ghosts. They won't let me sleep. Keep glidin' in and out, hoverin' over the bed. What can I do?" she wailed.

Augie Doggie strolled out and stood next to her, looking up at me with droopy eyes, his tail slowly wagging back and forth, almost brushing the ground.

I hugged her. "Want to sit out here?" When she nodded, I walked over to the porch swing on the end of the porch, and she followed. Over the summer, the ivy had regrown a protective cover over this end of the porch.

Once we were both seated in the swing, I pushed against the floor with my feet, and the chain creaked as the swing moved slowly back, and then forward again.

"Tell me what's happening with the ghosts, Trudy." I needed something to distract me from what was happening at the cemetery. Sam would share the results of the disinterment with me once he knew them, but that could take days. It would be a shadow hanging over both of us.

"Last night, they started in at dark, wandering through the house. And that man in the kitchen is the worst!"

I didn't tell her that if there really was a ghost haunting that kitchen, it was most likely that of either her half-cousin, or her grandfather. I had seen them die. But I had no experience with ghosts. Were they recognizable? Did they bear any resemblance to the human body they had formerly been attached to?

What was I thinking? I didn't believe in ghosts. My education in science provided no basis to believe in spirits inhabiting the earth. The man in the kitchen was affiliated with whoever was pretending to be Reba. Was it Bosque?

"Do they speak? Do they seem threatening?"

"My Liz wants to be with me, I think. She follows me around, and while she's there, the others stay away. Reba wants to talk to me, but she can't open her mouth. She shakes her head and acts sad. Did you tell Sam I've been seeing her?"

"No." I didn't plan to tell Sam. I was fairly sure he didn't believe in ghosts, but if he did, he didn't need to be wondering why his dead first wife was haunting Trudy in Elizabeth's old house. I didn't want to be wondering that, either. My nose itched. I rubbed it, and immediately sneezed.

"I like having My Liz around. Can you get rid of the others? Maybe if Sam came and Reba saw him, she'd be satisfied and stay away."

"Trudy, do the ghosts threaten you?"

"No, but when they are there, I can't sleep!" she wailed.

"Why don't you and Augie come back to Ponca and stay with Sam and me for a while. We have plenty of room." I knew Mother wouldn't be happy about having house guests, but I was concerned for Trudy's safety.

"But this is MY house. My Liz gave it to me. I can't leave!"

"I'm not talking about forever, only for a few days. Maybe if you're not here, the ghosts will go away." I sneezed again. My fall allergies had set in. Ragweed.

She shook her head. "They'll be here when I get back."

"Trudy, what do you want to do?"

"I want Sam to make them go away. Maybe he can get someone to talk to them and find out what they want." Trudy stopped the swing's motion with her foot.

A medium? I was unaware of anyone in Sam's circle of friends who claimed to have that ability.

"You can talk to Sam about it. But in the meantime, you and Augie come home with me. Sam has a busy week, it may be Saturday before he can come back over to Pawhuska." He hadn't mentioned having appointments with clients in his Pawhuska office this week.

"My cousin Mary won't be glad to see me. She doesn't like me." Trudy sighed.

"She does like you. Mother has a difficult time expressing her feelings. She comes across as if she doesn't care about people, but she does." I wasn't sure how to explain to Trudy about my mother. I'd spent most of my life thinking she didn't like *me*. She would never share her feelings or talk about herself. I had always believed she was either mad at me, my siblings, or my father. I was certain she had always projected that same persona when she was in Pawhuska, even years ago. "Mother doesn't share much of herself with other people, Trudy. She's hard to know. I've learned not to take it personally. She's not mad at me, and she's not mad at you. Maybe she's mad at life."

My mind flashed back to the September before Sam and I got married. We'd solved a decades-old mystery at Osage Hills State Park, and I'd learned something about my mother's early life that had contributed to her constant state of sadness and stifled emotions. Trudy knew nothing about what I had learned; my mother would not approve of sharing the story with her or anyone else.

Trudy sniffed. "Will she be mean to Augie Doggie?"

Mother hadn't exactly taken to Queenie and Zeus even though Sam and I had done our best to keep the dogs out of the kitchen and out of Mother's room. But they were curious hounds after all, and they followed their noses–and the scents they detected–everywhere.

"She won't be mean, Trudy. But Augie will probably have to spend some of the day outside with the other dogs. When Sam and I are at work, Mother usually puts them outside."

"Do they have water? And a cool place to lay?" Trudy's lips pursed, and her brow furrowed.

"Sure. We have a covered porch, and the water bowl is there in the shade. I've even put doggy beds out for them, although right now they prefer the cool concrete. They are happy outside, Trudy." My nose itched again. I rubbed it.

She sighed. "Okay. What am I going to do all day while you and Sam go to work?"

That was a good question. Mother would not like having Trudy there with her, disturbing the quiet. "We'll have to think about something for you to do. The library's not far away, and you could walk over there, or drive if you'd rather. And there's a big park right next to the high school where I teach. You could meet me for lunch."

If the weather stayed nice, Trudy could stay out of Mother's hair and away from the 'ghosts' at Elizabeth's house until Sam could get to the Pawhuska house with someone who could either 'commune' with Reba's ghost or get rid of them.

"I guess I should get ready. Should I take my car?"

"If you want to be able to drive around town, you should. Otherwise, you'll have to walk everywhere, or rely on Sam or me to take you." I sneezed for the third time.

"But where would I want to go besides the park or the library? And I won't be gone but a day or two. Right? Promise?"

"I promise. Let's gather your things. Augie doesn't need to bring anything. We have plenty of dog stuff already."

"Queenie will be happy to see me and Augie Doggie!"

I was certain that the dog would be. My uncertainty lay in my mother's reaction to two more living, breathing bodies sharing the house with us.

I led Trudy into the house. She headed upstairs, but I stood in the foyer, looking first into the study, then, the front parlor, and finally, down the short hallway to the kitchen door. This is where it all began, where I met Sam and felt that first little stirring in my heart. I closed my eyes. The smells of the house hung in the air: lemon oil, wood, old carpets. Nothing had changed since the house changed ownership.

Upstairs, Trudy hummed as she packed her overnight bag. 'Take Me Out to the Ballgame.' Memories, both good and bad, swarmed over me.

I crossed the entry to the stairs and studied the old carpet runner that snaked up to the second story hall. A long, red thread had come loose from the carpet binding; the edges were fraying. The carpet itself was probably over seventy years old, and bare spots had worn in the center of each step. Trudy, or someone, had no doubt vacuumed recently, but bits of grass were visible on several lower steps. Augie Doggie's contribution?

I knelt to brush the grass off the carpet, and then lifted the end of the runner to uncover the bottom step. Elizabeth had kept her earliest diary in the hidey hole constructed in that step. The first diary had revealed the horrific event that dictated the pathway of the rest of her life. I pushed the hidden latch on the step, and the wooden top piece popped up. The hole was not empty.

"Jamie? What are you doing?" Trudy called from above me on the second-floor landing.

"There's something in Elizabeth's hidey hole. Have you been using this secret place, Trudy?" I reached for the packet of envelopes that filled the small space.

"Not me. No sir. I haven't looked in there since I took that book from it, the one my daddy put away for My Liz."

My memory flashed back to the day I'd found the hole in the bottom stair. Cleverly concealed with a trick latch, and covered by the carpet runner, it provided a perfect place to hide something while also keeping it easily accessible. As far as I knew, Trudy and myself were the only living people who knew about the hiding place.

"But there's something here." I pulled the packet out of the hidey hole.

The top letter was addressed to 'SAM.'

Chapter 16

Trudy hurried down the steps, hugging a soft-sided carry-on suitcase. "What is it?" She frowned at the envelopes I had moved from the stairs to my lap.

"Some letters. The top one is addressed to Sam."

"Why are there letters to Sam in the hidey hole?"

"Maybe Elizabeth put them in the step before she died. Or maybe Vera?" I suggested. But why would either one of those women have written to Sam? They saw him several times a week, if not every day.

I pulled off the rubber band that secured the envelopes together and flipped quickly through the bundle. The name on the front of each letter was *Sam.* I untucked the flap of the top envelope and pulled out a folded note. The small, cramped writing slanted downward across the page.

Please, Sam. Please, please listen to me and don't tell me it's not possible. I know her, and I know what she's capable of. She won't want me to have this baby. She's going to do something to harm the baby, or to harm me. I need to see you, face to face. Tonight.

"What does it say, Jamie? Who's it from?" Trudy plunked her suitcase down on the floor.

"The letters are to Sam, maybe from Reba."

"What are they doing here?"

I resisted the impulse to pull open each note, one by one, and read the progression of thoughts that had led to this final one. If the notes were from Reba, they told me three things. She was either paranoid or sensing danger from another woman; she believed her pregnancy was real; and she and Sam were not living together at the time they were written.

"Jamie, what are those letters doing here?" Trudy asked again.

I tucked the note back into the envelope and slid it under the rubber band with the others. "I don't know, Trudy. Maybe Elizabeth put them away?"

Trudy considered the possibility, her mouth twisting as she pressed her lips together. Her eyes widened, and she focused on me. "If they're from Reba, then she brought them here. The ghost brought them here!" Her hand covered her mouth and she looked at the small stack of letters with horror.

"No, Trudy. A ghost didn't bring these. A human did." I inspected the hidey hole in the stairs again. No spider webs, no bugs, no dust. The hole was clean. Whoever had placed the notes there had done so recently. I studied the envelopes. The edges weren't discolored; they didn't look as old as they had to be. But then I wasn't sure what such a note would look like if it had been in a protected place for ten years.

Trudy shivered as she leaned closer. "That ghost put 'em here. And she's been wandering around, wanting someone to find them. Wanting me to find them. She's been on the stairs, trying to show me."

I doubted there had been a ghost on the stairs. But there might have been a person on the stairs. Someone had been coming into the house, someone who knew about the hidey hole. Someone who'd used the hiding place and wanted Trudy to find something she'd placed there.

But that was impossible, I argued with myself. Who outside the immediate family knew about the hidey hole? The only explanation was that Elizabeth had put the notes there before she passed away.

"Trudy, you say you see ghosts. Have you been keeping the doors locked?"

She nodded. "Like you told me to do. I check 'em ever' night before I go to bed." She crossed her arms and frowned at me.

"But do you lock them when you go in and out every day? When you leave the house for any length of time, do you lock the doors?"

"Why should I? If I'm walking Augie Doggie, or going to the store, there's no need, is there?"

"Yes. There's a need. Someone could come in the house anytime you are gone, not only at night."

"Oh." Trudy uncrossed her arms and sighed. "You think someone left the letters while I was at the store, or at Vera's?"

"Maybe."

And then they had waited in the house until dark, and made Trudy think she was seeing ghosts. I patted her hand. This was scary, and Trudy might be in real danger, whether she realized it or not.

"Trudy, when we get home, let's not say anything to Mother about the ghosts in Elizabeth's house. It might upset her." Truthfully, I wasn't worried about Mother being upset, I was worried that what Mother might say would upset Trudy. Mother didn't 'suffer fools,' and Trudy's conviction that the house was haunted would slide her right into that category.

"I wouldn't want to scare her. But you don't have ghosts. Why would she care if I do?" Trudy scratched her head.

I didn't want to answer that. I sneezed again.

Halfway home to Ponca City, my cell phone rang. The Caller ID read: *Ellen.* My sister was calling, and that usually meant there was trouble in her life. At least I didn't have to wonder if something had happened to Mother, since she was in Ponca City with us.

"Hi, Ellen. Everything okay?"

"Harry's had a heart attack. He's in the hospital, and I know I should go see him there. But I can't, Jamie. I can't. He'll think I want him to come home, and I don't. I'm done this time. I really am."

My jaw clenched. I was sure from her loud, emphatic tone that she *was* 'done' this time. Ellen's affection for Harry had been up and down for the past twenty years. I couldn't remember how many times she'd kicked him out and then taken him back in. It made sense that she took him back in, what didn't make sense was why *he* wanted to come home to her.

"How serious is it? Is he in ICU?"

"Yes, but they expect to transfer him to the heart unit tomorrow. I don't want Mom to know. She'll tell me how much he needs me right now and to go visit like a good wife."

"He does need you." The man had stuck with Ellen all these years, despite her OCD and other idiosyncrasies.

"But I can't take it anymore. It's my house, too, and he's constantly wanting to watch his TV programs, or have his friends over, not to mention the snoring and the thrashing at night. I can even hear him from the guest room, Jamie, it's that loud."

"Ever hear of ear plugs?" I asked.

"Don't start. He's the one with the problem. He's the one who should fix it. He never thinks about me. Never considers how his actions and habits affect me."

"Do you consider how your habits affect him?" The words were out before I could stop them. We had circled around this issue for years, but Ellen refused to believe that her relationship with Harry involved give and take on both sides. I knew the only reason they had not divorced was because Harry still loved Ellen and was willing to put up with her occasional rants. So far, it seemed he had been doing all the giving in the relationship, but it wasn't enough.

"Stop! I guess I won't get any understanding from you or Mom."

"She's doing okay, by the way, even though you didn't ask."

"I didn't ask because I have too many things going on here. Besides, she's with you and I'm sure she's fine. You are the responsible one. And you've got Sam."

This conversation was taking the usual track.

"Is there something I can help with, Ellen, or were you only letting me know what had happened to Harry?

I'm actually on the road, driving home from Pawhuska."
I smiled, hoping to put some cheer in my voice. I didn't
want to argue with my sister.

"I thought you would want to know. I guess I was
wrong. Don't tell Mother. I'll call her in a day or two.
Goodbye." The phone went dead.

I glanced in the rearview mirror. Trudy was
following closely in her car. Augie Doggie was probably
in her lap. She was probably scratching his ears and
whispering to him as she drove. Thank God she had the
dog for companionship and comfort.

Chapter 17

"Where have you been?!" Mother shrilled as Trudy and I came into the house through the garage door.

Queenie and Zeus barked and bolted to meet us. Augie's long tail thudded against the wall as the other dogs greeted him.

Mother stood in the center of the hallway, arms crossed, glaring from me to Trudy and then at the dogs.

"Mother, I drove to Pawhuska after work. Trudy had another frightful night last night. I don't think she should stay in that house alone until we've been able to go through it completely and figure out what's happening there."

"What? She's a grown woman. And there are no such things as GHOSTS!" Mother scowled at Trudy and stomped back into the kitchen.

Trudy hung her head. "I knew Cousin Mary wouldn't be glad to see me. No one believes I saw those ghosts. But I swear I did. Augie knows I did." Trudy reached down to pat the dog's head, but Augie and the two other dogs were in a pile on the floor, wrestling.

"Let's take your things to the bedroom, Trudy. Then you can go with the dogs to the backyard. I'll talk to Mother." Trudy followed me down the hallway and past the kitchen.

"Mother, you're not helping," I said, a few minutes later after Trudy had gone out into the backyard with the dogs. "Trudy is frightened. And even though you don't believe she's seeing ghosts, she must be seeing something. This weekend, Sam and I will figure out what's going on. Meanwhile, could you please be nice?"

Mother pulled a casserole out of the oven and eased it down onto a cooling rack. She slipped off the oven mitts and dropped them onto the counter. "I've never been a person to put on a false front, Jamie. You know that. I call it like I see it. And that woman is like she's always been. Nutty as a fruitcake."

I winced. It would do no good to explain to Mother once again that Trudy was different from us, and it was no fault of hers. She was as aware as I was of Trudy's history, the facial deformity caused by forceps during her birth and her difficulty communicating. "I'm not asking you to forego your principles, Mother. I'm asking you to be considerate of her feelings. We're all upset about many things, not to mention that we're all adjusting to change."

She glared at me. "Change? This is more than simple 'change.' I'm adjusting to an entirely new lifestyle. How you and Sam can exist in such an unorganized world I don't know. Everything is loosey-goosey. The phone rings at all hours of the day, cars rumble by and honk, the dogs bark. I can't focus on my reading or my crosswords. There is no peace. And I'm too upset to sleep. I miss my bed, and my room, and my house." She paced the short space between the stove and the island, working herself into a frenzy.

When I reached out to hug her; she shoved my arm away. "Don't try to coddle me. I'm going to my room. Maybe I can find some peace and quiet there." She marched out of the kitchen. "Don't bother me."

I paused at the island, listening to her loud footsteps and then the slamming of her door. We'd been living together in the house less than a week. I wasn't sure it would last a full month before somebody said something unforgiveable.

From the kitchen window, I watched Trudy in the backyard, hunched over on the bench near the trees. All three dogs sat at her feet, listening as she talked, their tails slowly wagging. My cousin had a rapport with animals unlike anyone else I knew. She had a sweet nature, and rarely said a cross word. I didn't understand why my mother refused to cut her any slack.

Something flashed behind the bushes near Trudy. I focused on the spot, expecting another flash. Had it been a reflection? Was someone standing back there, in the alley? If someone was there, the dogs would be having a fit, wouldn't they?

The flash didn't repeat.

I turned away and pulled plates from the cabinets. Trudy and I might as well eat. In the silence of the moment, I thought about the notes to Sam that I had found in the step hidey-hole at Trudy's. What would Sam say when I showed them to him? Had he seen them before? Had he been the one to put them there? If not Sam, or Trudy, who?

It was already 7 p.m., and Sam was not home yet. I expected him to drag in dog-tired like he had last night. He wouldn't want to talk about those notes, and, depending on his mood, I wouldn't want to upset him by bringing them up. It could wait until tomorrow night.

From the shelter of the back hedge, only a few feet away from the woman, the Watcher listens.

She's talking nonsense to those dogs. All about ghosts. *The Watcher smiles.* That part of our plan is working and it's going to get worse, not better. There will be justice of the highest form. Prison for one. And Death for others.

The Watcher's hand covers the Watcher's mouth, but a little laugh escapes. One dog turns his head.

Does he see me? Hear me?

The Watcher's breathing slows, and the figure stands motionless, blending into the shrubs and trees, part of the landscape.

"Trudy? Come on in for supper," Jamie calls.

The Watcher waits until the animals and people are all inside and the door is closed before slipping through the back gate and out into the alley.

Chapter 18

Thursday

After school, I headed down the hallway to the drama classroom in the far west wing of the high school for the weekly meeting of the Drama Club.

Several students were already there, perched on tables and chairs, speaking in low whispers. As I entered the room, conversation stopped, and every student looked at me. Brooklyn lowered her head and mumbled to Zeke, who sat next to her. I smiled at them and made my way to the front of the classroom, where Romy was talking with another student on the small stage.

As I moved toward Romy, her conversation ended, too, and the boy she had been talking to left the stage. He nodded at me, and smirked. Romy frowned.

"Still no news about Caleb, I guess." I leaned against the podium, turning so that I could see the classroom. The students had resumed their conversations, heads down, but several of them had their eyes on me. "Is that what they are all so busy discussing?"

The drama teacher cleared her throat. "Probably, that and the latest gossip." She drew in a deep breath. "It concerns you. You were tutoring Caleb, weren't you? Science or something?"

"Yes. The administration approved the tutoring. What's the problem?" Maggie Dent had given me a heads-up about this. I knew what was coming.

"Word is out that you were among the last, if not THE last, person to speak to him on Sunday. You know how these kids blow everything up. Too many crime dramas on cable. Too many stories of teachers having sex with students." She lifted her eyebrows and stared at me.

"They think Caleb and I were having a relationship?" I was fairly certain that's what most of the school–students and teachers alike–thought.

"He told one of the students that an adult in the play wanted to hook up with him. He didn't say who. The students are filling in the blanks." Romy grinned slyly and raised her eyebrows.

"It wasn't me. And I'm happy to clarify things with this group," I said firmly. "Is this gossip going to be a problem?"

"Not if we don't make it one. Let's go on as if everything is normal." She glanced at the students again and then led me over to her desk, where papers were spread everywhere. "We're working on sets today, and I need your advice. You went out to the Camp. You saw the way we'll stage the production. All sets need to be flat panels that can be moved to the stage using those curtain tunnels they plan to set up. Explain that to the kids. We'll get some ideas about what we need to build, and what props you need to find that aren't already on your list. Got it?"

"Business as usual."

Romy turned to face the students and cleared her throat. "Okay, let's get started. Lots of work to get done in our two-hour slot today. Gather round the tables."

After I'd explained the staging at Wentz Camp, we read through the play, discussing scene changes and props. Other than a few curious glances from a few of the boys, the students seemed focused on the tasks.

As the students gathered their belongings two hours later, I jumped into the fire.

"Before we adjourn today, I want to address a rumor. I was tutoring Caleb in Science. We've been working together in my classroom once a week for about a month. Our relationship was strictly that of student and teacher. You can help me by refusing to listen to, or pass on, any false rumors you hear. If you have any questions, ask them now."

The students looked at one another, and I saw some eye rolls, winks and shrugs. One student smirked; I called on him.

"Jessie, is there something you'd like to say? I'm all ears."

His mouth dropped open. "Um, no, Mrs. Mazie. I believe you, but I'm pretty sure Caleb wasn't kidding when he said an adult wanted to hook up with him. He didn't lie about stuff."

Other students, including Zeke and Brooklyn, nodded.

"If there was someone from the cast who was trying to do that, the police will find out. Meanwhile, if you can help the police in any way with information about Caleb, please call them. I'll see you all tomorrow."

If another adult in the cast had made an overture to Caleb, it had to be someone from the community playhouse group. Who?

Chapter 19

A nondescript, dark sedan sat in my driveway when I returned home after the drama club meeting. On the front porch, Chase Longhorn stood talking to Sam. If their conversation was about Reba's disinterment, which it most likely was, I didn't want to disrupt them. Sam would want privacy. He would tell me what had been said when he was ready.

I pushed the garage door opener as I turned into the driveway and pulled into the garage. When I opened the backdoor, an undercurrent of cinnamon wafted through the air along with the scent of bread baking.

A cabinet door slammed in the kitchen and a pan clattered to the floor. Outside, on the back porch, a cat yowled. I peeked through the laundry room window. Trudy sat, head in her hands, on the bench under the arbor. All three bassets were stretched out at her feet. No sign of the yowling cat.

Mother pitched her pot holder into the sink as I came into the kitchen. "This – isn't – working. These animals. And that Trudy. There is no quiet. There is no peace. I can't think. How you expect me to function in this environment, I don't know."

I glanced around the kitchen, ready to clean up a mess or wash any dishes she'd dirtied in the process of cooking, but there was nothing for me to do. The room was spotless. "Has something happened?"

"Happened? The whole day 'happened.' I'm literally at my wits end. I can't even think to start supper. I've made a cobbler, that doesn't require following a recipe ... But if you expect me to have supper on the table by 6 o'clock ..." she glanced at the wall clock and I followed her look. 5:45.

"I'm not expecting anything fantastic, Mother. If you could tell me something specific that has you upset, maybe I can deal with it. And supper doesn't have to be at 6. Really, if you'd rather not cook, we can always go out."

She glared at me. "That's not the point. You've got to do something about – THEM!" She jerked her chin toward the window, and the backyard beyond.

"I know you didn't expect us to have company so soon after moving in, but Trudy needed to get away from Pawhuska. The dog is part of the deal."

"Trudy is seeing ghosts. She believes in the spirit realm. A spiritualist under my roof. I can't live with that, Jamie."

"Mother, she's not a spiritualist. But she is sensitive. I think someone's scaring her intentionally, and Sam and I have got to find out who is sneaking into the house, and why. It's been a busy week and we haven't had a chance to talk with her yet. We'll go back to Pawhuska with her on Saturday and get to the bottom of things. Can you handle it for one more day?"

Mother placed her hands on her cheeks and closed her eyes. Her lips moved but she didn't say anything. Was she praying?

"It will be all right soon. I promise." I crossed the room and patted her stiff shoulder, then grabbed a glass and went to the refrigerator's water spigot. "I saw Sam on the porch. Have you talked to him?"

She opened her eyes and dropped her hands, as she turned back to the stove. She pushed the pilot for the front left gas burner and the gas jets roared. "I heard a car, and expected him to come in, but he didn't."

"He's on the front porch. Chase Longhorn is with him."

"That detective? What does he want? The whole thing is ridiculous. Disinterring Reba Mazie because of the word of a convicted felon. They won't find anything, and they'll have spent taxpayer money for nothing."

She pulled the cutting board from a lower cabinet and set about chopping carrots.

"So, you don't want to go out to eat? What are you going to make?" I asked from the safety of the other side of the island.

"A chicken dish. Breasts with vegetables and mashed potatoes. Cobbler for dessert. It's baking now."

"I smelled it when I came in. Sounds delicious."

"Maybe. I was so distracted when I made it, I may have left something crucial out. I've never cooked under such conditions before."

If she meant conditions like having another adult around and a few dogs in the backyard by 'conditions,' I didn't know why that would affect stirring a few ingredients together to make a cobbler. But then, what did I know about cooking? My experience was limited. And I certainly didn't understand my mother's moods.

"Go on now, Jamie. You better see what that detective wants. He and Sam could be arguing. Go referee."

I headed for the front door, expecting to hear raised voices if an argument was in progress. Instead, all was quiet. When I opened the door, Sam was standing alone, and Chase Longhorn was climbing into his car at the curb.

Sam's face was pale; his dark eyes were deep and unreadable.

"Honey? What did Longhorn want?" I asked, clasping his hand.

"They exhumed Reba. Yesterday."

"I thought that was what they might be doing when I drove past the cemetery on my way to Trudy."

He squinted at me. "Why didn't you say anything last night?"

I shrugged. "I wasn't certain."

He pulled his hand from mine and ran his fingers through his hair. "I can't believe they've done this. I can't believe they think her death was anything other than suicide."

"They won't find anything, Sam. And it won't make any different what anybody says. If there's no proof, no evidence, there's no murder."

"I wish it was that simple."

"You mean it's not?"

"They would have to prove me guilty to send me to jail. But there's also the court of public opinion, Jamie. I'm already being judged there. Two of my appointments cancelled today. One from Fairfax and another from Shidler."

"You're telling me that people have judged you and think you're guilty? But they know you. And if you've known them a long time, they knew Reba. They would remember, wouldn't they?"

"It's not that simple. You don't know everything about me." He faced the street, staring across at the red maple tree where a gusty evening wind was whipping the leaves.

"Of course, I don't. And you don't know everything about me. But, specifically, what should I know, Sam? What would make these people turn on you so quickly?"

He looked up at the evening sky, where wisps of cloud tinged with pink raced across the blue. "Before law school, I drank too much. People remember."

Something stirred in my memory, and a voice with an intense Southern drawl, scoffed in a stage whisper, 'he sure gets ugly when he's sauced.' It had happened nine years ago, in my great aunt's house, where friends had gathered while she was in the hospital in a coma. That night, I'd wondered about what Pawhuska Mayor Martin Wells had said. He had tried to insult Sam, but Sam had stayed cool and been kind to me. I was already a little bit in love with his dark looks and his solemn manner. I'd dismissed the words and not thought of them since.

"You were young. It takes time to find yourself." My brain wondered, *what did he do?*

"You know it was worse than that. I am an alcoholic. Once an alcoholic, always an alcoholic."

I threw my arms around him and hugged him. He faced me, and, for a moment, he laid his head on my shoulder. Then, he inhaled deeply and straightened. He peered into my eyes. A spark glowed. "I can't imagine losing you. Especially for something I did when I was much, much younger."

"Key words. Much, much younger. I'm sure hoping you never get wind of some of the things I did in my wilder youth." A series of quick memories flashed past, mostly from the years when I dated—and then married—my first husband, Rob. Much of my twenties, before I had my children, included some crazy parties and stunts urged on by my free-spirited mate. "I love you, Sam. I'll stand with you, no matter what people say. I *know* you."

"You do, Jamie. As much as anyone lets anyone know them. Thank God there are no mind readers." He closed his eyes. "Longhorn came to tell me that the forensic examiners with the FBI at the University of Central Oklahoma in Edmond are examining the remains. He promised to keep me updated."

"That's reassuring, isn't it?"

He nodded slowly. "He also wanted to ask me about something they found in the coffin." His lips pressed together in an anguished look, and his eyes were wet.

"What?" My mind raced.

"My wedding ring."

My front teeth bit into my lip. I thought about the necklace I'd worn for many years, Ben's wedding band on a silver chain. I'd cherished that ring. Even now, it was in my jewelry box upstairs, one of my fondest possessions. "Did you put the ring there?"

"Yes."

I had an idea of why, considering Reba's mental state, and the fact that she had lied to him about the baby and then decided to end her life. But I needed him to tell me. I looked up at him, quizzically. "Why?"

"Many reasons. She was dead. And our marriage, in my mind, was dead. Her deceptions had killed it long before she killed herself. The fact that there was no baby, when it had given me hope that our marriage might heal and be whole again, was too much. I put my wedding band inside the coffin as a finality. The Reba I knew and loved had been dead to me for a long time, if she ever really existed. Her body died, too. Why keep the ring?"

His face drooped. My husband was exhausted. He hadn't been sleeping; he would leave our bed to wander the house. I assumed he was sleeping on the sofa, where his restless tossing wouldn't bother me, but it was also likely that he paced the living room until his body wore out and he collapsed into the recliner.

I hugged him again. "Who could blame you? I had no idea, Sam, that things were so far gone between you and Reba." I had wondered a few times why Sam had no communication with Reba's family, but I had assumed that because there were no children of that marriage, the family had not kept in touch. Once again, I hadn't asked.

Sam closed his eyes. "These past few years with you, I realized that what drew me to her in the first place was that she reminded me of you—my 'lost love' from childhood."

We'd spoken of this so many times, of the summer weeks we spent together in Pawhuska while I was growing up. Aunt Elizabeth had gathered playmates for me and my siblings and Sam was included in the group as well as Trudy, Vera and Toby Green.

"Like you, she loved butterflies. But her chrysalis shriveled before she grew wings. She never flew. And in the end, she hung from the garage rafters." He opened his eyes, but they were unfocused and dark with sadness.

I shivered at the image Sam had painted: Reba, an undeveloped butterfly. Her life had held promise. Sam had seen it, believed in it. But she was unable to grasp her future and was unable to take wing. It was overwhelmingly dreadful.

I needed to shake off the feeling. "I think I'll take the dogs for a walk. Mother's fixing supper. Do you want to go with me?"

Sam shook his head. "I need time alone, to think."

He kissed me quickly. I left him there and went inside the house to get the dogs.

The Watcher lowers the automatic car window three inches and stares at the house. Inside, lights come on. Drapes are closed. A glow from the television in the front living room flickers.

The front door opens. Jamie emerges, holding several leashes. Three Basset hounds pull her forward, eagerly sniffing the ground, the bushes and the sidewalk.

The Watcher considers the dog breed. **Not particularly protective. Scent hounds. Hard to train. Independent. What were the chances that if a stranger approached the group as they walked down the sidewalk of the tree-lined street, the animals would rescue their owner?**

If there was only one dog, perhaps a 50-50 chance that the animal would react. But with three of them, would they have more interest, and more courage? Would they react to Jamie's fear once she realizes the danger?

Too many unknowns.

The Watcher waits until Jamie and the dogs disappear around the corner a block away, and then turns the car around and drives slowly down the wide street through the neighborhood.

There will be another opportunity. Soon.

Chapter 20

By the time I returned home with the dogs, the muscles of my arms hurt from grasping the leashes to keep the hounds in check; my ankle throbbed. There was nothing like hanging on to three dogs that wanted to sniff in four different directions. Halfway through the walk, I had promised myself I would never do it again.

I had no one to blame but myself. I'd wanted to give Trudy time alone with Sam. She wanted to tell him about Reba's ghost. When that conversation was over, I would tell Sam about the letters I had found. Hopefully, he would tell me what they said, and shed some light on why they had been hidden in the stair's hidey hole.

I keyed in the alarm code on the panel beside the garage door and punched it in again by the backdoor before the dogs and I went inside. Ever since the robbery and murder at the gas station two miles away, I'd been thinking about home security. Mother was here by herself much of the day, and I would never forgive myself if someone committed a home invasion while we were gone.

She'd complained about the security system for the first few days. She was nervous about turning it off if she wanted to go out into the backyard. She was nervous about turning it on when she came back inside the house. What if she punched in the wrong code and accidentally summoned the police or the fire department? Would she be fined? I assured her that both departments were probably used to false alarms from home security systems. The security firm itself would call first, before sending the fire department or police.

As I came into the house, the television blared in the living room. I peeked through the doorway into an empty room, and then strolled into the kitchen. The hot casserole dish rested covered on the stove; place settings were on the table. I listened for telltale sounds that would reveal where the members of my family had gone, but the only sounds came from the television and the clicks of the dogs' toenails as they followed me through the house.

I stepped out onto the back porch. The dogs raced across the yard to the metal bench beneath the spreading limbs of an old oak tree where Trudy and Sam sat. As I moved towards them, Trudy frowned, her eyes dark in a white face, tears running down her cheeks. Sam shook his head.

"What's wrong?" I asked.

Sam stood. "These ghosts that Trudy is seeing. I don't believe it. Even if I did believe that spirits were haunting the house, Reba would have no reason to be there. She never visited Elizabeth's home. Not with me, and not by herself."

"I'm not lying to you, Sam. You've got to believe me." Trudy pleaded, lifting her hands toward Sam.

"Trudy, I believe you feel Elizabeth's presence in the house. It is possible. But all these other ghosts, these men you are seeing ... it's too much."

"But won't you help me get rid of them? Can your medicine man come and talk to them?"

"If I'm not convinced that these spirits are having a mass haunting at your home, how will the shaman be convinced?"

"Sam, can you talk to your mother? Maybe she will convince the–uh–shaman to chase away the evil spirits."

"I refuse to believe you are being visited by Reba's ghost." Anger filled his dark eyes.

I laid one hand on Sam's arm. "Trudy, let me talk to Sam for a minute. I haven't told him about the letters. Maybe that will make a difference."

"Please, Jamie. Tell him now."

"What letters?" Sam rubbed the back of his neck and sighed.

"Remember that hidey hole in the lowest step of Elizabeth's front stairs? Where we found her first diary?"

"Yes. Was she using it again before she died?"

"Someone was. When I went to get Trudy last night, I noticed the carpet runner was unraveling near the bottom of the stairs. I pulled the carpet up and checked the hidey hole. I found a packet of letters, addressed to you."

"Where are these letters?"

"In my school bag. I'll get them." I dashed inside to the kitchen and grabbed my satchel from the kitchen island. When I returned, Sam was pacing the yard and Trudy remained slumped on the bench. Evening shadows were deepening. I held out the packet of letters, bound together by the red ribbon.

Sam took them and pulled out the top one. "You found these at Elizabeth's, in the stairs?"

"Yes."

"Did you read them?"

"No."

He flipped through the stack, and then pulled the letter out of the top envelope, tucking the remaining envelopes between his left arm and his body. As he read what had been written, his face blanched and his eyes widened. He stuffed the page back into the envelope and opened the second one, read it, then opened the third. The pages and empty envelopes fluttered to the ground.

"My God," he breathed. He continued to open the letters, dropping each one as he finished reading it. The last letter dropped to the lawn.

"Sam? Who are they from? What did they say?" I asked, although I suspected they were all from Reba.

"My God," he repeated. He slowly moved to the bench and eased down next to Trudy.

"Sam? What's wrong?" I asked.

He shook his head and closed his eyes.

"What did the letters say?" Trudy asked.

"I have never seen those letters before," Sam mumbled.

I stepped over to the bench and rested my hand on his shoulder. "Who were they from? And how do you think they got in Elizabeth's house?"

He rubbed the palms of his hands on his jeans and straightened, blowing air out and then sucking in a deep breath. "The letters are from Reba. It's her handwriting."

I remembered the text of the first note, the only one I had allowed myself to read. *Please, Sam. Please listen to me and don't tell me it's not possible. I know her, and I know what she's capable of. She won't want me to have this baby. She's going to do something to harm the baby, or to harm me. I need to see you, face to face. Tonight.*

"The two of you weren't living together at the end?" I wanted to know this most of all, but I wasn't sure why.

"No. She'd moved in with her sister, and that arrangement wasn't going well. I thought her sister was feeding her paranoia, certainly someone was. Here's the proof. Maybe someone did kill her or have her killed."

"We need to give these to Detective Longhorn."

Sam leapt up from the bench. "No. Not yet." He bent down and gathered up the letters and envelopes.

"But in the last note, she's afraid of someone. It's not you. She wants to see you." I retrieved one of the notes that the wind had carried a few feet away.

He nodded. "Yes, and that's what the police will see. She wanted to meet with me. She came to my house and killed herself in the garage of the place where we had lived together. And maybe the police will think I paid someone to make it look like a suicide."

"Reba left these notes," Trudy wailed. "I told you she did. Do you believe me now?"

"Oh, Trudy. Give Sam a minute to think." I stood next to my husband. "If you've never seen these notes before, where have they been for the past nine years? And who put them in Elizabeth's house?"

"That's what I need to figure out before I can give them to Chase Longhorn."

I chewed at my lip. "You said Reba lived with her sister. What about the sister? Is she still around? You thought she was provoking Reba's mental problems?"

"I didn't want to believe it at the time. Reba and Sharon, her sister, hadn't gotten along for several years. I was surprised when she left our home and went to live with her sister."

"Where is Sharon now?"

Sam shrugged. "I haven't been in touch with any of her family. Haven't seen or heard anything about Sharon since Reba died." He pulled in a deep breath and tossed his head to flip his hair out of his face.

I fixated on Sharon. Why would this sister want to break into Elizabeth's house and frighten Trudy, pretending to be Reba? It made more sense that the intruder was Bosque, but why would he bring the letters, and know where to hide them?

Sam stared up at a jet contrail that had caught the last bit of sunlight from the sinking sun, leaving a silver streak across the darkening sky. "They didn't look alike. Reba had dark hair, Sharon was a blonde. Reba was tall and thin, Sharon was several inches shorter and on the plump side. They even talked differently, Reba laughed easily, and was rarely serious until the later years, but every time I saw Sharon she was sulking." Sam dropped his look to the ground. "I can't imagine that she had anything to do with these notes. I doubt Sharon was the person Reba wrote about."

"Who else could it have been? What other women could have been influencing her?"

"Her mother, certainly, but she would never have provoked Reba. She was concerned about her, and supportive of our marriage."

"What about a friend? Someone she trusted?"

"There's no one else. She didn't have a lot of girlfriends, only acquaintances from school or work. I can't think of anyone who might have even had access to those notes, not to mention leaving them in your aunt's house."

Trudy wailed. "It was Reba! I know it was. Why don't you believe me?" She stood up, stomped one foot and charged off to the house. Augie Doggie raced after her. Once she and the dog were inside, she slammed the door.

"I don't blame her for being upset. You could have humored her a little." I patted Sam's shoulder. "She's upset."

"I'm not going to humor her about ghosts. It's her imagination, and we only encourage her by telling her that it's okay for Elizabeth to be haunting the place. And this idea she has that Reba's ghost left these notes ... it's impossible. I'm not sure I can believe anything Trudy says anymore. And I wish you wouldn't either." Sam scowled.

He was far more upset than I thought he should be. "She asked you to talk to your mother. Will you?"

"I won't pull my mother into this. She believes in the Ancestors, spirit guides that help our people. She will encourage Trudy, not push her to accept reality." He sat down on the bench.

I sat beside him. "We're at an impasse, then. What's our next step?" Queenie settled on the lawn at our feet while Zeus rolled over on his back and thrashed in the grass.

"Maybe it would be good for me to contact Reba's family. See if I can find out who she was close to before she died."

"Do you know where they live?"

"Ever heard of Google? If they are on the social internet sites, I'll find them. And if they aren't, I can check property and tax records and pin down where they live. I should have some answers by early next week if I put a friend of mine on it. He's the closest thing I know personally to a private eye."

In the kitchen, Mother was dishing up her plate. The chicken dish steamed, and the aroma of herbs and butter filled the kitchen.

"Trudy! Supper is ready," I called. The living room television was on, and I suspected that Trudy and the dogs were camped out in there, watching the news.

"I'll be eating in my room again. It's peaceful there," Mother announced. She grabbed silverware and a napkin after buttering a slice of bread.

I sighed. "Mother ..."

"What? Aren't I entitled to some peace? It's the least you can allow me." She tramped out of the room before Trudy and the dogs could arrive from the living room.

"What's with your mother?" Sam asked.

"She wants peace. She's not finding it living here," I said. I dished the food onto my plate and carried it into the dining room, where I waited for Sam and Trudy to join me.

Outside, in the white Honda, the Watcher sits, watching the windows of the house across the street. Lights come on in the front bedroom, while three people have gathered around the table in the dining room.

The Watcher's fingers tap nervously on the steering wheel.

So, the woman comes running back to Sam and his wife. I didn't expect that. It throws the plan off another day or two, at least until she gets back to the old house.

The Watcher unwraps a candy bar, and eats it in three big bites, chewing loudly, and following the treat with a swallow of diet cola from the convenience store.

I want it to be over, *the Watcher shouts into the empty car.* Sam has lived his perfect life long enough.

Chapter 21

Friday

When I woke at 5 a.m., the other side of the bed was empty. Queenie's bed in the corner was also empty, as was Zeus' bed beside hers. Sam was either already up, or he'd never been to bed. I didn't remember him sliding in between the sheets, only that he'd been in the family room at his desk, reading some documents, when I called it a day about 11 p.m.

I pulled on my robe and went to search for him. The house was quiet and dark except for a soft blue light coming from the coffee maker in the kitchen. I peered out the window over the kitchen sink. The streetlight two houses down cast tree shadows over most of the yard.

I stepped out the back door and onto the patio. Chill air sent a shiver down my back, and I pulled the sides of my robe closer together. Damp air held a hint of fall, that odd mixture of growth and decay, moisture and dryness, that was exclusively autumn.

"Woof!" Queenie trotted over to me from the glider, where Sam was stretched out with a pillow under his head. He lifted one hand and gave a little wave.

"Morning. Did you sleep out here?" I picked my way around the plant-filled pots and furniture that no one had yet organized to create a friendly backyard space.

"Hmmm." Sam's low voice answered.

"Was that a yes or a no?"

"I didn't really sleep. But it's nice out here. A little breeze. Reminds me of home. My brother and I used to sleep outside most of the year."

"You've never mentioned that before. And not that much about your brother." Sam, however, knew all about my siblings, the ins and outs of Ellen's marriage, the struggles with Randy's PTSD and mental disabilities. Once again, I was reminded of how little I knew about some of my husband's relationships.

I lifted his outstretched legs and scooted under them to sit on the end of the glider. "Tell me about him."

His brother had come to our wedding at Osage Hills State Park, along with two dozen other relatives, most of whom I had seen again at various holidays over the past years. His family was scattered throughout northeastern Oklahoma and southeastern Kansas, but a few of them, like his brother Lucas, had moved to northwestern Missouri, the original tribal lands of the Osage Nation.

The biggest memory I had of Lucas at the wedding was the wide smile on his face. He'd slapped his younger brother on the back more times than I could count and grinned at me. Their family resemblance was evident, the same dark hair, expressive brown eyes, and intelligence. But he was five years older, six inches taller, and a hundred pounds heavier. From what I'd read of historic Osage warriors, Lucas had the build of his warring ancestors.

Sam rubbed my hand. "You know about sisters. You and Ellen. So, you can guess about Lucas and me." He paused, and I studied his brown eyes.

"Go on. I know about siblings."

"We fought each other as hard as we played together. Everything was a competition, fishing, hunting, whatever. He was always bigger, heavier. But I could hold my own. My dad said I was a 'scrapper.'" A little grin lifted the edges of his mouth. "I was a high school sophomore when he enlisted. But you know all about that."

"You told me before we got married. I think you wanted me to be prepared when we met at the wedding. I remember you told me that he came home changed. I think all soldiers do."

"He came home and didn't care much about anyone but his Army buddies."

"But he got married. And he's still married, unless you've been keeping something from me."

"I went to his wedding and he came to mine. I don't know much about him now."

Light poured into the yard from the kitchen window, and seconds later the back door opened. "What are you two doing sitting out here in the damp dawn? You'll catch cold," Mother scolded.

"We're grownups. If we want to sit outside on our porch and watch the sun come up, we can. I'm not worried about catching a cold." I wrapped my robe tighter around me.

"You should be. The older you get the easier it is to get sick. Immune systems disintegrate. I read about it." Mother stood stiffly in the doorway, one hand holding the door, the other on her hip.

Sam, always the diplomat, changed the course of the conversation when he said, "It's a beautiful morning, Mary. You should grab a cup of coffee and join us."

"I'm not dressed for it." She pulled back into the house and shut the door, but not before Augie Doggie had wiggled his way through it, dashed across the porch and tried unsuccessfully to leap up on the glider with us.

I reached for the puppy, grabbing his solid body and lifting him onto my lap. Was Trudy up? If she was, she'd soon join us on the porch. I didn't expect Mother to encourage her to linger in the kitchen.

"Look," Sam said. He pointed at a beautiful black and yellow caterpillar, inching its way across the patio.

"It's a monarch caterpillar." I bent over the dog to watch the insect make its way toward the closest boxwood. "There must be some milkweed in the yard somewhere. Did you know that's the only thing that it eats?"

Sam nodded. "I heard that on the news not long ago. It's almost time for the annual migration, isn't it? Happens in September?"

"Yes. I've scheduled lessons on the monarch butterfly in my general science class. If people were more aware of how important butterflies are to pollinating plants of all kinds, and how rapidly they are disappearing, I'm sure they would appreciate them more. I don't know anyone who doesn't enjoy seeing butterflies."

"But not like you do, Jamie." He smiled sadly, and I knew he was thinking about Reba's love of butterflies, as well as mine.

I was a butterfly fanatic. I'd been known to stop the car and pull off the road when I spotted monarch butterflies flying south in the early autumn months. A few years ago, in early October, I literally stopped traffic in Pawhuska when a large flight of butterflies flitted their way through town.

"One good thing about buying a house with an already established yard is that the former residents have usually planted bushes and trees. Landscaping makes such a difference, especially if it's done with wildlife in mind." I gazed around the yard. The sun was nearing the horizon, and the outlines of the bushes and trees had come into focus.

"You're preaching to the choir, Jamie. I have no doubt that you'll be headed out to the local landscape nurseries before long to fill in whatever gaps in animal habitat you find around our yard."

"You know me well." I placed the pup on the ground and rose from the glider, suddenly intent on finding the milkweed and the butterfly bushes that this insect would feed upon as a caterpillar and drink from as an adult. The caterpillar was only days away from spinning its own chrysalis, where, in two or three weeks, it would quickly develop its wings in preparation for its annual flight to Mexico.

Behind us, the kitchen door creaked open. Trudy stepped outside.

"Is my Augie out here with you?" she peered into the semi-darkness. Augie 'woofed' at her and raced to dance around Trudy as she crossed the porch.

"Morning, Trudy. You're up early." I rested my arm on the back of the glider to make more room for the three of us.

"Can't sleep. I keep thinkin' 'bout those ghosts in my house. Are we going to make them leave tomorrow?" She stroked Augie and the dog grunted with pleasure.

Sam nodded. "Yes, Trudy. We'll go to your house tomorrow and check things out. I'll change the locks. You're going to have to remember to lock the doors whenever you leave, even if you're only walking Augie around the block." Sam reached across me to pat her leg for emphasis.

"We should call Vera and have her meet us there. She'll need a new key," I added.

"Will your mother come, Sam? Will she talk to the ghosts?"

"Trudy, I will talk to her about it. But I can't decide that for her."

"You promise to talk to her?" She glimpsed the horizon, where an orange glow signaled the imminent rise of the sun.

Dishes clanged inside the house. Mother had started breakfast.

"I'm off to the shower," Sam said. He pushed up from the glider, then bent and kissed the top of my head before going inside.

A mockingbird sang nearby, and a crow flapped overhead, cawing as it flew.

"Jamie, I want to go back to my house, but I'm scared. I wish you and Queenie and Zeus could stay with me."

I thought about that. Queenie might add an extra layer of protection. Her keen ears always alerted me to visitors before they knocked or rang the doorbell. And she would warn Trudy if someone had entered the house.

On the other hand, so could an alarm system. I made a mental note to talk to Sam about the addition of a security system to Trudy's house. Would Trudy remember to turn the alarm system off and on as she came and went during the day? If she couldn't remember to lock the door, how would she remember to turn the alarm on? Too many false alarms and the system would be useless in the face of a real emergency.

Chapter 22

Soon after I arrived in my classroom Friday morning, Romy Vaughn pushed the door open and stormed in. "Did you hear the news?" she asked in a high, breathless voice.

"I guess not. What?"

"The police found Rusty Clement, the playwright. Hit and run. He's dead." Romy's voice broke and she covered her face.

"Wha-at?" I came around the lab table from the storage cabinet to stand beside Romy.

"Rusty jogs every morning. One of his neighbors found him in the street. I can't believe it."

"Neither can I." My thoughts raced. I recalled my own narrow escape with a car days ago. "That's so awful."

"Yesterday he told me he was going to rewrite the play's ending, and that it might alarm some people in the community," she said in a shaky voice.

"How so?" Rusty had told me about the new ending at rehearsal, but not what the results would be. Now, we'd never have that conversation. He was dead. Numbness settled over me.

"He had a theory about the crash at the final Ponca Grand Prix race. You know, the race car driver that died was his brother. Writing this play was his way to go public with what happened–or what he *thought* might have happened that day."

"Did he tell the police his theory?" So, this was Rusty's real intent in writing this play, to reveal his theory about his brother's death.

"Nobody put much stock in it. He was a minor and he'd been drinking beer."

"Did he see something?"

"He told me his brother was infatuated with a girl. He said I'd have to wait to read the play, and that he'd send me a rough draft." She pushed her graying hair off her face and rubbed one finger under her eye where her eye liner had smeared.

"Did he send it?"

Romy blinked. "I don't know if he meant email or postal service. I haven't gotten anything. I heard the news on the radio on my way here."

"When you get the draft, Romy, send it to the police. If it names a possible suspect, that might be a lead as to who wanted Rusty dead."

Romy stared vacantly out the window. Suddenly, she rushed from the room.

After the last class period of the day, I waited in my classroom the required thirty minutes in case any student wanted to discuss an assignment with me. My head buzzed. How could so much go wrong at one time? Two murders and a disappearance, not to mention Sam dealing with Reba's disinterment. And I was at the center of two nasty rumors.

When thirty minutes had passed, I drove to the Target store, needing the distraction of shopping. I'd promised Sam after breakfast that I would get new locksets for Trudy's house. Three for outside doors, and one for Trudy's bedroom. She would feel much safer if she could lock the door. And hopefully, it would keep the 'ghosts' out. If it didn't keep them out, we had a bigger problem with Trudy's imagination than I believed.

I pulled into a parking space, grabbed my cloth bags out of the back seat, and headed for the store. All I could think about was Rusty Clement. The local radio station had been running clips about his death, but so far, no witnesses had come forward. The car that ran him down had left no skid marks, making it appear the incident was intentional. His death had been classified as vehicular homicide.

Someone fell into step beside me as I walked toward the store.

"Hi, Jamie. I guess you heard the news about Rusty. The play's off. I'm so bummed," groaned Belina, the blonde vixen in the play.

"I can't believe it." All day, I'd been waiting to hear from Romy about the script. If Rusty had sent it, there could be clues in the final scenes. And if he hadn't sent it, the information might be on his computer. Surely, the police would check the computer once Romy had told them Rusty's intent to write the possible true-crime ending of the play.

"Do you think they'll come up with another fundraiser for the drama students? Another play we can do jointly?" Belina asked.

I shrugged. "I'm more concerned about Rusty's death, and how my students are going to deal with this. Drama class doesn't meet on Fridays. Add this to Harwell's murder and Caleb's disappearance, and it seems like we might have a serial killer on the loose."

Belina stopped. "You really think so? You think that kid was kidnapped, and those two guys were killed because of the play?" Her eyes widened.

"What other connection is there? I heard Rusty was writing a new ending to the play. He was going to accuse someone of his brother's death in that Grand Prix race. And Davis Harwell, the shop teacher, had been at that race, in his brother's pit crew. The two of them were more than collaborators on the play."

Belina didn't respond. Eyes downcast, she trudged beside me, her mouth in a determined line. "It's coincidence, that's all. I don't believe it's anything more."

We pushed through the doors and into the entry area adjacent to checkout. Belina stopped. "Well, guess I won't see you again. Unless the high school does another joint production with the Playhouse. Good luck." She hurried toward the interior of the store.

I stared after her. At the rehearsal, she'd been friendly, almost pushy. She seemed to want to be friends. Today her reaction was 180 degrees off.

I didn't look closely at the mail after I scooped the envelopes and circulars out of the curbside mailbox when I got home. Inside, Mother stood waiting in the hallway. I braced myself for another tirade like last night's.

I'd already picked up that she spent most of her days in the recliner in the living room, watching out the front picture window. She had a clear view across the street at the neighbor's side-by-side driveways and knew when they left their homes. And she'd already memorized the types and colors of cars that belonged to families on our block.

Mother's behavior reminded me of Mildred, my neighbor in Las Vegas, New Mexico, who had kept a running journal of every vehicle that traveled the street in front of our houses for many years. She'd been a big part of my life there; it was hard to believe that she had died right in front of me, in a horrific conclusion to the mystery of my husband Ben's death. I didn't like thinking about Mildred.

With Mother tapping her foot, relaying information about the neighbor's comings and goings that I didn't care to hear, I dropped the mail, my purse and work satchel on the kitchen island and started for the bedroom to change into comfort clothes.

"Doesn't that strike you as strange? The same car passing here five times?" Mother followed me down the hallway. "And that's only the times I was looking out the window. No telling how many other times they drove by."

"We live on a busy street, Mother. The side streets in this neighborhood all feed into our street. People drive by. Going to work, coming home for lunch, going back to work ... Do you really think we are under surveillance? Is that what you're worried about?"

"I wouldn't have taken notice if they didn't slow wa-a-ay down, like they were looking to see if someone was home," she huffed.

"Man or woman driving?"

"Who can tell these days? I think they had one of those hoodies on. That's suspicious, I think."

"Everyone wears hoodies, and if I remember, the morning was cool."

"Well, I think it's suspicious." She stopped in front of her bedroom door, arms crossed.

"Where's Trudy, Mother? Have you been nice to her today?"

"She was here earlier. Made a sandwich for lunch. Said something about going to the library. Was her car on the driveway?"

"No. She's been gone quite a while, then."

Mother shrugged. "At least she's not talking about ghosts. She'll come back when she's hungry." She stepped into her room and closed the door.

"I'm going to walk the dogs," I called. They could use the exercise, and so could I. At the word, 'dogs,' dog toe-nails sounded on the hardwood floor of the hallway. All three of the animals followed me and waited at the bedroom door, wagging their tails as I changed into sweatpants and an old football jersey.

An hour later, I was washing my hands in the hall bathroom when the backdoor slammed and Sam called, "Did you grab the mail, honey?"

"It's on the island," I hollered back.

When I entered the kitchen, Sam stood at the island, an open letter in his hands. He placed the letter on the island and looked up at me.

"Bad news?" My mind raced through possibilities, like overdue bills.

Sam wiped the palms of his hands on his jeans. "There's going to be an inquest. They want me to testify."

I sucked in a breath. I had hoped that Reba's disinterment would provide results consistent with suicide. Did this mean that it didn't? "When?"

"Next week. In Oklahoma City."

"So soon? Do you need an attorney?"

"Don't you think I'm capable of defending myself?" He snapped.

"It's not that." I closed my eyes and shook my head. I'd never seen him so tense. "You're too close to this. You need some advice, and someone to be there with you."

"After all this time, I can't believe ..." His voice dropped off. "And based on the word of a criminal. How can they put this much weight on anything that Bosque says?"

Sam's words struck me. If evidence showed that Reba had been murdered, wouldn't he want to know who did it and why? I moved to the refrigerator and pulled out a bottle of water, stewing on Sam's comments. Could anybody attend an inquest? I should be there.

Sam stomped out of the kitchen. Questions crowded my mind, but Sam didn't want to talk about it.

The dogs barked in the backyard. Trudy's car had been parked in front of the house when we returned from our walk, and the dogs had been eager to go to the backyard when I released them from their leashes. They were probably playing catch with Trudy now.

Princess leaped up onto the island. "No, cat." I gathered her up and set her on the floor. She flicked her tail and slunk across the room and under the table.

I wasn't in the mood for conversation. It seemed that no one in the family wanted to talk to each other. The dogs were the only beings who wanted to interact.

Chapter 23

Standing by the kitchen window watching Trudy and the dogs, I sipped my water and watched yellow leaves flutter down from my neighbor's cottonwood.

The dryer rumbled in the laundry room. Mother had taken over one of my least-favorite household chores–laundry. She actually liked to iron and fold clothes. She called it 'creating order out of chaos.' It was hard for me to imagine anyone enjoying that chore.

Princess padded out from under the table and circled my legs, leaning against them and purring loudly. I stooped to stroke the cat's long, silky fur, and she stared up with huge green eyes and meowed.

"I haven't seen you much this week," I told her. My independent feline spent a lot of time off to herself, sitting in a sunny window, curled up on the top level of her carpeted tree house, or roaming the rooms, watching Mother and Trudy from a distance. Very unlike the dogs which were constantly underfoot, eager for human contact.

I picked up the cat and cuddled her in my arms until she squirmed and leapt to the floor. Princess scampered out of the kitchen and disappeared as

Mother stomped in from the adjacent laundry, arms crossed.

"Jamie, what was the name of that murdered teacher?" She scrutinized me, her eyes narrowed.

"Davis Harwell. Was there something on the news?" I refilled my water bottle from the spigot in the refrigerator door.

"Did you forget that the two of you had been corresponding?" Her look bored into me.

I pulled in a quick breath and choked on a sip of water, then cleared my throat. "Corresponding? With Davis Harwell? No ..."

"Oh. So, you've forgotten you were flirting with him." She slammed a short stack of folded papers down onto the granite island.

"What? He was a teacher at my school and a dinner theater cast member. We weren't corresponding, and I never flirted with him." Where had Mother come up with this idea?

"This looks like correspondence to me." She tapped the pile of papers. "I raised you better than this, Jamie. Does Sam know?"

"What on earth are you talking about?" I picked up the stack of notes and unfolded the top one.

You make my day. Excited to see you later. The brief note was signed, *Davis.* The handwriting was unfamiliar.

"Where did you find these, Mother?" I opened another note and read: *Been loving you in my mind all day. Davis.* "I've never seen these before." I whirled to face her. "Tell me where you got them. And who wrote them?"

"Jamie. Don't lie to your mother. If you haven't seen them, how did they get inside your denim jacket pocket?"

My mind raced. How did notes from Davis Harwell end up in the pocket of the jacket I wore yesterday?

"I noticed a stain on the front of the jacket. You left it on the mudroom bench. I treated the spot, then found these in the pocket. I'm ashamed of you." She folded her arms and glared.

"I've never seen these before." I pitched them back onto the island. One fluttered to the floor.

"Well, when you decide to stop lying to me, I'll be in my room. You can finish your own laundry." With a final glare, she marched off to her room.

I stooped over and read the note that had fallen to the floor. *You are so sexy. Tonight will be crazy fun! – Davis*

I cringed. Obviously, Davis Harwell was having an affair. But not with me.

I'd worn the jacket to school yesterday. Anyone could have placed the notes in my pocket. I stuffed them into the junk drawer next to the pantry. Had someone killed Davis because of an affair? An angry husband, or jilted ex-lover? His wife? Maybe it wasn't a robbery-gone-bad at the gas station after all.

Who would want to make it seem that I was his lover? The notes should go to the police, but Detective Blaise would no doubt believe they really were *mine*. He wouldn't accept someone else had slipped them into my pocket if my own mother didn't believe it.

With both Sam and Mother unapproachable, I went looking for Trudy and found her in the backyard with the dogs. She was trying her hardest to keep three balls moving for the three dogs, tossing each ball as soon as one dog brought it back to her. Ears flopping, the dogs raced around the yard on short legs. Trudy had been at it long enough that she was out of breath, and the dogs' tongues hung out of their open, drooling mouths. Her face and neck glistened with a fine layer of sweat.

"Whew, you dogs are wearin' me out," she complained, grinning. She dropped to the ground and the dogs swarmed her, licking her face and hands. Augie Doggie backed away from her and barked, challenging her to throw the ball one more time.

"No, Augie. That's enough. I'm pooped!" She rolled to one side and clambered up.

Tails wagging, all three dogs circled her, and then dropped to the ground to roll in the grass. They caught sight of me and gazed over with big, brown eyes, their long tongues lolling out of the sides of their mouths. I wished I had my phone with me to snap their picture.

Trudy noticed me and waved. "Hello."

I crossed the yard to the bench under the trees and Trudy hurried across the grass to sit beside me. "Augie and me are ready to go home and get rid of those ghosts. Will we go early in the morning?"

"Sam and I haven't talked about it yet. I don't know what he has to do first, before we go." I looked up and glimpsed a Monarch butterfly battling the breeze, lifting and then dropping as it winged its way in a southwesterly direction.

"Where is he? I heard his car pull into the driveway a long time ago, but he hasn't come out to say hello. And then I heard Cousin Mary yelling at you. Did you do something wrong?" Trudy pulled her knees up and wrapped her arms around them.

"She wasn't yelling. She was expressing her opinion, and it was completely wrong." My temper still simmered. Mother didn't know me very well if she thought I would flirt with another man and have an affair when I loved Sam with every ounce of my being.

"What was she wrong about?" Trudy tilted her head and eyed me.

"It doesn't matter, Trudy. Sam's not happy tonight, either. I think I'll order some pizza for supper. We can go pick it up. Supreme or Meat Lovers?"

Trudy's mouth twisted as she thought. "Neither. What's that one called with pineapple in it? Does Sam like that one?"

"The Hawaiian? No, he doesn't, but I can get two pizzas."

She nodded. "Yum." Trudy licked her lips. "Has he talked to his mother about going with us tomorrow? She needs to come to the house and then get her medicine man to make those ghosts leave."

"Sam said he'd talk to her. Ask him about it at supper. I'll call in that pizza order."

"Let me feed our dogs and I'll be ready." Trudy bolted off the bench and jogged to the house in front of me.

As the sun drops in the September sky, at the side of the house, behind a mature twenty-five-foot evergreen, the Watcher waits. Minutes pass. Finally, Jamie's car backs down the driveway.

She's not alone. That woman is with her.

The Watcher's fists clench and then, minutes later, relax.

That's okay. I can wait. No need to rush her death. I like my other plan, and I'll stick to it.

The Watcher nibbles at a fast food burger, finishes it, then wads the wax paper wrapper into a ball and pitches it into the back seat, laughing.

The mother's reaction was priceless! I'd wanted Sam to find the notes. But the mother is almost as good. One more chink in their trust in one another. They're wrapped in the webs I'm spinning around them.

The Watcher smiles and settles back into the seat of the Honda.

Chapter 24

Saturday

"Is it time to go yet?" Trudy hurried into the kitchen where Sam and I sat at the island drinking our morning coffee.

"Are you in a hurry? I didn't think you'd be that anxious to get back to the ghosts," I said.

"I'm not, but Sam's mother will be able to help. She'll make them go away. And then Augie and me will be safe again."

"Is Theresa ready for this?" I asked Sam. Although we'd talked briefly about his mother going with us, he'd never told me if she had agreed to go.

Sam set down his coffee cup, crossed his arms and leaned back. "Mom has agreed to go. She is apprehensive."

"Will the shaman meet us there, too?" Trudy asked.

"Not today. Once Mother has experienced the situation, she will decide whether the shaman needs to be involved."

Trudy frowned. "But the shaman needs to come. I told you, Sam. Why don't you believe me?"

"Why don't you get Augie ready to go?" I suggested. Sam had become increasingly short-tempered this week, and Trudy could quickly try his patience today.

"But ..."

"The faster you get ready, the sooner we can go." I smiled my encouragement.

She dashed toward the dog feeding station in the mudroom, calling for Augie. Queenie and Zeus answered her call, too, woofing in unison. All three dogs raced toward their food bowls. Mother appeared in the kitchen doorway, her face pale and her eyes wide. She turned and went back the way she'd come. We couldn't leave the house soon enough for her, I was sure.

She'd refused to talk to me last night, secluded herself in her room and ate her supper alone. I would have to address the so-called affair soon, but I didn't want Sam to overhear our conversation. He had enough on his mind without having to worry about why someone was implying I'd had an affair.

Thirty minutes later, Sam and I pulled into the narrow driveway of the retirement community cottage his mother had purchased six months earlier. Trudy had followed in her car, and it sat idling several yards down the street.

Theresa stood on the small porch, a plaid shawl draped around her shoulders. After Sam parked the truck, I slid out and moved into the back seat. She could talk with Sam better if she was sitting beside him, and she had more room to stretch her legs.

A minute later, after Sam had offered his arm and walked her to the truck, she scooted onto the front seat, glancing at me. "Morning, dear."

"How do you feel about this ghost adventure today?"

She shook her head. "I feel much the same as Sam does. Why would these ghosts appear to Trudy? There is human influence here, without doubt." She settled against the seat and fastened her seatbelt.

"I agree. I hope you can help us figure it out. I'm glad you came."

"I will do what I can, Jamie."

The ride to Pawhuska was quiet. What would we find in the house? Would there be evidence that other people had been there? Would Sam's mom be able to detect the presence of spirits? Or would the house be as Trudy and I had left it on Wednesday? Periodically, I checked the driver's side mirror to make sure that Trudy was following in her car. I could see her head, and above the wheel, a smaller dog-sized head. Augie was sitting in her lap.

I thought about Davis. I remembered distinctly the first time we'd met, at a faculty meeting. He'd been standing with a group of teachers Gail was introducing to me. He'd stepped forward to shake my hand, the women nodded and smiled. His blue eyes had twinkled above rosy cheeks and a trimmed beard. He wasn't my type, but he seemed nice, and genuine.

Our second meeting, at a combined gathering for the Playhouse crew and the high school Drama Club, was less formal. We'd chatted briefly at the table where someone, maybe Romy, had placed a container of cookies and a jug of tea. I didn't remember what we talked about, but, as we chatted, Davis had said hello to several students, calling them by name. It helped me put names and faces together.

Two meetings, and now the word was that we were having an affair. It was ridiculous. I switched off my thoughts and focused on the pastures and scrubby prairie trees that flashed past the truck windows.

The old house that had belonged to my great aunt appeared the same as usual from the outside, well-kept flower beds and the porch clear of all but a few leaves blown in by early autumn winds. Ivy still crawled up the west side of the house, but the trim around the windows and doors looked freshly painted and the porch looked like a shady retreat.

Trudy pulled up behind us in the narrow driveway as we climbed out of the truck. Augie Doggie leapt from the car and raced up the steps to the porch, where he stood, barking ferociously at the front door. Trudy frowned and hurried after the dog.

"Trudy, wait," Sam called. He helped his mother out of the car and took her arm as she shuffled up the sidewalk toward the house. Her fall the previous winter had slowed her steps considerably. She had lost her confidence and moved slowly to compensate. At the bottom step, she paused and observed the house. "We must be careful now. There is ... something."

Trudy waited until all four of us were on the porch before she inserted her key in the lock and shoved the door open. Augie dashed in, barking.

We peeked inside, then stepped one by one into the dimness, waiting in the dark hallway until our eyes adjusted to the interior. Trudy flipped the light switch. In unison, we gasped.

Chapter 25

The small Tiffany-style lamp which usually sat on the entry hall table, lay on the wood plank floor, the beautiful shade of leaded glass in shards. The table drawers hung open, and the notepads and pencils they usually contained were haphazardly strewn beneath the table.

I turned toward the study. The room where my great aunt had spent so many hours reading and sewing was in disarray. The contents of the bookshelves had been thrown about the room and rested upside down, covers open and pages crumpled. Elizabeth's sewing notions box had been turned over, her spools of thread and extra buttons scattered over the area rug.

"Oh, no!" Theresa groaned from beside me. She braced herself against the frame of the wooden pocket door to the study.

I dashed across the hall to the dining room, my pulse racing and my heart sinking. Every inch of the elegant walnut table and the floor was covered in shards of my aunt's beautiful china, each piece shattered and left to lie where it fell.

Behind me, Trudy began to sob. I threw my arms around her and stopped her from following Sam and his mother into the kitchen. Once again, Augie took the lead, growling and barking.

The dog yelped. Low voices reached us in the hallway. Sam appeared, carrying Augie. A dishcloth had been wrapped around the dog's foot and secured with a long green twist-tie.

Sam handed the dog to Trudy, his face pale and his mouth pressed into a grim line, and then rushed up the stairs. Theresa Mazie appeared in the kitchen doorway, using the walls for support. Once in the hall, her hands lifted to cover her face.

A chill passed through me. I hurried across the hallway and into the kitchen, ready, I thought, for whatever disaster I found.

The cabinets, where plates, cups and kitchenware had been stored, were now empty. Everything they had once held was broken on the floor. Scrawled in enormous black magic marker across the bare countertops was written:

He Killed Me. Send Him to Hell.

Behind me, Trudy screamed. I wanted to scream, too, but I whirled and drug her from the kitchen to the front door to get her out of the house.

We all had to get out of the house. Someone evil had been here, someone with tremendous anger. I glanced upstairs, where Sam rushed in and out of the bedrooms, emerging from each with a grim look, his face growing darker with each step and his eyes flashing with rage. He pounded down the front stairs.

In the entry hall, he pulled out his cell phone and punched in a number.

"Toby? Get over to Trudy's right away. Someone has vandalized the house." He ended the call and touched my arm. "Take Trudy and Mom over to Vera's. I'll wait for Toby."

He punched another number into the phone, and as I followed Theresa and Trudy down the porch steps, Sam said, "Vera? It's Sam. I'm sending Trudy over there with Mom and Jamie. Trudy can't stay in the house. Jamie will explain."

Vera's was the logical place to go. A distant relative of Trudy's, she was also her best friend. Although Vera and I had gotten off to a rocky start when we first met, I now considered her one of my closest friends. She would offer the comfort that Trudy needed after seeing the ruined house. Her calm demeanor would help settle us all.

Trudy wailed during the short drive in her car to Vera's house, only a few blocks away. Sam's mother huddled in the front seat, her hands covering her face. My whole body quivered. The destruction of Trudy's house was personal and was directed not at Trudy, but at my husband. Who had done this?

I *knew* Sam. We'd had issues before with his silences and his reticence to tell me things I had every right to know. Was there something horrible he had not yet told me?

"Theresa, I don't understand what's happening here," I said to her as I drove. "Someone is accusing Sam. Reba's body is being disinterred. Can you help me understand?"

Sam's mother let out a deep, throaty groan. She stared through the windshield. "Sam was not responsible for Reba's death. Someone evil is at work. This is not the end of it."

I glanced at her pale face. "Do we need the shaman?" I asked.

She closed her eyes. "It isn't spirits we need to worry about."

Chapter 26

"Why do you think this is happening now? And who is behind it?" I asked Theresa as I pulled the car into Vera's driveway and parked. Theresa stared out the window, her eyes unfocused. In the backseat, Trudy sniffed.

"Why did Reba's ghost do this? It's my house, not Sam's! Why did someone destroy my things?" Trudy asked in a raspy voice, her face buried in the scruff of Augie's neck.

"Sheriff Toby will help us find answers," I reassured her.

If anyone could, it was Toby Green. He knew this community inside and out. In the eight years I'd known Toby, he'd always been logical, intuitive and trustworthy. As he often said, solving a crime was a matter of pulling together the scattered pieces of a jigsaw puzzle.

"Reba was troubled at the end," Theresa abruptly said. "She was different. Confused, moody. Not like the happy little girl I had known for years. I tried to talk to her, but I didn't want to be a meddling mother-in-law."

She watched Vera descend the front steps of her house. "I know when to speak and when to stand aside and watch. I was watching. I didn't believe Reba would kill herself. She was not committed to die."

"Are you saying that someone killed her?"

"It is one explanation. But if someone did kill her, it could not have been Sam. There is no violence in Samuel. Not like in my son Lucas."

I remembered my conversation with Sam earlier in the week. He'd talked about his brother Lucas for the first time in a long while. Had the situation reminded him of Lucas's violent tendencies, too? Surely Theresa didn't think Lucas had something to do with Reba's death?

As Vera approached the car, the three of us and the dog climbed out. Vera took my hand and pulled me toward the house in front of the others. "What happened?"

In a low voice, I explained what we had found at Trudy's.

Vera ran her hand through her graying hair. "How horrible. Who would do such a thing?"

"I'm open to any ideas."

Trudy stepped up, her face wet with tears. She sniffed loudly, and Vera embraced her.

"We all want to know who did this, and why," I said.

In the house, Trudy collapsed onto the sofa while Theresa and I stood, arms crossed, in the center of the living room. Augie jumped up on the sofa and crawled into Trudy's lap. After licking her chin, he laid his big head on her leg, sighed and closed his eyes.

"I knew about Trudy's 'ghosts' but I didn't believe they were dangerous," Vera said. "I haven't seen them."

"Ghosts didn't do this, Vera." I was certain of that, and everyone but Trudy was also convinced that someone truly evil had entered the house and destroyed Trudy's things. What I couldn't imagine was why they had done this to Trudy; the message was directed at Sam.

"They could be poltergeists, right?" Trudy leaned forward, elbows on her knees.

"I'm not a ghost expert. But, I think this was done by a living person." I rubbed the back of my neck and shivered. The inside of Vera's house was not much warmer than the outside air.

Vera hurried over to the thermostat and adjusted the dial. A floor furnace roared to life as Theresa clutched her shawl tight around her shoulders. A slight odor of natural gas rose up from the heater as the burners caught fire.

"Trudy, Sam and I are devastated about this. Your home insurance will replace most things of any value. But I know some were irreplaceable." I swallowed hard, hesitant to voice what I'd been wondering ever since we found the wreckage in the house. "Maybe someone isn't happy about the disinterment of Reba's body."

Trudy nodded. "Reba's ghost!"

"Someone wants you to think it was Reba's ghost," I said firmly. "Vera, I need to use your phone book. The door locks must be replaced. I'll make a call to see if someone can meet me there this afternoon. You three can stay here, and I'll go back to the house."

Vera and Theresa nodded, their expressions grim and their faces pale.

Marlon Little Sparrow, the locksmith, agreed to meet me at Trudy's house in thirty minutes.

The senseless vandalism was an extreme act, full of anger and maybe even vengeance. Why destroy the beautiful china? And books? The value of those items rested with the fact they were Elizabeth Graham's things, collected throughout her life, and then given to Trudy. They were Trudy's heritage. Elizabeth had come to that house in Pawhuska essentially destitute, an unmarried teenage orphan with a child. Trudy, Vera and I were her closest living relatives. What did that have to do with Sam and Reba?

Toby Green's vehicle, door panels stenciled with 'Osage County Sheriff,' sat in front of Trudy's house with another car and Sam's truck. I let myself in the front door and followed the sound of voices to the kitchen, where the destruction was the worst.

The third person already in the room was India Merchant, an insurance representative whose company held Trudy's insurance policies, as well as Sam's and mine. "Hello, India. Toby."

The sheriff crossed the room and hugged me. "Jamie. Glad to see you, but sorry it's because of this." He gestured toward the room. India was snapping pictures with her phone.

"Hi, Jamie. This is awful. I'm so sorry." India trotted to the back door and then turned, jockeying her camera to get the best angle of the room for the photo. "I'll take pics of the study and the dining room next. And as soon as possible, if you could make a list of any specific things of value, that would be very helpful."

With Trudy's help, the list would be ready in a few days, but I dreaded compiling it. Years ago, I'd spent nearly five months living here with Elizabeth as she recovered from an attack that left her fighting for her life and in a coma. I knew this house, and I knew the items stored throughout.

India left us in the kitchen. I looked at Sam, and his woeful eyes stared back at me. I crossed the room and rubbed at the writing on the countertop with my thumb. The words were written in permanent marker. The only way to erase the damage was to remove the countertop.

Toby took out his phone and opened the camera app. He snapped a photo of the countertop. "You've really upset somebody, Sam," he said. "But I guess we know where to start. I saw Bosque at the Mini Mart yesterday. Shouldn't be too hard to find out where he's staying and bring him in for questioning."

Bosque? The convicted felon who had told the authorities that Sam hired him to kill Reba. Did Toby think he had something to do with this? I retrieved a broom and dustpan from the mud room and began to sweep up the mess on the kitchen floor.

"He's here? Since when?" Sam had grabbed a scouring pad from under the sink and was rubbing the old linoleum counter, successfully removing both the words and the color of the countertop material as he worked.

"Not sure. One of the deputies saw him come out of Patti Granger's house a week ago." Toby took a picture of the back door, and the smashed pitcher that lay on the floor in front of it.

"Is that the Granger that used to hang out with Sharon? Reba's sister?" Sam stopped scrubbing and looked at Toby.

"One and the same."

"Have you seen Sharon around here lately? Or her mother?"

"The mother, maybe five years ago. She lived at Fairfax for a while. Looked different. Her hair was graying and long. And she'd lost weight."

Belina had said her family was from Fairfax. What were the chances that the two women knew each other? Fairfax wasn't a very large town, and it was likely everyone there was acquainted or related in one way or another.

"I'm done with the pictures," India announced. She surveyed the kitchen one more time. "I sure hope you catch the devil who did this, Toby. Such a shame. Family heirlooms, I bet."

I nodded. "I'll get the list done and will send it in an email as soon as it's ready."

"Excellent. And will you tell Trudy I'm sorry. I know how attached she was to some of those figurines." India stowed her camera in a large handbag.

And so did I. How many times had I seen her take the collection of Hummels down from the shelves and dust them? She'd do it all again the following week on cleaning day.

India opened the back door and exited as Marlon Little Sparrow entered.

"Hello, Marlon," Sam said. "Thanks for coming so quickly."

Little Sparrow carried his tools in a metal box. He set it by the door and then noted the disaster around the room before he whistled low and long. "Jiminy, what happened here? Burglary?"

"Vandalism. Didn't take anything, senseless destruction," Toby Green chimed in.

"Forced entry?"

"Don't think so. No signs of that. Perp either had a key or got in when the house was unlocked." Toby's phone beeped. He pulled it out of his pocket and checked it.

"Was Trudy hurt?" Marlon asked.

"No. She was in Ponca City with us. We brought her back today and found this," Sam explained.

"In Ponca? Last night?"

"Yes. Why?" Sam continued to scour at the countertop. Most of the writing–and countertop color–had disappeared.

"I drove down this street last night, about ten. My daughter was studying at a friend's house a half-block away. When I picked her up, the house lights here were all on. I thought Trudy must be having company."

"Did you hear anything?"

Marlon shook his head. "Sorry. Car radio was on."

"I'll ask around the neighbors. Maybe somebody will remember something," Toby said. He slipped out the back door.

Marlon picked up a lock set and opened the package. "Best get to work, then. I figured three sets to change out. That right? Need an inside door changed too, huh?"

Chapter 27

After promising I'd return to help with the cleanup, I left Sam with the locksmith and drove the short distance back to Vera's. A brisk wind had picked up, and brown leaves danced circles in the streets. Inside the house, I found Vera, Theresa and Trudy seated at the kitchen table. Augie Doggie's long tail wagged back and forth while he waited for me to come closer and pat the top of his head.

Vera carried a pot of tea from the kitchen and refilled the three cups on the circular dining table where the women had gathered. "How are things?"

"Lots of cleanup to do. I'm going back over there. Could Trudy and Theresa stay here for a few hours while I help Sam?" I asked.

Trudy looked at me with her wide-set eyes, her mouth quivering in a frown. "All those beautiful things," she wailed. Her hands gripped the arms of the chair like claws.

"But they are only things, Trudy. I know they meant a lot to you, I don't mean to imply that they don't have value."

Her face crumpled in grief. My heart hurt. She needed something to focus on, but the task I needed her to do–making a list of all the destroyed items–might only deepen the pain in her heart.

"Trudy can stay here. I think she could use a nap." Vera tilted her head toward Trudy and then patted her friend's hand on the tabletop. "Maybe Theresa would like to rest, too."

Trudy sniffed. Theresa smiled and nodded. Her eyelids drooped.

"Is that okay, Trudy? Do you mind staying here with Theresa while Vera helps me at the house?"

Trudy closed her eyes. "I would like to rest. And snuggle with Augie."

"I'll stretch out on the bed while you're gone, Vera, if that's okay." Theresa rose to her feet, a bit unsteadily. Vera rushed to help her to the nearby bedroom.

After both of us were in the car, Vera asked, "Who would have done this Jamie? And what do you think about these ghosts Trudy keeps seeing?"

"I don't believe in ghosts. Someone is trying to scare her. I'm so glad the locks are finally being changed." I was still kicking myself for not having it done when Trudy first mentioned the ghosts. I started the car and backed into the street.

"But why would they destroy Elizabeth's possessions? What is the message?" Vera pulled a tissue from her pocket and blew her nose. Slightly reddened eyes told me she was still battling the cold or virus she'd been struggling with all week.

"You would know that better than I would. I don't have the history, but it involves Sam and Reba. Do you remember much about their relationship? Or her family?"

Vera ran her fingers through her hair. "I didn't know Reba very well."

"Sam says she changed over time. Became depressed and moody. To me, the personality shift could signal drug use. But I'm surprised Sam didn't pick up on that."

Vera regarded me and chewed her lip. "You want me to be honest?"

"Of course. I haven't ever known you to sugar coat things. Remember the first few months we knew each other?" I chuckled.

"Do I? You were something. So naïve." Vera smirked and then peered up at the sky; mid-afternoon clouds roiled, multiplying into the possibility of a storm.

"'Clueless' is what you said." I remembered all too well that our relationship had a difficult start. When it became apparent that I needed Vera's help to learn who had attacked my aunt and why, I had to convince her she could trust me. Eventually, we had become friends.

"Clueless, yes. And truth be known, you've always been a bit clueless about your husband. Blinded by love?"

"Both of us have things in our pasts that we haven't wanted–or needed–to share," I admitted. "I know Sam is an alcoholic. He's never hidden that from me, and he hasn't slid back into those old habits. This thing with Reba, the cold case investigation, has shaken him. I don't seem to be much help."

"He probably wouldn't let you help. He's always carried such guilt about her death. And anger. She lied to him. He felt, and still feels, betrayed."

"And now to have to face it all over again. And to have the question of a hired killer hanging over his head."

"A hired killer?" Vera stared.

I parked the car in front of Trudy's home. "I thought you knew about the cold case investigation. The disinterment."

She shook her head. "What are you talking about?"

Vera listened intently while I explained the situation. Then, she slammed the heel of her hand against the dashboard. "That's the most ridiculous thing I've ever heard. Sam hired a creep to kill his wife? Sounds like the plot of some idiotic made-for-television movie."

"Yeah. And Sam and I have starring roles."

Vera stared out the windshield. "That was so long ago." Her voice pinched.

"What do you remember about Reba?" I didn't recall Vera ever talking about Sam's first wife. Our conversations had never strayed much into our pasts. She was close-mouthed about many things, and I respected her privacy.

Vera shrugged. "I knew her because of Sam. But I knew 'of' her before that."

I waited for her to say more. A flock of birds dipped as they flew across the street, fighting a gust of wind. Vera's eyes darted about and her fingers twitched.

"Reba had a reputation," she finally said with a sigh.

"What kind of a reputation?" My mind considered what that word could mean.

"She and her sister were on the wild side. They did crazy things, as well as smoked pot and drank, like a lot of us. Like I said, we weren't friends."

"Was that small-town talk or do you think the bit about 'crazy things' was true?"

"Some rumors might be small town talk. Gossip rules in small towns like Pawhuska and Fairfax, where everyone knows everyone."

"Separate fact from fiction for me. I'm leaping to conclusions. Who might have wanted Reba dead? Might have hired someone to kill her?"

"There was some story about her and her sister at one of those 4th of July races in Ponca City. A car crashed, and a racer died."

A splash of ice water to my face wouldn't have shocked me more than her words. Vera was talking about the Ponca City Grand Prix, the race featured in my high school drama club's fundraiser, and the death of the playwright's brother.

"Were they blamed for the accident, or witnessed it?"

Vera shrugged again. "Without a doubt they were there. But as for anything else, I don't know. You should talk to Lucas. If anyone might know, it would be him."

"Lucas? Sam's brother?"

"Yeah. If I remember correctly, he was the one who took Reba and her sister to the race that weekend."

Chapter 28

Sam, Vera and I worked for several hours to sweep up the broken ceramics and dishes. Vera placed books and unbroken items back onto the shelves in the study, Sam did the same in the parlor, and I tackled the kitchen.

So much was broken and useless. Our extra kitchen items, boxed up when we moved, were still stored in the garage. I would bring them for Trudy, supplemented by a new set of dishes and glasses.

Marlon Little Sparrow trudged in and out of the house with lock sets and tools stuffed into the pockets of his tool belt, working on the exterior doors. His whining drill and pounding hammer provided background noise for my racing thoughts.

When Marlon had finished replacing the locks, he handed over three sets of two keys for the outside doors, and two keys for the interior lock. All three outside door knob locks were set for the same key, as were all three exterior deadbolts. At Toby's recommendation, Little Sparrow had also replaced the locks on several ground floor windows, making it more difficult for anyone to get the window open from outside. After I paid him for his work, he drove away in his panel truck. Sam locked the house and the three of us left for Vera's.

At Vera's home, she and I went inside to check on Trudy and Theresa. Trudy was asleep on the sofa, a crocheted afghan pulled up to her chin and Augie Doggie stretched out beside her, snug against her body. The dog's eyes opened, then closed. He snored softly.

Theresa sat at the kitchen table, finishing a cup of tea.

"We're ready to go back. How are you feeling?" I slipped into the chair across the little table from her.

"Ready to go. I'm tired. And we didn't accomplish what you wanted."

"You mean, about the ghosts?" I offered a small smile.

"There are spirits in the house, Jamie. More than one. But it is the sense of some living evil there that bothers me more than the spirits."

"An evil person in the house?"

"The one who destroyed Elizabeth's belongings. Such rage." Theresa placed her empty teacup carefully on the saucer and scooted back her chair. "I'm worried about Trudy. She shouldn't be there alone."

A few minutes later, after Sam arrived at Vera's, Theresa, Vera and I walked quietly to the front door and out onto the porch. Sam waited in the truck, engine running.

"I'm going to talk to Sam about that race while we drive home," I told Vera.

"You can try. It all happened a long time ago." Vera crossed her arms and hugged herself against the blustery, damp twilight air. "More than fifteen years."

"But someone died. That's not something you forget," I observed. Theresa took my arm, and the two of us descended the steps to the sidewalk.

"Let me know what you find out," Vera called after us. "I'll phone you when Trudy decides to go back to the house. And I'll probably stay with her the first night."

"Thanks. We'll talk soon." I escorted Theresa to the front passenger door of the truck and then climbed into the back.

How would I begin this conversation with Sam other than blurt it out? It would have to wait until we had dropped Theresa at the retirement village. She had enough on her mind without recalling what had happened at that long-ago race and bringing up Lucas's possible involvement.

Vast pasturelands, eerily gray in the dimming light of the day, flashed past beside the highway as I considered possible ways to start this conversation. Sam didn't like to talk about Reba. It was possible he didn't know anything about what had happened at that race. But I had to ask. We were halfway home when Theresa's head dipped and bobbed. She'd fallen asleep.

"Sam, Vera and I were talking ... she didn't know about the disinterment," I said softly. "Or about the inquest."

"I figured everyone in Pawhuska knew," he said wryly.

"I guess some people don't." I paused. I had to be cautious about what I said and how I said it. Otherwise, Sam might shut me out.

The lights of Ponca City lit up the horizon, and soon the neighborhoods of southeast Ponca City, the area they called 'The Osage,' closed in around us. Sam drove through town and out to Theresa's complex, then parked once again in her driveway. While he escorted her to the cottage, I climbed out of the back seat and into the front. I waited.

Eventually, Sam hurried back to the truck, slid in and started the engine. "Mom's not feeling well. I think it was the stress of finding Trudy's house vandalized."

"Did she say anything about 'ghosts'?"

"No. But she did say something about an evil spirit. There are plenty of those who aren't dead."

I shifted sideways to face him as we drove. "She told me the same thing, earlier." I picked at a small flaw in the denim of my jeans, then chose my words carefully. "Sam, Vera said Reba had a reputation as a teenager. And something about a Grand Prix race in Ponca City where someone died."

Sam visibly jerked. He looked at me quickly, then back at the street. "Why did Vera bring that up?"

"We were talking about why someone might have wanted to kill Reba."

"That was so long ago. Years before she died."

"But if someone was still angry about something that happened years before, maybe they wanted revenge. Vera told me Lucas was with them at the race."

Sam's mouth pinched into a grim line. Bad memories? My heart pounded in my throat, and I was beginning to think he wouldn't tell me any more when he said, "Yes. My brother took them to the races."

My brain extrapolated that they'd all been drinking. That Lucas had perhaps seen whatever had happened. That maybe all three of them had been drunk. "Did they talk about any of it after they got home? The accident? The death of the driver?"

Sam seemed lost in thought. Nearly a minute passed before he turned his head toward me and spoke again. "I wasn't at home that summer, so I didn't go to the race. Lucas enlisted not long afterward, and I left for law school. Why would Vera think of that? It was so long ago."

"But she did think of it. We should ask Lucas."

"Maybe." He flicked on the radio, even though we were only a few blocks from home.

For now, anyway, the subject appeared to be closed.

Sam stopped in the driveway and I got out. "I'll grab the mail and be right in," I said. The garage door lifted, and Sam drove in.

The mailbox was jammed by a large overstuffed yellow envelope. The envelope bore no return address, and I assumed it was a catalogue, or something related to our medical insurance. I carried the mail through the garage and into the house, stopping in the mudroom to hang up my jacket.

I opened the fat envelope and pulled out a sheaf of papers held together by a thick rubber band. The top sheet read; *Race to Death, a play by Rusty Clement.*

I carried the thick envelope into the kitchen.

A pot of beefy stew simmered on the stove. Carrots, celery and potatoes were cooking in the bubbling broth along with the meat. The aroma of baking cornbread rushed out of the oven when I opened the door to peer in. In the living room, the television blared; Mother was probably watching her favorite Saturday night game shows. I slipped onto a bar stool at the island and flipped through the pages of the play.

I'd never read the play line for line and hadn't listened closely during the blocking work at rehearsal last week. A few weeks ago, I'd scanned the italic pre-scene materials and the dialogue, looking for items needed as props, then I'd used those notations to create my prop list. Now, because of what I'd learned about Reba and Lucas being present at the race, I was curious about the play's plot, and the story Rusty had wanted to tell.

About mid-way through my scan of the document, several notations had been made in pencil on the backside of one of the pages, and a few lines of dialogue had been struck through with black marker.

Rewrite. Mention other racer by name. Lucas Mazie. I sucked in my breath. Lucas had been driving one of the race cars? I focused on the words. Had Lucas been involved in the crash? There was nothing about Lucas in the actual lines of dialogue.

I found another notation, and another paragraph struck through by the marker.

Rewrite. Mention the two drunk women seen before the accident. Why are they not named anywhere?

A chill slipped down my back. Hurriedly, I flipped through the remainder of the three-act play, stopping on the final page where black marker had scratched out lines and more notations had been written on the side margin. The notations were cryptic and unclear. Something about 'drunk bystanders' creating problems. Someone who had been at the race might be able to make sense of these notations. I wasn't sure who that would be.

Howard DeKalb had seemed familiar with the race, as had the Wentz Camp director. But neither were willing to talk about it.

Rusty Clement had been killed in a hit and run on Friday, and Davis Harwell, Rusty's source for details about the race and the original gardener in the play, had been killed last weekend. Was this play the reason they'd been killed? If so, the so-called accident at the race had been murder, and two people very close to Sam had probably been involved.

I gathered up the script and slid it back into the envelope. Why was this happening now? Sam needed my support, but my time was being taken up with this play, and now with reading the script. Granted, I should have read the play long before, maybe then I wouldn't feel so blindsided by current events.

I closed my eyes and worked through the questions in my mind. The logical sequence of events seemed to be: Rusty writes a play, focusing on the Ponca City Grand Prix, with Davis Harwell's help. Davis' brother was killed in a final race. And Sam's brother Lucas also participated in the race. Davis was dead, and now Rusty was dead.

Someone didn't want this story told. Had the race car driver's death been covered up? Called an accident when it wasn't?

My thoughts sparked. Like Reba's death had been called a suicide, when it wasn't?

I pulled my attention back to the play, and the race. More than 15 years had passed. Who would still be concerned that the truth might come out? Obviously, the killer, if the driver's death had been intentional.

Two drunk teenager girls. *Sharon and Reba?*

Outside the kitchen window in the dimming twilight, the Watcher stands stiffly, staring.

That idiot playwright sent the play to *Jamie*?

Eyes narrowed, the Watcher sees Jamie pull back from the document, her eyes wide, her face white. Jamie straightens the pages, then stuffs them back into the envelope. She tucks the package under her arm and rushes out of the kitchen. Light flicks on at the other end of the house. The bedroom?

So much for taking my time, letting things unroll like I'd planned. This drama must end – SOON!

Chapter 29

Sunday

Someone pounded on the bedroom door. I pinched my eyes shut and turned over, pulling the thick comforter over my head. I reached over to Sam's side of the bed. It was empty. After a restless night, I'd hoped to be able to sleep in, but someone—it had to be Mother—had other ideas. Sam would never wake me up. He was the morning 'lark,' not me.

"Jamie? Are you still sleeping? I've been up for hours. You promised we'd go to Muskogee to see Randy. Get up!" Mother shrilled.

I shoved the covers off and rolled out of bed. One glance at the light pouring in around the Roman shades, and I knew it must be mid-morning. If I hurried, we could still be at the Veterans Hospital in time to have the noon meal with my brother. That is, if he was willing to eat, and if he knew who we were. He never wanted to eat with strangers. At the hospital in Albuquerque, he most often ate in his room, unless he was having a good day and was willing to share his time with other people. He was not willing 98% of the time.

"I'm up, Mother. I'm getting dressed," I shouted toward the closed door.

"I'll be in the kitchen, waiting. I'll heat you up one of those egg and cheese biscuits you like, and you can eat it in the car."

"Thank you." I hoped for some coffee, too.

Thirty minutes later we were on the highway. I nibbled the biscuit sandwich as I drove, and Mother chattered about the television programs she'd watched the night before. Game show after game show, featuring contestants from all over the country. Each person seemed crazier than those on the previous show. Unique individuals seemed to be attracted to those types of programs.

My mind churned over the script while Mother talked. Had the other cast members read through it? Surely Romy was aware of the accusations the playwright made. Why had she chosen this play for a dinner theater fundraiser? Obviously, Rusty, the playwright, had an axe to grind with somebody. I couldn't help but think that someone had known Rusty's intent to suggest a killer and had killed him because of it.

"Are you listening?" Mother demanded.

"Yes, I'm listening. Are those people on the game shows that desperate for money that they'll go on national television and make fools of themselves?"

"Most of them are very smart. They earn the money they win." Mother picked a piece of lint off her slacks.

"But not everyone wins. Most of them go home with very little, except embarrassment."

"Being on a game show is nothing to be embarrassed about. They take tests and show themselves capable of competing before they're accepted. It's hard to get on those shows, Jamie. They don't pick just anyone."

I nodded. Enough said. This was one of those hopeless conversations where she would have a retort for anything I said. No way she would ever change her opinion, or even consider mine.

"Did you watch anything other than game shows last night?"

"Oh, yes. There was the sweetest movie on the Hallmark Channel. You see there was this businessman who didn't have time for a personal life. He was unapproachable, and he kept firing his personal assistants. Then this small-town girl came to the big city and got the job. Well, things went up and down after that until finally ... Jamie, are you listening?"

"Let's turn on some music, Mother. We've got about another hour until we get there. We've only just gotten on the turnpike." We had little in common to talk about. Even now, with a great opportunity to become closer and talk about things that mattered, our conversations remained about the mundane.

Mother crossed her arms. I positioned the XM radio dial to an Easy Listening channel and tilted the driver's seat to a more relaxed position. When I glanced in the rearview mirror at the toll booth, I noticed a dark blue sedan. Was I crazy, or had the same car gotten onto the highway right behind me south of Ponca City?

My brother Randy was asleep when we arrived at the Veterans hospital. According to the nurse, sometimes

173

he slept all day. Was it easier for the facility to cope with his occasional bouts of uncontrollability if they drugged him so he'd sleep?

Mother sat beside him and held his hand, talking to him as if he was awake, telling him about her move and about the house. She even made a few snide comments about what it was like living with Sam and me, and then cut her eyes over to me. I stroked his hand and spoke to him once Mother gave me an opening and prodded me to speak. Not long after, abruptly, he flipped over on his side and buried his face in the pillow.

That was our cue to leave.

Back on the turnpike again, a dark sedan followed too closely. The car crept closer, and scenes from cop shows flashed in my mind. Would the car run us off the road? If so, I wouldn't be able to help the police with any description of the vehicle. The car had no front license tag and no identifying features. I wasn't even sure what kind of sedan it was.

Finally, the driver changed lanes and the car flashed past and down the highway.

"Well, it's about time!" Mother exclaimed. "I've been watching that car tailgate us for miles. Thank goodness they're going on. Made me nervous."

"You've been watching them? I seem to remember a dark car behind us on our way here. Do you?"

"Oh yeah. But they weren't tailgating like this one. Not sure if it was the same car. Could have been."

Sam's truck wasn't in the garage when we got home. Mother and I walked into a silent house. Instead of being greeted by two energetic dogs, only the cat appeared, flicking her tail and complaining in rapid consecutive meows.

"Princess, where are the dogs? Did Sam take them for a walk?" I asked, before noticing that the dog leashes were hanging on their hook above the mud bench. At the kitchen window, I glanced into the back yard. No dogs.

"I think I'll take a little rest before supper, dear. I'll be in my room." Mother headed down the hall.

I checked the other bedrooms for the dogs. Had they gotten trapped behind a closed door? "Queenie? Zeus?" Princess scampered ahead into each room, then looked at me, her luxurious tail arching over her back. Her green eyes blinked. "Not here, are they?" she seemed to say before she bounded from the room and into the hall.

At the front of the house, I hurried through the living room to the entryway. The wooden front door stood open and the storm door wasn't locked. Princess leapt effortlessly onto the console table near the door and sashayed around the lamp and the potpourri bowl.

Everything looked to be in order in the living room, and as far as I could tell, nothing was missing. But I was sure Sam wouldn't have left the storm door unlocked and the front door standing open.

I stepped out on the front porch, closing the storm door quickly so Princess couldn't dart out of the house. "Queenie? Zeus?" I scanned the lawns on both sides of the street. No sign of the dogs. I chewed at my lip. If the dogs had gotten out, they could be anywhere, following their noses. A block away, a mile away–no telling. And I doubted they could find their way home; they were far too easily distracted. On the off chance that I might have missed seeing them earlier in the backyard, I sprinted around the house to the backyard gate.

A piece of trash flitted across the grass in a gust of wind. I picked it up and carried it to the trashcan. Monday was trash day, and the can was jammed full of garbage-filled plastic bags. A blue glimmer, reflecting a ray of the afternoon sun, caught my eye. I shifted a trash bag to one side and saw an empty blue vodka bottle.

Was Sam drinking again? I wanted to reject the obvious answer but couldn't think of an alternative. Neither Mother nor I drank, except for an occasional glass of wine or champagne on special occasions. The current situation might be enough to drive anyone back to alcohol. Had Sam given in?

An empty house, an unlocked door, and now a vodka bottle. If Sam wasn't to blame, who was? Had someone been inside our house? And where were my dogs?

Chapter 30

I called Sam's office and got his answering machine; his cell phone was rolling over to voice mail. It wasn't like Sam to be out of touch with me. And I was worried about the missing dogs. I paced the living room.

When the house phone rang, I jumped. Usually only solicitations came in on that phone, but the caller ID read *Mazie.* I answered, "Sam?"

"Jamie, this is Theresa. The doctor called in a new prescription today, and I need Sam to get it for me. He's not answering his phone. Is he there?"

"No. But I can get that for you if you need it tonight." It would give me a chance to look for the dogs as I drove to the pharmacy a mile away.

"Yes, it's something for my stomach. Ever since Friday, it's been acting up. Would you mind? They close at 5 on Sundays."

"Not at all. I'll run out right now. Walmart Pharmacy, right?"

I grabbed my purse, told Mother where I was going and left the house. Both dogs had collars with tags bearing our new address. But they were hounds. One scent would lead to another, and another, and another.

When would they decide to come home? And would they make that decision before someone picked them up off the street? Dognapping had become commonplace, even for dogs of mixed breed.

The pharmacy would close in ten minutes, and when I arrived, a small group of last minute customers had gathered in front of the pharmacy counter. I got in line. As I waited, my mind raced. Sam, Reba and the script's notation about Lucas. I hadn't seen my husband all day. Had he been at the office? At the forefront of his mind, no doubt, was the inquest, and a possible murder investigation.

A woman in line behind me jostled me with her purse, and I inched forward.

"I tell you, it's frightening," she whispered. "Two murders in one week, and that high school boy missing. Can't help but wonder if they're connected, can you?"

Her companion continued the conversation, a little louder. "On a different subject, I heard something else today, about that new attorney from Pawhuska. I heard he's under investigation for the murder of his wife 10 years ago."

"Seriously? Are you talking about Sam Mazie?" the first woman exclaimed.

"You know his wife teaches science here. I haven't met her yet. What a shock for her," the second voice responded.

"I imagine so. He's a good-looking man. Big dark eyes. Has that sensitive look. You never know what that kind are really thinking."

"I know what I'd like him to be thinking," the second woman chuckled.

"I can help whoever's next," the pharmacy clerk called.

I cleared my throat and stepped forward, then gave Theresa's name in a low voice and explained what I needed. A few minutes later, with the pharmacy bag in hand, I hurried away from the counter.

"Hey, Jamie?" A voice called as I neared the exit. Belina glanced at the pharmacy bag as she rushed up to me. "Making a drug run?"

"For Sam's mom. How are you?" The last time I'd seen her, she'd acted as if we wouldn't see each other again, and didn't seem to care.

"I'm great. Glad to hear the play is back on. Aren't you?" Belina grinned and offered her hand in a high-five.

"I haven't heard that news." I lifted a limp hand and let her slap mine. How could that be? The ending to the play was not written, and never would be now.

"Romy Vaughn called this afternoon. Said she had received the final scene from the playwright, apparently mailed before his death, and that she wanted to go ahead with it. Rehearsals are back on for Tuesday," Belina bubbled. "Have you got time for a coffee tomorrow night? I'd like to go over some things with you before the rehearsal. And to talk. Seems like we have things in common, and I could use a new friend." She tilted her head and smiled.

My feelings were mixed. She was being nice and reaching out. I also needed a friend, and a confidante. Any reason it shouldn't be Belina? Could I get away from school in time to meet for a few minutes before rushing home to supper? I considered my response for only a second. "I think I could do that. About 4:30?"

"At the Coffee Spot downtown? I love their Salted Caramel Mocha." Belina smacked her lips, glanced into the store and then at her watch. "I've got a few more things to grab. See you then."

I dropped the medicine off at Theresa's. She looked ill, and said that she planned to take a dose of the new prescription and go to bed. One of the nurses who worked for the complex had come by to see her, given her some aspirin and suggested she put her feet up and let the medicine work.

As I left her house, I tried Sam's cell again. Still no answer. A niggling worry began. I couldn't remember a time since we'd been married when I had been out of touch with him for so long.

On the way home, my cell phone rang, and I jumped to accept the call, thinking it was Sam until I saw the caller ID. It was Romy.

"Hello, Romy," I said.

"Jamie, I'm so glad I caught you. I have some terrific news. Looks like we'll be able to go ahead with the fundraiser as planned."

"Did you get the script?"

"No, damn it. He must not have got around to it before he died. But I've looked at the copy I have, and I think we can skip that last scene. It's actually a logical place to end, anyway, although it doesn't get into the mystery of what happened later at that race. Notes on his rough draft could imply that the crash wasn't an accident. Maybe he intended to point the finger at someone. Too late now. We'll make it work without it. Rehearsal at 6 p.m. Tuesday. Be there!"

The phone clicked off before I had a chance to ask any questions, or even to admit that the script had been mailed to me. By mistake? I intended to spend some time with the play tonight, trying to decipher the notes Rusty had written on the final pages. Our last conversation, at last week's rehearsal, had left me uneasy. He'd been concerned about the consequences of his revelation. Had he been killed to prevent the revelation from being made?

Romy had decided on an ambiguous ending. There would be no revelation. And two people were dead.

At home, Sam's car sat on the driveway.

I rushed inside and found him in the kitchen, talking to Mother. He folded his arms around me in a hug and kissed my forehead. Queenie and Zeus tapdanced into the kitchen and stopped beside us, their tails wagging.

"Dogs! Where have you been?" I squatted and scratched their ears. Queenie grunted, but Zeus tried to give my face a lick.

Sam squinted at them. "Were they gone?"

"Yes. When Mother and I got back from the hospital, they weren't here."

"They were here when I got home," he said.

Mother shrugged. "They were in the backyard. They barked and I let them in. Maybe ten minutes after you left."

I would have sworn the backyard had been empty, but I didn't search it thoroughly after finding the vodka bottle. It was possible the dogs had been sheltering under the bushes. Was there another explanation?

"How was your day?" Sam asked. His eyes were dull and a little bloodshot, and his shoulders drooped.

"Made the trip to Muskogee. Where have you been all day?"

"At the office, mostly."

"Mother probably filled you in on our trip to the VA Hospital. I picked up some medicine for your mom and took it over to her. She's not feeling well."

"Thank you for doing that. I forgot to charge my phone last night." He glanced at Mother, who had her back to us; she was stirring something on the stove.

"I was getting a little worried since I couldn't get hold of you."

"No one came to arrest me, if you were wondering." He frowned.

"That is the last thing I would expect to happen. Are you worried about that?"

He leaned against the island. "Not at all," he scoffed. "I'm not guilty of anything, so what could I be arrested for?"

I shrugged. "Nothing." I stepped over to the stove and glanced into the pot. A tantalizing aroma of something beefy with rice and tomatoes was bubbling as Mother stirred. "Smells good."

"Hope so. Biscuits in the oven. Soon as they're done, we're ready to eat." She replaced the lid and set down the spoon.

"Thanks for fixing supper. I'll go freshen up, and be right back."

The dogs followed as I hurried to the master bathroom to wash my hands and face. In the bedroom, I stooped to pet them. "Where did you go, dogs?"

They didn't answer. I was sure they had not been in the backyard when we returned, but somehow, they'd come home safely. I crossed the room to the nightstand, intending to take the script to the dining room. When I'd finished eating, I would study it and try to decipher the notes in the margins.

I had tucked the script in the nightstand drawer when I turned off the lamp last night, but when I pulled the drawer open, the large envelope wasn't visible. I pawed through the contents, old birthday cards and yet-to-be-used birthday and sympathy cards. The envelope was gone.

Had I put it somewhere else? If so, it didn't register in my memory. Where would that be? The nightstand was my go-to place to stick something, if I didn't leave it on my makeshift desk in the dining room. I hurried through the house to the dining table. My filing system for the moment consisted of piles of related papers. The oversized envelope wasn't there.

"Missing something?" Sam asked from the doorway.

"Yes. A large yellow envelope. A copy of the script for the play." I flipped through a file box on the floor.

"Haven't seen any envelope. And I didn't move any files today, so there's no chance it ended up at my office by mistake. Your mother says supper's on the table."

I stood in the center of the room and searched my memory. Where had I tucked the manuscript? My mind was blank.

Earlier, we'd come home to an open front door. Maybe I'd only thought nothing was missing.

Chapter 31

The three of us stood side by side at the sink, washing and drying the supper dishes. Mother had always been funny about using the dishwasher. Even now, if there was any food stuck to any plate or cookware, she insisted it be scrubbed, washed and dried by hand. Sam and I had agreed that arguing with her about this was pointless.

When my cell phone rang, I dried my hands and crossed the room to retrieve it from my purse. The Caller ID read: *Gail.*

"Jamie, you've probably talked to Romy. The fundraiser is back on. She'll need to find a student to take Caleb's part. He's in pretty bad shape, but at least he's alive."

"Caleb? He's been found?" A tightness in my chest eased. The student's fate had been on my mind all week. I'd been afraid for him.

"It's been on the local news all day."

"I've been out of town. Haven't even had the television on. Did the police find him?" I chewed at a fingernail, anxious to hear what had happened and to learn of his condition.

"He showed up at his house late last night," Gail explained. "The television reporter said Caleb has no memory of the past week. His mother took him to the hospital, and the spokesperson there noted that Caleb was in good condition. But we can't expect him to do the play."

"Of course not."

"I'll talk with Romy. She probably has a drama student in mind."

Gail hung up and I sank onto the bar stool. Caleb was all right. Where had he been? What had happened? The police would talk with him and eventually, maybe the rest of us would learn the details. Meanwhile, all I could do was speculate about what had happened. If it was true that he was 'dating' someone in the play, it would come out.

After cleaning the kitchen, Sam retreated to the space he used as a home office in a corner of the living room, while I headed for the dining room table and my makeshift office. The weekend had been consumed with family issues, and I hadn't reviewed my planner for the week to see what I'd scheduled for my students. I flipped on my computer and quickly located my classroom planning schedule. A mix of class assignments and experiments, I had made careful notations so that a substitute could follow the plan without deviating from the materials the students needed to cover to satisfy local and state requirements as well as my own personal requisites.

I was reviewing my sixth period lesson plan an hour later, when a message popped up in the corner of the screen, notifying me of a new email from 'A Friend.' I ignored it. A message from anyone I knew would pop up with their name, not that phrase. Five minutes later, the message appeared again. And five minutes after that. I closed my class planner software and opened my email. The three emails showed in my inbox, one after another.

Subject: *I Know What You Did*
Subject: *I Know What You Did*
Subject: *I Know What You Did*

And what exactly was that? The message space of each email was blank.

Sam and I were both lost in our thoughts as we readied ourselves for bed. He showered, and I cleaned my face and brushed my hair. Finally, I reached for my toothbrush in the ceramic holder by the sink. It wasn't there.

"Sam, have you seen my toothbrush?" I called. The running water stopped.

"Toothbrush? It's not in the holder?' Sam reached out of the shower and grabbed a towel from the rack.

"No." I dug through the drawers beneath the vanity top, and then checked the floor beneath the vanity and the nearby wastebasket. "Not here."

"Maybe your mother cleaned the bathroom after you two got back today and threw it away," Sam said.

"It wasn't that old." I searched the same drawers again. "That's crazy."

"It'll turn up. Don't you have a replacement somewhere?"

"I keep extras in the linen closet, in case someone needs one." I crossed the room and rummaged through the bathroom supplies until I found an unopened toothbrush package. I tore it open and returned to the sink to brush my teeth.

A missing toothbrush, a missing envelope, and an open door. Had someone been in the house while Mother and I were gone? Maybe. Was anything else missing? Should I have called the police? Should I tell Sam? It seemed so inconsequential. *He has enough to worry about.*

"Sam, how are you feeling about the inquest on Wednesday? We haven't talked about it recently. Has your PI friend had any luck finding Reba's sister, Sharon?" I asked after I brushed my teeth.

At his sink, Sam squeezed toothpaste onto his toothbrush. "He's searching for her. Last known whereabouts were in Tulsa, around nine years ago. He thinks she might have changed her name."

"Why would she do that?"

He shrugged as he brushed his teeth. He spat and said, "Maybe she got married?"

That seemed logical to me. "I hope he can find her."

"Me, too. Thing is, there is no way to know whether she'll be a character witness for me, or against me."

"Against you? Did the two of you have issues?"

He wiped his mouth with the towel. "It wouldn't be the first time two sisters had an issue with the husband of one of them." He hung the towel back onto the rack and stepped into the bedroom.

In the backyard, the Watcher stands hidden within the thick arborvitae hedge. At the far end of the ranch-style house, a light clicks off.

Cozy evening. First, they're in the kitchen, doing the dishes. Next in the dining room/office. And then the bedroom.

The Watcher chuckles, and peers through the fragrant branches of the evergreen. Earlier, neighborhood kids had been slamming their skateboards down on the cement and jumping their bicycles over the curbs as the unseasonably warm night pressed against their skin. But all is quiet now.

Glad I was here to witness her finding that bottle in the trash. Has she mentioned it to him yet? Wish I could be a fly on the wall to hear that conversation. I'm missing out on a lot. I need cameras and hidden microphones. But getting them into their house, with that old woman there all the time, will be harder than the house in Pawhuska. I didn't even need electronics for that part of my plan.

The Watcher yawns, and stoops to walk out of the bushy evergreen.

Tomorrow is another day. And it won't be long, now. This week.

Chapter 32

Monday

I stepped into the high school, sluggish from lack of sleep. The smell of floor wax hung in the air, as well as the scent of bleach. Amazing that all schools smell the same, no matter where they are. The halls were empty but scattered classrooms were lit up, indicated some teachers had arrived early, like me.

At my classroom, I reached around the doorframe to the light switch. The lights flickered on to illuminate Detective Blaise, leaning against my desk, his arms folded.

"Good morning, Mrs. Mazie. Did you have a good weekend?"

I crossed the room to the closet and hung up my jacket. "There's really no need for chit-chat. I heard that Caleb is back. Is that why you're here?"

"Where were you this weekend?" He maintained his casual pose against the desk.

I suspected that he knew where I'd been, that it was either Blaise or one of his cohorts who had followed us in a dark sedan throughout the weekend. But I knew better than to be belligerent. Policemen in general are friends of the public. I didn't really believe Blaise was a bad apple. "I drove to Pawhuska on Saturday with family. We were gone all day. Sunday, I drove to Muskogee with my mother to visit my brother at the Veterans hospital. It was a busy weekend." The kernel of a headache that had begun in my head after I woke up, blossomed.

"Yes, it was a busy weekend. But somehow you found time to get Caleb back to town, leaving him with a permanent reminder of your affections, right?" His cold blue eyes drilled into mine.

"I don't know what you're talking about." I circled the desk and stood behind the chair, bracing myself. "I heard he had come home. What happened to Caleb? Where has he been?"

"So that's how you want to play it." The detective straightened and loomed over me. "Caleb had ligature marks on his neck and his wrists. And burns from what was most likely a cigarette. And he'd been branded. Don't tell me you've forgotten incising your initials on his wrist?"

"What?" I clenched my fists, not believing what I was hearing. "That's horrible."

"J.M. was carved into the flesh on the inside of his lower right arm. J.M. for Jamie Mazie."

I gripped the back of the chair as my classroom did a lazy spin. "That's crazy. Why would I do that? What did Caleb say?"

"He has no memory of the last seven days. Doesn't remember where he was, how he got there or how he got home. But I think you know."

"I was with a family member every minute of the last two days. Ask any of them." I pulled my planner, graded homework assignments and two text books from my satchel and stacked them on the desk.

"I probably will. And I may also ask them about your friend, Davis. Some letters have surfaced. Evidence of your affair. Are you still denying it?"

Letters? Like Mother had found? My mouth went dry. "I hardly knew him." A student appeared in the doorway, lingered for only a second and then slipped back into the hall.

The detective pulled a folded paper from the inside pocket of his jacket. "Does this look familiar?" He opened the paper revealing my monogram at the top of the page. The note below it looked to be printed on a computer.

It was my stationary, with the letter 'J' in a fancy script centered at the top. "Where did you get that?"

"It was sent anonymously to my office this morning."

Words wouldn't come. I had no answer as to how my stationery had ended up being sent to the police. I kept it in a drawer of the buffet cabinet, near my makeshift 'office' on the dining room table. My tongue felt like sandpaper.

"I didn't write it."

"The text was printed on a computer using Times New Roman, a very common font, as you know." He folded the paper again and slipped it back inside his pocket. "And there's one more thing. I'm going to need a DNA sample. A toothbrush was recovered from Davis' home during another search of the premises last night.

It's possible it belonged to his lover. I'd like to take a sample of your DNA."

It probably was my missing toothbrush. My initials carved into Caleb's wrist, my stationery with love notes written to Davis, and my toothbrush in his bathroom. Someone had been in my house yesterday. They'd taken the script I'd been sent, my stationery and my toothbrush.

When I climbed into my car after school, I couldn't remember much about the day. It had passed in a blur. I had handled the lessons and experiments by rote, and as the buzzer sounded at the beginning and end of each class, I fell into zombie mode. One half of my brain remained frozen, unable to comprehend or accept what the detective had told me.

The text notification dinged on my phone. *R U still meeting me for coffee?*

I closed my eyes and grasped the steering wheel. Belina was a stranger, but I was badly in need of a sounding board. I needed someone to share this with, someone to help me decide what I should do. Mother couldn't handle it, and neither could Trudy. And Sam was too involved in his own dilemma to pull him into mine. Belina was reaching out in friendship. Should I let her into my life?

I texted back, *On my way.*

At the Coffee Nook, Belina waved from a table in the corner and then took a sip from a large mug. Steam rose up around her head.

I placed my order at the counter: a latte with an extra shot of espresso. I needed a boost to get through the rest of the day.

She smiled as I reached the table. "Thanks for coming. How was your day?"

"I've had better." I slipped off my jacket and hung it on the back of the chair.

"Students giving you a hard time? I can't imagine teaching high school. Those kids are on a hormone high. And science? I bet most of the kids don't give a flip about that." She grinned and tossed her hair.

I couldn't argue with her assessment. I forced a smile. "You're probably right. But the ones who want to get into college are interested or pretend to be. And with the new emphasis on technology because of all the high-tech gadgets being developed, there is relatable information in science class."

"Sure there is. Davis said the same thing about geography." She frowned at her coffee cup. "I wanted to ask you something. I heard a rumor."

A queasy feeling settled in my stomach. I blew on my latte, and then took a sip.

"You remember that I'm from Fairfax? People there like to talk."

I nodded. Was this going to be about Sam, or me?

"I heard they dug up Sam's first wife. And that there's a cold case investigation? Is that right?" She peered at me through the steam of the coffee and lifted the cup to her mouth.

"It isn't a rumor. It's true. The inquest is Wednesday."

"That's awful." Her shoulders slumped. "I mean, just because Sam had a reputation as a party boy in

high school ... As if you don't have enough to deal with."
She set her cup on the table and traced the rim with
one finger. "There's another rumor. About you and
Davis. Is that one true, too?" She stayed very still,
waiting for my response.

Sam, a party boy? That didn't sound like the Sam
I knew. I opened my mouth to refute her statement but
closed it and kept silent. He was an admitted alcoholic,
after all. But I had to respond to this second rumor, not
run from the cafe like I wanted to. That wouldn't help
matters. She would think that the second rumor was as
true as the first. "No. that's not true. Someone is setting
me up. I hardly spoke to Davis. We didn't meet until the
first rehearsal."

"You didn't see one another at school?" Belina
tilted her head and watched me.

"No. His classroom was in a different wing of the
building, on a different floor. And I have no clue what
lunch period he was scheduled to supervise. I didn't
know him."

A sigh eased through her slightly open mouth.
She nodded. "I believe you."

"Why does this matter to you, anyway? You and I
hardly know one another." I fingered my cup and dented
the thick paper sleeve of the cup holder with my
fingernail.

"We could be friends. If there wasn't suspicion
between us." She rolled her eyes.

"Suspicion?" I wasn't suspicious of her, why was
she suspicious of me?

She folded her hands on the table top. "I had such
a crush on Davis. He flirted with me, and I thought he

might ask me to go out with him, but then he was murdered. I'm still not over it." Her lower lip trembled.

"I'm sorry. It's troubling that after more than a week they haven't found his killer." And troubling that the police seemed to suspect *me*.

"I have my suspicions about who did it, but no proof." Belina pushed back in her chair and closed her eyes.

"Who do you suspect?"

She gritted her teeth and hissed, "Romy."

"Why?"

"She always interrupted us whenever I tried to talk to him. She wouldn't leave him alone."

I didn't recall any interactions between Romy and Davis at the rehearsals, only general cast instructions during the blocking session. "But I don't remember–"

"Of course, you don't. You weren't around. You weren't watching." Her eyes widened and glittered. Her lips pressed tightly together. She looked like a completely different person from the smiling woman who'd been sitting at the table when I arrived.

"Have you mentioned this suspicion to anyone else?"

"Why would I? But I trust you. I don't think you're the kind who would let a murderer get away with it."

"Whoa. A murderer? How did you get from flirtations to murder?"

"He turned her down. She couldn't take it. She didn't want another woman to have him." Belina's eyes sparked.

"I guess that's possible." I gulped my coffee.

Belina's chest heaved and her face reddened. She seemed close to tears.

"Did you hear that Caleb is back?" I said, changing the subject.

Belina settled her wide eyes on my face. "The missing student?" she asked in a deadpan whisper.

"Yes. The police don't know where he was, and he has no memory of the past week. He's in the hospital."

She swirled the liquid in her cup and stared into it. "Glad to hear it."

We sat in silence for a few seconds. She didn't seem glad about Caleb. And she thought Romy was a killer.

My cell phone rang. The Caller ID listed a local number I didn't recognize. I glanced at Belina, but she seemed lost in thought.

"This is Jamie Mazie," I said into my phone.

"Mrs. Mazie, I'm calling from the Ponca City Hospital. We have your cousin Trudy here. Her friend listed you as next of kin on her admission papers and asked us to call you."

"What happened?" I pulled in a quick breath.

"She was attacked in her home. She's in the ER right now."

"I'll be right there." I clicked off the phone. It must be something serious if they brought her to the Ponca City hospital. "I have an emergency, Belina, I've got to go."

She glanced up from her coffee cup with red-rimmed eyes. "Hope it's nothing serious. See you at the rehearsal tomorrow?"

I hurried out of the coffee shop, my mind in turmoil. What had happened to Trudy?

Chapter 33

The smell of antiseptic flooded out of the Emergency Room doors of the Ponca City Hospital as I rushed inside. A triage nurse acknowledged me with a nod but continued to speak with the elderly couple at the check-in window. A volunteer pouring water into the coffee machine glanced up at me.

"Are you looking for someone?" she asked.

"My cousin, Trudy O'Day. Someone called me to say she was here."

"Give me one minute and I'll find out where she is." The volunteer poured the remaining water into the machine, then rushed down a hallway and through a door. A minute later, she came through another door into the waiting room and motioned to me. "She's in Cubicle 7. You're Jamie, right?"

I followed her through the doorway and into another hallway where white full-length curtains closed off a dozen cubicles. The volunteer led me to cubicle seven and drew back the curtain. Trudy was stretched out on the narrow bed. Vera sat in the extra chair on the far side of the narrow room, one hand patting Trudy's shoulder.

Trudy groaned. White bandages covered half of her forehead and her left cheek and one hand was wrapped in thick gauze. Her left eye was swollen shut; the deep red bruise would be purple tomorrow. Her right eye opened.

"Jamie!" she wailed. "The ghost attacked me!"

"Oh, Trudy." I rushed to her and touched her gently. "I'm so sorry." Then I looked at Vera. "What happened?"

"We're going to step outside for a minute, honey." Vera patted Trudy's arm. "We'll be right back. You try to rest."

"Don't leave me!"

Vera patted her again. "For just a minute. I need to talk to Jamie."

"The ghost beat me up. I was so scared." Trudy thrashed on the bed.

A male nurse entered the cubicle. "We've got a room assignment, and the orderly will take you up in a minute." He noticed me. "You're the cousin? We have some paperwork for you at the desk."

"Let me take care of this, Trudy. I'll be right back." I patted her hand and left the room.

As much as I wanted Vera's insight into what had happened, it could wait until Trudy was in her room. On my way to the desk, I asked the nurse about Trudy's condition.

"She has some bad bruises and lacerations. Nothing required stitches. She definitely took a beating."

At the desk, I signed the paperwork for her admission. A 'ghost' attacked Trudy. Whether she truly believed it had been a ghost or not, she must have been terrified. I was terrified, and I knew that her attacker was *not* a ghost.

"She insisted on going home last night," Vera said, leaning toward me from her chair in the waiting area nearest Trudy's new hospital room. "You know how Trudy is when she makes up her mind."

I did. She was like a dog with a bone, unwilling to be diverted. "So, you let her."

"Of course, I let her. And she didn't want me to stay."

"This happened last night?" I asked. The nurses were still in Trudy's room, getting her settled in the bed and checking her vital signs.

Vera threw her hands up in the air. "I'm not sure when it happened, and neither is Trudy. I called her at lunch time today, I'd planned to bring her a barbecue sandwich and fries. She didn't answer the phone, so I drove over but she didn't answer the door, and it was locked. Augie didn't bark. I figured they'd gone for a walk, or to the store. I ran some errands and went home."

"Was she inside the house, hurt?"

Vera shook her head. "I don't think so. I called her a little later, and she still didn't answer the phone. I drove back over. This time, the front door was unlocked, and when I went in, I found her in the kitchen." Vera shook her head. "She was all bruised and bloody. I don't know what the hell happened."

"What did she say?"

"She moaned, 'the ghost', over and over. And 'where's Augie?' She insisted I look all over the house for him, and in the backyard."

The dog wouldn't leave Trudy's side willingly. He was never more than three feet away from her. "Where is Augie now?"

Vera shook her head. "Augie is gone. I told her we should go to the Ponca hospital, since you and Sam were here. I don't know what's going on at that house, Jamie, but she can't stay there."

"Did she say who attacked her?" I rubbed the back of my neck, where goosebumps had formed. Trudy had been in real danger, and none of us had seen it coming. Correction, I thought: Theresa had known.

Vera shook her head. "She can't get past the 'ghost' part."

"Did you call Toby?" I wondered if the sheriff's investigation into the vandalism had turned up anything.

"Yes. He was at the house when we left. He'll probably call you soon."

"I hope so. He needs to get to the bottom of this." Surely Toby had some leads. Had he interviewed Bosque? The convict had to be behind this.

When the nurses left Trudy's room, one of them stopped beside us. "I've given her a sedative, and an IV. Tomorrow she'll be free to go home, but I'm sure she'll be sore. Talk with the discharge nurse in the morning, please."

Vera and I stepped inside the room. Trudy lay on the bed, eyes closed, jaws clenched.

"Trudy?" I leaned over her.

Her right eye flicked open, and then shut.

"You need to rest, now. I'll come back with Sam after supper. Okay?" I reassured her. She didn't respond. The medicine had already kicked in.

"I'll stay for a while, Trudy," Vera said. "Get some sleep. I'll drive back to Pawhuska later." Vera perched on the side of the bed.

The fingers of Trudy's right hand worried the edge of the bed sheet, and then eventually lay still.

Chapter 34

"Mother? Sam?" In the house, the aroma of something beefy cooking floated on the air. Leftover stew, I expected. My nose led me straight to the kitchen, where both dogs were studying Mother as she stirred a pot on the stove. Princess pranced across the small kitchen table and jumped to the floor at my feet. I knew her tricks. Since the dogs were preoccupied, she could grab my undivided attention.

I stooped to pet her as she wound her way through my legs, flicking her tail like a feather against my calves.

"Sam's not here. Hasn't called. Thought I might be having supper alone." Mother glared at me. "Don't know why it's so difficult to let me know when you'll be late. Do you two ever manage to eat together?"

I thought about my answer. With the two of us, Sam and I had never kept a regular suppertime. It happened when it happened, and often one of us picked up supper and brought it home so that no one had to cook and there were no pots and pans to scour. Bringing a third person into the mix had made suppertime much more complicated.

"Supper isn't the major deal it was years ago. And it's always just been Sam and me. We are flexible about eating."

"And I'm not, huh?" She slammed the spoon down on the counter. Drops of brown sauce splattered the granite. "It's a matter of common courtesy to call. Courtesy. Does no one practice that anymore?"

"I'm sorry."

She grabbed two pot holders out of a drawer.

"Mother, I'm late because Trudy's here in the hospital. I should have called, but ..."

"What has she done now? That woman has always been accident prone, and you know it. From the day she was born." She lifted the pot off the stove and carried it over to a trivet on the counter, shaking her head.

"It wasn't an accident. Someone attacked her."

Mother placed the pot on the trivet then whirled to face me. "Attacked her? Where?" She dropped the pot holders.

"In her house."

"I thought you had the locks changed?"

"We did. I don't know the details. Trudy's bruised, but no bones were broken."

"Who did this?" She leaned against the island, her fingers splayed against the granite.

"I don't know. Toby will investigate. I'm still waiting for him to call." I pulled dishes out of the cabinets and silverware from the drawer and arranged the place settings on the bar side of the kitchen island.

The oven timer dinged. Mother grabbed the pot holders from where they had fallen on the floor and retrieved biscuits from the oven. "I don't know what to think about this place, Jamie. Bad things happen here. Maybe I'll go back to New Mexico." She slid the biscuits off the baking sheet and into a woven basket. "No one is safe here," she muttered.

It did seem that way. Ever since Mother had arrived, not even two weeks ago, our lives and our new city had been in constant turmoil.

Mother ladled the stew into two bowls. My phone rang.

"Jamie, it's Toby. Have you been to see Trudy?" My sheriff friend's voice was brusque and to-the-point.

"Yes. At the hospital. But we didn't have a chance to talk. Tell me you know what happened and who's behind this. Trudy wasn't saying much."

"We figure Trudy left the house to walk the dog and left the back door unlocked. There was no sign of forced entry. She must have been on that walk when Vera stopped the first time. The intruder probably assaulted her when she got home. There's still no sign of the dog."

"And no eye witnesses?"

"None of the neighbors saw anything."

"What are we dealing with here, Toby?"

"All I know for sure is that real fists made those bruises, Jamie."

"If this is about Sam, as the writing on the countertop said, why attack Trudy?"

"We won't know that until we find the perpetrator. I'll keep you posted."

I clicked off my cell phone and laid it on the countertop.

"No answers, I take it," Mother huffed.

I shook my head. "No. This is very frightening. What if they shift this mischief here, to our house?"

The doorbell rang, and the dogs dashed for the door.

"Why is it the doorbell rings whenever we're sitting down to supper?" Mother groaned.

"It's a rule of nature," I called over my shoulder as I hurried down the hall.

The man who waited on the porch was tall and muscular, with dark hair and eyes, like Sam's. He was familiar. I opened the wooden front door but waited before opening the glass storm door. When he smiled, I was certain of his identity. Only one person in my wedding photos had that wide, bright smile.

The dogs woofed and rushed out onto the porch to sniff Lucas Mazie's pant legs. He extended an open hand for them to nose.

"Hello, Jamie. Sorry to stop in unexpectedly." Sam's brother straightened.

I hugged him quickly and turned back to the house. "Come in, Lucas. What a surprise. Sam's not home, but Mother and I were about to eat some supper. Please join us."

"Late day at the office, huh?" He followed me into the house and slipped off his jacket. I took it from him and hung it on the coat tree in the corner of the entry hall.

Lucas looked lean and fit. Like Sam, he had aged into an attractive middle-aged Native American man, but more muscular and taller than Sam.

"Yes. The work days are often long right now." I peered up at him. "Join us for supper?"

"If you insist. How much later will Sam be?"

"No way to know." I led the way to the kitchen. Other than at our wedding festivities, I had never had a conversation with Lucas. I'd only been around him that one weekend. "I'll call and let him know you're here."

"Don't bother. I want to surprise him."

For Lucas to appear on our doorstep after eight years was more than a surprise. And the timing, with the disinterment and investigation into Reba's death, made me wonder if that had influenced Lucas to visit.

Mother looked up from her stool at the bar as we came into the kitchen. Her eyebrows lifted.

"Lucas, do you remember my mother, Mary Jamison? Mother, this is Lucas, Sam's older brother. You met at my wedding."

"Oh, Lucas. How nice to see you again. We weren't expecting company." She glanced from the pot holders to the dirty spoons and pots that cluttered the stove and the counters.

"Please, Mrs. Jamison. I'm family. It's kind of Jamie to offer me supper. I should have called first."

"Mmmm." Mother slid off her stool and went to the cabinet where she grabbed another bowl and saucer. "Sit here, please." She indicated the small breakfast table and relocated the two place settings from the bar to the table. Then, she rummaged in the silverware drawer. As Lucas scooted his chair up to the table, she spooned up another portion of stew.

"What brings you here?" Mother asked. She wasn't one to beat around the bush, and I was glad she was taking the initiative to get the conversation going. I had a lot of questions for Lucas, but I needed an intro to that conversation.

Lucas smiled and picked up his spoon. "I'm sure you know my mother. She called yesterday, and although she didn't say so, I could tell she wasn't feeling well. And she was upset about the disinterment." He studied the steaming bowl in front of him, stirred it, then pulled a biscuit from the basket and buttered it. "I decided I needed to drive down to see her."

"That's an attentive son. I hope your mother appreciates you." Mother pushed her chair up to the table and picked up her spoon.

Lucas tackled the stew and biscuits as if he hadn't eaten all day.

"This is very good, Mrs. Jamison. Did you make it?" Lucas wiped his mouth with his napkin, and then scooped up another spoonful.

"I did. They don't cook."

"Too busy, I'd imagine. I like your house, Jamie. Fitting for two professionals." He nodded at me and kept eating.

"Thanks. We're not quite unpacked. As you probably suspect, life has been stressful with the move and the Pawhuska event."

He nodded and scraped the last of the stew out of his bowl. His brow furrowed as he placed his napkin and utensils on the table. "I've been turning things over in my mind about Reba. Both Mother and I are concerned about how this reflects on Sam. He wasn't at fault, you know."

Mother stood, grabbed all three plates and bowls and carried them to the sink.

"I never thought he was." I played with my napkin. Why was Lucas here? I'd told Sam last night that we needed to talk to him, and now here he was. Had Sam called his brother, too?

"It is natural to have doubts. To wonder. I have the benefit of an outside view."

"You were in the service. And lived elsewhere. What could you know about their marriage, or what happened in their relationship while you were gone?"

"Maybe nothing. But I knew them before. I know what their relationship was built on, how it began. There is insight there."

"Probably."

"Would you like some dessert? Or coffee?" Mother asked.

"Coffee. Black, please." Lucas pushed back his chair. Zeus padded over and stuck his nose on the chair seat, then waited for Lucas to rub his nose.

"You knew Reba when she was younger?" I asked.

"Yes. And her sister, Sharon. Sharon and I briefly dated. Sometimes the three of us went places together."

"Like the Grand Prix Road Race here?" I stood and crossed the room to the window. When I faced Lucas again, he fixed his eyes on me.

"How do you know about that?"

"For now, let's say I learned it from a playwright. Tell me more about Reba and her sister."

He got up from the table. "First, let's get this cleaned up."

The three of us loaded the dishwasher. Then, Lucas nodded toward the living room and led the way to the other room.

"Sharon was the wild one," Lucas remarked as he perched on the edge of a living room chair. "When I was young, I was drawn to that type. It was only luck that allowed us to survive." He got up and leaned against the wall, tucking his hands into the front pockets of his jeans.

"Sharon and Reba were close?"

"They fought, like siblings do. Reba always stood up for herself. She didn't let Sharon bully her, at least not when I was around. Then I went to Boot Camp."

"You and Sharon broke up when you left?"

"I wouldn't say there was an official breakup because we weren't officially together. She could get a little too crazy, even for me." Lucas ran his fingers through his hair.

Should I press him for specifics of Sharon's craziness? Maybe, but I wanted to know more about Reba. "Sam's trying to find Sharon. He hopes she can shed some light on why Reba killed herself and put this murder-to-hire rumor to rest."

"I'm not sure Sharon is the one to do that. She'd like nothing more than to send Sam to jail, I'm afraid."

"Why?"

"She blamed him when we stopped dating. And I'm not so sure she didn't feel that he'd rejected her, too."

"You went into the Service. How can she blame Sam for that? And what do you mean about Sam rejecting her?"

Lucas shrugged. "Who knows why Sharon did anything. I learned eventually that she has no conscience. In popular terms, she's a sociopath."

"That was years ago. Any idea where she's been since?"

"She hasn't contacted me."

Mother carried a mug of coffee over to Lucas and he thanked her.

I settled onto the sofa. "Please sit. Surely Sam will be home before long."

"How's Sam doing with this, anyway?" He sat in the wingback chair near the window.

I thought about that. We'd hardly spent any time together since moving in. Sam had been busy arranging his office and tending to his clients, while I'd been preoccupied with my teaching, unpacking and the play. Then there was Trudy and the ghosts. I'd promised to check in with Trudy tonight, but visiting hours would be over in another hour. "I'm not sure. I'm worried, actually."

Lucas cocked his head. "He's not drinking, is he?"

I checked myself before I answered. I wanted to be true to Sam. I didn't know for sure the bottle I'd found in the trash can belonged to him. Considering an intruder had been in our home and taken things of mine, wasn't it possible they had left something else behind?

"Jamie? Is he?" Lucas prodded.

"I found an empty vodka bottle in the trash can, but I'm not sure it has anything to do with Sam. We haven't had liquor in the house for years. Even then, it was wine I'd bought for our guests."

"Vodka wasn't his drink of choice. Maybe someone else in the neighborhood used your trash can."

"That's possible, and even likely. It's not the only weird thing going on around here."

Chapter 35

"Explain." Lucas pushed his body deep into the cushions of the chair and stretched his arm across the back.

In as few words as possible, I told Lucas about Davis' murder, and about the dinner theater play based on the Ponca City Grand Prix. When I told him the playwright was dead, a victim of a hit-and-run, he swore and stood up.

"Damn it. They're still hashing over what caused the crash?"

"Lucas, I heard you were there. And the script had a note on it, saying you were a driver that day. Did you see what happened?"

He ran his fingers through his hair, a gesture Sam often used when he was agitated, and paced the room. His face ran the gamut of emotions; surprise, anger, concern and even disbelief. When he finally stopped, he looked at me with uncertainty.

"Jamie, I've never talked about this. Not with anyone. I'm not sure I want to talk about it now."

"Could two people have been murdered because of what happened that day? And what are the chances that someone else will be hurt if this dinner play actually goes on?" This had become a real possibility in my mind, and I was worried that someone else I knew might be injured or killed. My stomach churned.

Lucas swiped his hand down his face and blinked. "I'll tell you."

"I'll listen, and I won't judge." My heart pounded in my throat, I was afraid of what Lucas was going to say.

"I was young. We were all young."

"And sometimes we do things we later regret," I said. There were several things from my past that I wouldn't want made public.

He nodded. "I do have regrets. I took Sharon and Reba to the races that day. Reba followed Sharon around, watched her flirt. Not that she didn't already know how to do a pretty good job of it herself."

"You drove in the races?" I shifted forward in the chair.

Lucas nodded. "I'd been going to that annual Fourth of July race since I was a kid in the '70s. After they held the race in '87, I decided I wanted to enter the street stock class. So, I found a Camaro at a junkyard. Took me two years to fix it up and add the required safety equipment, another year to learn to compete. In '91, I entered the race."

He paused and took a long drink from his coffee cup. "Fixing that car kept me out of trouble. But when I started driving that Camaro, it fed my need for speed. Country road races on dark nights. I wanted to be in the Grand Prix more than anything."

"I don't know much about the race," I interrupted. "The play is mostly build-up before the race and includes only a few details. The script ends before the final race day begins." I didn't tell him about the ending that Rusty had been thinking of writing before he died. I was sure the play, when it was performed, would end as the original script had been written, prior to the final races. My leg twitched, and I pulled it up under me. I needed to know what happened.

"The final races were thirty laps at an average speed of 93 miles per hour," Lucas explained, "and there were over twenty divisions of cars, racing in eight or so separate races. We had to qualify in a 10-lap preliminary on Saturday, prior to the finals on Sunday. I remember, that year, 1992, 145 drivers pre-registered. That's a lot of cars, a lot of drivers." He peered at me. "You've been out there and seen the track?"

"I've been to Lake Ponca and driven the road on the east side, around the old concession stand and the lake offices." I squirmed in the chair.

"Then, you've been on the track. Not quite an oval, almost like the head of a golf club driver. Sharp turns at the bottom and the top, but a good straightaway to pick up speed. Nightmare number 6 turn at the bottom, then back up to the pits." He closed his eyes. "I still dream about that turn. Saw more than one racer plunge into the lake there, didn't matter how many hay bales and barriers they stacked up."

"But someone died that day." I leaned forward again.

He studied his hands, shaking his head. "I saw the dust ahead of me. Knew someone had gone off on the Number 2 turn. Red flags came out. The race stopped. I didn't know the details until I was back at the pit."

"What happened?"

"A volunteer claimed that a woman or girl had run across the road in front of the first-place race car as it made the turn. The car flew off the track, into the grass and hit a tree. When the crews got there, the driver was dead. Strange thing is, no one else saw the female who supposedly caused the crash."

"That's terrible." Images filled my mind and I shivered, but not because I was cold.

"Took hours to get things cleaned up. Eventually, they ran the final races."

"Did you place in the race?" I stood up and walked over to the window.

"Didn't finish. Loaded up the car and headed home after the accident." He took a deep breath and brushed at his jeans with one hand. "Sharon and Reba wanted to leave. Reba was feeling sick."

"After all your work?" I whirled to face Lucas, not believing what I was hearing. "You packed up and drove home without racing in the finals?"

He shrugged. "Yes."

"And then you left and enlisted in the Army."

"Yes."

"There's more to this story, isn't there, Lucas?" I couldn't believe it was as simple as he'd told it. Was there another reason the girls wanted to leave? What had made Reba sick? A knot in my stomach meant I might already know the answer to those questions.

He cleared his throat and looked at his watch. "Doesn't look like baby brother is going to make it home, and I'm sure Mom is waiting on me. I'd better go."

"One more question, Lucas. Who was the racer who died?" Tension held my body still as I waited for the answer.

"Royce Harwood. He was from Blackwell, or Tonkawa maybe. His brother was the one who claimed some girls were involved. But he couldn't identify them, and there was no other proof."

My heart pounded and sweat beaded on the back of my neck. Puzzle pieces were falling into place. Rusty Clement was the playwright, and Davis Harwell had been helping him with authenticity details. Davis' brother was the racer who died. Had Rusty and Davis both seen what happened right before the crash?

"Jamie, I promised Mom I'd get to her place before she got ready for bed. I should head that way." As he stood up, he rubbed the palms of his hands on his jeans.

"Sam's probably tied up at the office, or ... something." My head spun with this latest information. But there were missing details. "I'm glad you stopped by and we had a chance to talk." I had a feeling I would learn nothing more. Either he couldn't tell me, or he wouldn't.

"It was good to see you. I'll catch up with Sam tomorrow. We'll talk again before I go back to St. Louis," he promised.

I walked Lucas to the door and watched him stroll down the sidewalk to his car.

A driver had died because of a 'female.' My mind filled in the blank space left by what he hadn't said. A woman ran across the track. Had Sharon or Reba been that woman?

Lucas's red taillights disappeared down the street. The ticking of the living room mantle clock pulled me back to the present.

Visiting hours at the hospital were over. I grabbed my cand called Vera. She picked up on the first ring.

"They gave Trudy something to help her sleep, and as soon as she dozes off, I'm headed home. I take it you're not going to make it here tonight."

"Sorry. Weird thing happened. Lucas Mazie showed up, unexpectedly. He just left."

"Did you ask him about the race?"

"Yes. Interesting story." More than interesting, but what other word could I use?

"And Sharon and Reba were with him?"

"He was racing. But he took them there."

"And?"

"Nothing definitive. Hopefully, I can talk to him again tomorrow. He's in town to see Theresa."

My phone buzzed; another caller was on the line. Sam? "I've got to go, Vera. I'll visit Trudy first thing tomorrow morning. When you take her back to Pawhuska, can she stay with you until we can give the house a thorough check?"

"My shift at the grocery tomorrow is 8 to 4. I'll be back at the hospital by 5:30 to pick her up. Neither of us are setting foot in that house until someone figures out what's happening there."

"Toby is working on it. Thanks, Vera." I clicked off and tried to switch to the waiting call, but the second call had gone to voicemail.

In a few more seconds, I was able to listen to the message. "Heading over to Mom's tonight, Honey. Sorry I missed you. I'll call in the morning. Love you."

Sam's voice, low and gravelly, sounded tired and stressed. Theresa was ill, ill enough that she'd asked Lucas to come home, and Sam to spend the night with her. Did Sam know that Lucas was going to be there? Why would she need them both? How ill was she?

A new worry ached in my stomach.

The Watcher stares through the front window into the brightly lit living room.

Lucas Mazie. I wouldn't have believed it if I hadn't seen it myself.

A slight change of plans. Maybe I can take care of Sam and Lucas at the same time. With his history, it won't be hard to weave him into Reba's death tale.

The Watcher steps back into the deep shadows, shivering with excitement. Hands tucked into the pockets of the black hoodie, the Watcher turns and strolls away under the shadows of the oaks.

Chapter 36

Tuesday

Visiting hours at the hospital began at 8 a.m., and I was one of the first through the doors. I stopped at the gift shop to buy a card and a bouquet of carnations, then rode up the elevator to the second floor.

Trudy was watching the national news on TV when I entered her room. The bruise on her cheek had deepened to dark purple, and her eye was swollen shut.

"How are you feeling?" I crossed the room to her bedside.

"They gave me something, so I slept. At least in the hospital I don't have to worry about ghosts attacking me, even though people die in hospitals."

Trudy needed to accept that a ghost had nothing to do with what happened to her. "Toby said you took Augie for a walk and left the backdoor open. That's how the person who beat you up got in."

Trudy blinked, and kept one eye on me. "Ghosts beat me up."

"Trudy, a person did this to you. They probably got in through the back door when you left it unlocked. We talked about locking the doors last weekend. Remember?"

Her look shifted to the television, and her chin jutted towards it as she clenched her jaw. "Why doesn't anyone believe me?"

"Did you give a description of your attacker to Toby Green? What did your attacker look like?"

Her eye shifted lazily back to me. "It was Reba's ghost. She had dark hair and wore a wedding dress with a long white veil over her face. She whispered her name, then hit me." Trudy closed her eyes and shivered.

I squeezed her hand. "It could have been anyone in that dress. Not necessarily a ghost."

"Reba's dead, isn't she? Why would the ghost say she was Reba if she wasn't?"

"I don't know." And I didn't. Why would a woman dress up like a dead person and assault someone? The only connection Reba had to Trudy was through me, because of Sam. It didn't make sense.

This time I used side streets and cut through neighborhoods to get to Lake Ponca. The car plowed through swirling leaves. Squirrels rushed across the streets, then leapt from yard to yard in their autumn frenzy to put away nuts for the coming winter. More than once, I slowed down to give the animals time to cross the street.

The drive gave me a chance to clear my head and think about something besides the ghost. Lucas had told me about the race, and I needed to see the location again. Hopefully, Howard DeKalb would be at Wentz

Camp, as well as Pamela Monroney. Both might have been in the area when the races were held. Maybe one of them had been there the day of the last race.

I parked the car at the locked entry gate and called the camp office on my cell phone. Howard answered.

"Howard, it's Jamie Mazie from the high school."

"Hello, Jamie. Rehearsal tonight, right? I'm glad the play is back on, and glad that boy is home safe and sound," Howard said.

I didn't think Caleb was 'sound' exactly, his injuries were severe, but at least he was safe. "Me, too. I have a few questions about the race."

"Don't I recall that the play ends before the race takes place?"

"As currently written, it does. But I'm curious about what happened during that final race. Can I talk with you? I'm out in the parking space by the front entry."

"I'll come out. Be there in a minute."

I leaned against my car and waited for Howard beneath the bright yellow sun. The wispy clouds overhead looked as if someone had taken an eraser to a blue chalk board and not quite obliterated the marks. I studied the clusters of small stone cabins on each side of the gates, and then the sloping lawn to the west. The lake must lie beyond the hill.

"Morning," Howard called. He unlocked the pedestrian gate and came through. "Let's walk that way." He jerked his head in the direction I'd been looking. "You probably haven't seen the caretaker's house or the rest of the grounds."

"There's a house down there?"

"You'll see it in a minute. No one lives there now. I would find it incredibly peaceful."

We came over the hill. The yellow bungalow, made of painted cement blocks and located near the lake shore, looked abandoned. The grounds had been cared for, but there were no curtains in the windows, or manicured flower beds.

The driveway that bisected the lawn ended at the lakeshore in a boat ramp. The morning sun shimmered; calm water lapped the shore. Across the lake, several small sheds with adjacent boat docks hugged the water's edge.

"So, the last race was the one in 1992? No races after that?" I stared toward the area where the race had taken place, on the other side of a small cove south of the caretaker's house.

"It was a funding issue. The sponsoring groups didn't make enough money to pay the expenses, and liability insurance costs hit the roof."

"That was about the time Americans became lawsuit happy, wasn't it?"

"Yes. And insurance deductibles and rates went sky high. Anyway, the races ended for lots of reasons."

"Was one reason the death of a driver?" I glanced at Howard.

His jaw tightened. "Could be. His death was most likely driver error. In a high-speed race on a short, curvy track, that's always a possibility."

A flock of Canadian geese flapped overhead, calling to one another as their v-shaped formation glided south. The birds dropped to the surface of the lake and folded their wings.

"Howard, do you know what happened when that driver wrecked his race car? Were you there?" I watched his expression and waited for his response.

He pursed his lips.

Ahead of us, a figure appeared on the lawn.

"Ah, there's Pamela. Maybe she can answer your questions," Howard said.

Pamela Monroney bobbed unsteadily toward us, her spiked high heels sinking into the thick lawn. She stopped and waited for us to reach her.

"Mrs. Mazie. Howard tells me the play is back on. I'm thrilled to hear it, but that means we must get right to work again, doesn't it? We've lost a week." Pamela turned and stepped unsteadily beside Howard as we walked toward the pool house.

"Jamie asked about that last race," Howard commented. "She's curious about the driver who died."

Pamela peeked around Howard to look at me. "Why would you want to know about that? It has absolutely nothing to do with our dinner play."

"But it does," I said. "I think that driver's death was the reason Rusty Clement wrote the play. He intended to revise the ending to include the crash."

"Oh, then we'd have an entirely different type of production, wouldn't we?" Pamela scoffed.

"What do you know about that last race?" I asked as Pamela led the way into the building. A whiff of heavy perfume hung in the air as we trailed behind her, something a woman might wear on a dinner date rather than to work.

"You seem to be obsessed with that driver's death," Pamela said as she sat primly behind a small desk in an alcove of the hall. She folded her hands.

"I've learned more about the race, from someone who was there." I sat in the visitor's chair; Howard leaned against the wall. "So, I'm curious."

"No one knows what happened. A racer, who was in first place at the time, lost control of his car on the Number 2 curve and crashed into a tree." Pamela shuffled the papers on her desk and then opened her desk planner/calendar.

"Was there an investigation into the crash?" I tapped my thumb on the wooden arm of the chair. I got the feeling Pamela did not want to talk about this.

"Yes, but there were no reliable witnesses. Most of the sightseers were on the straightaway, between points 4 and 5, or even 6. That's where the racers accelerated." She focused on the calendar spread she'd opened.

"Were you there?"

She glanced at me, then back at the calendar. "Enough about that. Can we talk about your prop list? What have you found so far? There's not much time."

I was certain that she had been there, and that she didn't want to tell me anything about what had happened. I cleared my throat. "I haven't checked my prop list in the past week. Any special suggestions?"

"That's what your mind should be on. Not that racer who killed himself." She closed the desk planner.

Startled, I shifted forward in my chair. "Killed himself? You think he did it on purpose?" This was a new twist.

"Figuratively, killed himself. Race car drivers take chances every day, and he knew a street track like the one here was especially dangerous. If you don't have any more questions about the props or the production,

I'm going to have to bring this meeting to a close. I have a full schedule this morning, starting with a meeting at the Chamber of Commerce in fifteen minutes."

I stood, and Howard pushed himself erect from the wall. "I'll walk you down to your car, Jamie."

Howard and I ambled down the drive to the gates, and my parked car.

"I'll see you this evening?" He asked. "I'm glad the play's back on. And, I'm glad it doesn't go into all that nasty stuff about the race fatality. The driver was popular. All the girls had crushes on him, and as I recall, he'd upset several young ladies that day when word of his engagement got out."

"He was engaged? That makes it even more of a tragedy. Was his fiancée present at the race when he died?" I leaned against the side of my car, hoping to encourage Howard to tell me more.

"Couldn't say. I wasn't there." Howard gazed toward the lake.

"Do you remember who his fiancée was? I wonder if she'd be willing to talk about that race."

He shrugged, and his face reddened. "Local girl, I think."

I unlocked my car and slid inside. He seemed to have lost his desire to talk about the race. I smiled up at him. "Thanks, Howard. I'll see you at the rehearsal."

"Yes, you will. Have a great day."

As I closed my car door, he stuffed his hands into his pockets and sauntered back toward the main building. I watched him go, and then climbed out of my car again. I wasn't ready to go to work, and I wanted a closer look at the lake and the caretaker's house.

The yellow cement blocks on the outside of the house needed to be cleaned. Algae, or maybe mold, had taken hold and was creeping across the face of the bricks. Bushes near the house's foundation had been cut back, some of them were little more than stumps, with stubby former branches lopped off waist high. I stepped up to the windows at the side of the house and peeked inside.

The wooden floors were bare, and lack of furnishing made the small rooms seem bigger than they probably were. The dingy beige walls could use a fresh coat of paint, but otherwise, the interior of the house seemed to be in good shape. I couldn't understand why the Camp wasn't making use of this house as accommodations for a live-in caretaker.

I circled the house and stopped to look at the lake. On the other side of a copse of trees was a boat ramp and a boathouse. Water lapped at the base of the pier; the water was far too shallow to allow any boat to utilize the dock or even travel into this northern arm of the lake. About all anyone could do was fish from the shore, or perhaps from a canoe or kayak.

A padlock secured the barnlike door of the boathouse on the lakeside, but a three-foot gap existed between the water surface and the bottom of the boathouse door. It would be easy to enter with a small boat, or for a swimmer to wade in.

Algae coated the surface of the water around the boathouse and the nearby boat ramp. The concrete ramp ended before reaching the low water level, revealing several feet of slimy mud. I peered into the water, looking for signs of fish or other aquatic life. A woodpecker hammered in a nearby tree, and a great blue heron stood on the opposite shore, one stilt-like leg bent. The water lapped, birds twittered, and far down the lake, a boat motor sputtered.

As I started back up the hill to my car, something moved in the trees near the far side of the caretaker's house.

I hurried up the hill and over to the house until I could clearly see the sloping yard between the house and the main building. The lawn was empty, but I was sure someone had been there. Whoever it was had now disappeared into the trees.

Chapter 37

In the car on the way back to the high school, my cell phone rang.

"Jamie, Trudy and I are heading to my house," Vera said. "I won't let Trudy go into her house alone. Anytime we go there, we'll go together. We'll stop to get some clothes and things she needs. We won't be in the house any longer than necessary."

"Thank you, Vera. And please call Toby. Let him know you are back in town. I think he should have someone watch your house, too. The inquest is today. I can't help but think all of this has something to do with that."

"Could be. Mostly, it's scaring Trudy and getting Sam riled up."

"Call Toby, okay? And stay together, until we know what's happening with the inquest." I pulled my vehicle into the faculty lot at the high school and drove along the row looking for a parking place.

"Jamie, I have to work my shift today. Do you think Trudy will wait in the grocery store snack area that whole time?" Vera asked.

"She's going to have to. Have her bring a book, or a crossword magazine. Maybe even a jigsaw puzzle. And we need to find Augie Doggie. Did you call Animal Control last night?" I circled the lot again. All the parking spaces were taken.

"He hasn't been picked up. I hope we'll find him on the back porch at Trudy's."

"Me, too. Trudy needs that dog. I'll call you tonight." I exited the lot and drove a block down the street to park.

As I hurried through campus to reach the building, I couldn't stop thinking about the racer who had died. Neither Pamela nor Howard had given the driver's name, but Lucas had. Royce Harwell. I would confirm with Romy when I arrived at the theater later, that Royce had been Davis's brother.

The day was full of odd looks from the students and the frozen faces of my fellow teachers. Sarah and Mark gave me sympathetic looks when I passed them in the halls, and Maggie patted my shoulder in the lounge during my afternoon break.

When the last bell rang, I was finally able to relax my tense shoulders. I cleaned up the classroom and waited the required time before I grabbed the bag where I'd stored my notes for the dinner theater. No students had stopped in. Either I was doing a good job explaining the science concepts we were covering, or no one wanted to talk to me.

I headed for the school office, hoping to learn of any new development with Caleb or the latest school gossip, but Gail had already left for the day. I was certain from the look I got from the student receptionist that there was new scuttlebutt about me in circulation. What was it now?

I drove to the Sonic Drive-in, pulled into a space and ordered a chili cheese dog and an orange soda. Mother would be fixing supper, but Sam probably wouldn't be home for hours. I needed time alone. I tuned my radio to an Eighties channel and focused on the music. I didn't want to think about Caleb or Davis or Rusty. And I didn't want to think about Lucas, and what he might know about what had happened at the Ponca City Grand Prix all those years ago.

But most of all I didn't want to think about Reba and what could happen at the inquest. My heart raced.

I pulled into a parking space in the lot near the Ponca Playhouse. Mother had not been happy when I eventually called her to let her know I wouldn't be home for supper. She had not heard from Sam, and the dogs were whining for their food.

"Put a cup of kibble in each bowl and set the bowls–and the dogs–on the back porch. That's all there is to it. I'll be home after rehearsal." When she started to protest, I disconnected.

Belina stood on the steps outside the rear entrance to the old theater.

"Hey, Jamie," she said as I walked up. "That old dude, Howard, is looking for you. He wanted to chat me up, but I'm not in the mood. Why would he think I was interested in him at all? Creepy."

Howard didn't seem creepy to me, only friendly. He was interesting, but way too old for either of us to consider a romantic involvement. "I like him, Belina.

Saw him this morning out at Wentz Camp. He was helpful."

"He wants me to flirt with him like I did with Davis." She bent over and shook her hair, then straightened, flipped her hair and smoothed a few wild strands into place.

"He didn't join the cast until after Davis died. How could he have seen you flirt with Davis?"

Belina glared and shrugged. She pulled open the door and walked stiffly into the backstage area of the theater.

It took my eyes a minute to adjust to the dimness. The house lights were up in the auditorium, but only a few spotlights lit the stage. Students lounged in seats here and there. Romy was deep in conversation with Gail on far Stage Left. They turned toward us as Belina and I crossed the stage. Neither woman smiled.

Romy's eyes narrowed. "Did you get a copy of the script in the mail?" She put her hands on her hips and frowned at me.

"I did. I wondered if the playwright sent it to me by mistake," I said.

"Why did he have your address?" Romy fired back.

"I don't know, Romy." I could see no reason for Romy to be so upset. Wide-eyed, Gail watched Romy.

"You and Davis, now you and Rusty Clement. Not to mention you and Caleb," Romy muttered in a low voice, her eyes glinting at me.

She might as well have slapped me. If there were rumors floating about, I had a good idea who might be behind them. Eyebrows raised, Belina stared at me. She had told me Romy was jealous of her and Davis, even though nothing had happened between them. Now Romy seemed fixated on me. And the look in her eyes sent chills down my spine.

"Why don't we begin the rehearsal?" Gail cleared her throat.

"Let's do that," I agreed.

As Romy turned away, her eyes flashed. What had provoked such a reaction? I had to agree with Belina, the woman had problems.

Two hours later, we had made one very rough read-through of the play, including character stage movements. Romy shouted at the adult cast members throughout, repeating their lines and correcting pronunciations. I worked on my prop list, noting which props needed to be moved during scene changes and working with the stage crew. As I meandered around, I caught Romy's glare more than once.

Howard was a ham. He played up his role as the gardener, reminding me of someone in an English crime drama. Romy sighed and rolled her eyes but didn't correct him. He was older and had a flair for the dramatic. I could see him being the comic relief for the play. The audience would love him.

When I dragged myself into the house about 10:30, Zeus met me at the back door, tail wagging. He gave a low 'woof' and accompanied me into the kitchen where Sam sat at the dining room table in the dim light, his head resting on his hands.

"Sam? Are you all right?" I dropped my satchel and purse on the island and hurried over to him.

"I'm not sure what's going to happen tomorrow. It's eating me up."

I hugged him. He smelled of fresh autumn air. He'd probably been sitting outside with the dogs most of the evening.

"Any word on Sharon's whereabouts from your P.I. friend?" I dropped into the chair next to him.

"The trail ran cold in Tulsa. She disappeared years ago. Nothing in any neighboring states."

"And her mother? Is she still in Fairfax?"

"Her mother disappeared about the time Sharon went off the grid." He stared down at his hands.

"Sam, you don't have anything to worry about. There are character witnesses plenty for you, and now that Lucas is home, can you get him to come to the inquest and testify for you?"

Sam got up so quickly that the chair fell back and hit the floor. He pulled it upright and then crossed the room to the kitchen counter. He leaned against it. "What did you tell him last night, anyway?" He stared at his hands.

"We talked about the car race. When he showed up here yesterday, it was the perfect opportunity."

"But that's not all you talked about. Did you tell him I've been drinking?" His look, filled with hurt and grief, lifted to look at me.

"I told him I found a vodka bottle in the trash. I don't know who put it there. Maybe Mother's been taking a nip on the side." I chuckled, hoping to break the icy atmosphere. Instead, Sam's arms dropped to his side and his fists clenched.

Mary Coley

"I haven't been drinking, Jamie. I made a promise, long ago. And I swore when I married you that it would never happen again."

I jumped up and headed for him, but he put one hand up to stop me from drawing near. "It is clear to me that someone is trying very hard to ruin my life. And it has spilled over to you, and to Trudy, and even to my mother." His hand trembled.

"You're right, Sam. It's spilling over to all of us." Sam thought I didn't trust him, that I thought he was drinking again. I couldn't deny that those thoughts had crossed my mind. I didn't want to believe them, but that wasn't the same as not thinking them in the first place. I took a deep breath and plunged in. "There is more I haven't told you. Rumors at school are that I was having an affair with Davis Harwell, and maybe Rusty, who wrote the play, and even that I was seducing Caleb, one of the students I tutored after school. Where is it all coming from? Who is behind this, Sam?"

His eyes widened, and he wiped his fingers across his forehead. "If I knew who was responsible, I would take care of it. But I don't know, Jamie." He ran his fingers through his thick, black hair, and focused on me again. "I have to go back over to Mother's soon. She doesn't want to be alone, and she wants both Lucas and me there. I will leave for Oklahoma City early tomorrow. The inquest begins at 8 a.m." He got to his feet and took a step toward the back door.

"Sam?" I reached out and stopped him. "I love you. Remember that."

His head drooped, and he closed his eyes. "And I hope you will always remember that, no matter what happens tomorrow, or in the days following, I would give my life for you."

A chill shook my body as Sam walked out the back door.

Near the kitchen window, the Watcher stands, one hand covering the glimmer of grinning teeth.

This is better than I ever imagined. They are falling apart! Another day or two and destruction will be complete. Victory is so sweet.

Slowly, the watcher backs away into the shadows of the giant oak tree. The light comes on in the garage, Sam's car backs out, the door rumbles down, and the light goes off.

Inside the house, Jamie settles in at the dining room table, pulls books from her work satchel, and spreads them on the table. She rubs her forehead with the tips of the fingers of both hands, making slow circles.

Erasing a headache? Erasing the stress of a marriage, and a life, on the rocks?

Chuckling, the Watcher steps deeper into the shadows and then strolls out through the backyard gate.

Chapter 38

Wednesday

Lack of sleep had taken a toll on my body. My head pounded as I rolled out of bed, and not even a cold shower revived my exhausted limbs. Sam was already on the road to Oklahoma City, even though the sun had yet to poke up above the eastern horizon. Queenie and Zeus followed me to the patio door and rushed out to roll in the grass while I turned on the coffee maker. Once the coffee had brewed, I sat on the porch glider, my legs tucked beneath me as I sipped hot coffee from a mug.

If Sam had asked, I would have gone to the inquest with him. Would that make any difference, having a second wife on hand while the court discussed the death, possibly murder, of the first? Probably not, but it would have given Sam support. It would have let him know that I truly did believe in him.

I didn't like the way our talk had ended last night. His declaration, that he would give his life for me, had not reassured me. What did that mean? My life wasn't in danger. Yes, weird things were happening, but it was

Trudy who had felt the brunt of someone's anger, not me. Did he really think the violence would extend to me?

When I walked into the school, I headed straight to the office. Hopefully, I was here early enough to catch Gail before another day of endless meetings and student interventions began.

I knocked on her partially-open door. Gail was at her desk; she waved me inside. "Jamie, come in. I was hoping we could connect today." The steaming cup of coffee on her desk increased my desire for another cup; fatigue was quickly settling over me.

"I wanted to talk to you about Caleb. How is he?" I asked as I settled into the visitor chair in front of her desk.

Gail clasped her hands together and steepled her fingers. "Caleb is … not good. Something very traumatic happened to him. He's not coherent. He hasn't told the police–or his parents–anything. But the cuts on his wrists–the initials–are very concerning."

"Detective Blaise told me about that. JM. My initials."

"Yes."

The pause lengthened until I finally spoke again. "You don't think I'd be stupid enough to carve my own initials on a student I had kidnapped, and then let him go?"

She shook her head. "No. I don't think that. But it's possible the kidnapper didn't let him go. What if he escaped, and the attacker never thought anyone would see those initials?"

My heart stopped. Were people really thinking I could do something like that? "Gail!"

"I'm voicing what the police are supposing." She frowned, shaking her head. "This is bad, Jamie."

"You've known me a long time. You know I would never do anything like that." I bent over, elbows on my knees, holding my head with my hands.

"No, you wouldn't. But the police don't know that. Someone did a number on that boy. I think the police are going to get a search warrant for your house in Pawhuska."

"Do they think I held Caleb prisoner in our old house? We don't own it anymore. The closing was held the Friday before we moved. The new owners are probably still unpacking like Sam and I are."

She sighed. "Thing is, Detective Blaise told me that the people who bought your place haven't moved in yet. It's a logical place for you to keep Caleb." Gail frowned.

Almost as if she'd summoned him, Detective Roland Blaise rapped on the door of her office and walked in. "Mrs. Strickland and Mrs. Mazie. Convenient to find you together. I won't have to repeat myself."

"Good morning, Detective," Gail said.

"Good morning." He frowned. "We have the DNA results. The toothbrush, and other DNA collected from Mr. Harwell's home, are a match to your DNA, Mrs. Mazie. At this point, you are officially a person of interest in that murder. Don't leave town, or we will have to issue a BOLO and bring you in."

Saliva stuck in my throat. My toothbrush, and other DNA. I was chilled to the bone. Someone HAD been in my house and taken some of my personal items. A deep anger ballooned inside me. I stood, and so did Gail.

"This is ridiculous. I've known Jamie for years, we worked together in New Mexico," Gail blurted. "She and Sam are happily married. I don't know why her DNA was found in Mr. Harwell's house, but I can assure you, Jamie herself didn't put those items there."

Blaise nodded and closed his eyes. When they flashed open seconds later, he drawled, "I'm sure she appreciates your vote of confidence. I'll notify the Superintendent that one of his teachers is a prime murder suspect. He can decide what to do." Blaise barreled out of the office as quickly as he'd come in.

I dropped back into the chair; white noise roared in my ears.

"Jamie, I'm so sorry. Is there anything I can do?" Gail hurried around her desk to stand beside me.

I pushed myself up from the chair and swayed, off balance. When the room straightened, I bolted for the door.

"I don't know what that would be. Someone is framing me, and I don't have the slightest idea why." The words echoed in my brain as I left the room.

Sam had said the same thing last night, about himself.

Outside Gail's office, the secretary waved at me. "A man left this for you." She handed me a folded paper. "You don't look well."

I could see my reflection in the glass door of the principal's office across from Gail's. I didn't look like myself. The clothing was familiar, but other than that, the figure was a medium-sized woman with a very pale face. And I didn't *feel* like myself either.

In the hallway outside the front office, I unfolded the note. The printed writing seemed familiar.

You have a target on your back. You and your husband may soon be dead.

My skin crawled.

A class bell rang as I left the office. A tall, dark-haired man rushed out the main doors of the school. I dashed toward the doors, but students poured from the classrooms and into the hallways, blocking my path. I pushed through them to the front of the building, pulled the doors open and looked for the man. He was gone. The parking lot and the nearby lawns of the big campus held nothing but more students.

It could have been Lucas. The man was the right size and had the right hair color. But, if it was Lucas, why had he left without speaking to me, and why would he have brought a warning to give to me at school?

Another name came to mind. Bosque?

Chapter 39

At the teacher's table in the back of the cafeteria, I bit into the sandwich Mother had made for my lunch and scanned the large room. Whatever else I felt about having my mother as a resident of my home, I very much appreciated her taking over the kitchen. Breakfast was ready when I was ready to eat it, my lunch was packed and waiting by my school satchel, and supper was cooking on the stove when I got home in the late afternoon or early evening. And, having Mother there to talk to when Sam was absent was comforting, whether I enjoyed the conversation or not. Sometimes, the adoring looks of my dogs and Princess's challenging stares, were not quite enough.

The clanging din of the high school cafeteria seemed worse than usual today. Voices hummed, and laughter erupted. Silverware clattered, and trays slammed as students dropped them onto the conveyor belt that carried them into the kitchen. This wasn't a place for quiet contemplation. As one of three lunchroom monitors–my job every-other Wednesday–I listened for nontypical shouts and violence, interrupted if needed, and kept the students moving along if crowds gathered.

Today, a huddle of boys near the tray return caught my attention. One of them stopped and scanned the cafeteria. His look landed on me. He snickered something to the boy beside him, and in a few seconds, the six teenagers had all turned to stare. I stood and ambled toward them. As I came nearer, one of them sauntered toward the exit and the others followed.

It was not hard to make the connection between what had happened in Gail's office this morning with Detective Blaise and the gossip circulating among the student body now. I made my way back through the maze of tables to my station. My lunch sack was gone.

I shook my head and glared at the cafeteria full of students, looking for a shifty-eyed, guilty person. No one stared back.

In my purse, my cell phone rang. The caller ID read *Sam*.

"Hi. How is the inquest going?" I asked in a low voice.

"Testimony was given this morning from the medical examiner, and from Toby as the Pawhuska sheriff. Toby wasn't sheriff when Reba died, but he was elected a year later when Sheriff Wofford died."

"Did anyone else testify?" I scanned the cafeteria again. More students were exiting the room as the minute hand of the wall clock clicked another notch closer to class time.

"I'm first up this afternoon, after lunch. We're expecting the judge to adjourn for the day about mid-afternoon. We'll reconvene tomorrow."

"Has any new information come to light?" I asked. I held my breath until Sam responded.

"No."

Relief flooded through me. I'm not sure what new information could be revealed from the disinterment, but the fact that there was none seemed like a good thing. "Was the man who accused you at the inquest?" I glanced around the cafeteria again. Only a few groups of kids remained, as well as an occasional loner staring at a cell phone screen. I thought again about the man who'd left the note in the office. If Bosque had been in Oklahoma City, he couldn't have been here.

"I don't expect Bosque to testify. This hearing is about the scientific information found after the exhumation, and comparisons with the original autopsy. They're looking for confirmation that the original cause of death was inaccurate," Sam stated.

"But, so far, nothing has been discovered that would lead them to believe the original determination of the cause of death was wrong?"

"No. However, if that is the conclusion of the inquest, a police investigation may take place where Bosque's testimony will be considered."

Bosque wasn't in Oklahoma City. Had he been here, at the high school?

I chewed a fingernail and glanced around the cafeteria again. I wanted the truth about Reba's death to be known. But if her death was confirmed as a suicide, I also wanted to know why she'd done it. I didn't think we would ever know the answer to that question. "Honey, I'm so sorry you are having to relive this again." The bell would ring soon, and the students would clear out. I moved toward the exit doors.

"What is happening there?" Sam asked. "I'm worried about you. I'm out of reach today, and again tomorrow."

I should have told him about the detective's visit to the school, and my new 'status' as a person of interest, as well as the note that had been left at the office, but instead, I said, "Today, I'll be searching for the rest of the props I need. Mostly automotive stuff, things a race car crew would have on hand in the pit."

"Ask Lucas for advice on that. He's staying the rest of the week at Mom's. When I talked to him earlier, she was feeling a little better, but she's very worried about Trudy and everything going on in Pawhuska."

"Trudy has gone home with Vera. I made her promise not to let Trudy go to the house alone, and to call Toby and let him know what's going on."

"Good advice. I'm sure he'll ask a deputy to keep an eye on the two of them, since he's here in the City for the inquest."

The bell rang, and the decibel level rose; voices and the clatter of flatware and trays drowned out Sam's voice.

"I've got to go," I blared into the phone. "Lunch hour is over. I'll be in my classroom and then shopping for props. Call me tonight, okay?

Sam probably responded, but the din was too loud. When I could finally hear again, the phone was dead.

Mid-afternoon, during my planning period, I left the school on my hunt for props. The play included two pitstop racetrack scenes. After researching body shops, maintenance garages and automotive stores, I made a few preliminary phone calls looking for loaner tools. Several shops seemed willing to provide the items I needed.

On the way to faculty parking and my car, two monarch butterflies flitted past. I scanned the sky for more but saw no others. I'd been reading that the number of monarch butterflies was constantly decreasing, and even though the migration was underway across the middle of the U.S., hundreds of thousands of the insects were dying along the way, unable to find the food they needed as they traveled. I watched the insects in their undulating flight and wondered how long each of them would survive. How many generations of their insect family would it take before they arrived at their destination in Mexico, or the less publicized site in southern California?

As usual, the science geek in me got caught up in wondering about the genetic programming so evident in animals of all types, whether insects, fish or mammals. Their lives were short and hard, as they struggle to stay alive until they can reproduce.

One monarch flitted near a large fragrant butterfly bush, circled back and dropped down to one of the bush's tiny dark purple flowers. The insect lingered, drinking the flower's nectar, and then took flight again, fluttering southwest toward the afternoon sun. I let out my breath, feeling like I was emerging from a dream. The quiet interlude had relaxed me more than a brief nap ever could.

At the maintenance garage a few blocks from the school, the manager was polite but adamant that his tools were in constant use by his mechanics, and he had nothing to spare.

My second stop, at the automotive store, had the same result, even though the person who had earlier answered the phone had seemed willing to consider my request.

"Occasionally," the manager said. "People exchange an old tool, usually to get a price break on a newer version. The shop owner doesn't always agree to that. Right now, we're out of used tools. Check at Woody's, on Lake Road."

I headed for Woody's. As I approached the office of the filling station/garage, a mechanic on the way into the office greeted me. His dark green coveralls were spotted with grease, and a red rag hung from his back pocket.

"I talked with someone on the phone earlier about borrowing some tools for the upcoming high school theater club fundraiser," I began. "The play is about the Grand Prix races that used to be held out at Lake Ponca. Can you help me?"

"You probably talked to Mitch, or maybe to Woody." The young man shrugged. "They told you it was okay?"

I nodded. "We only need the tools for a couple of days. Rehearsals, the dress rehearsal, and then the performance. I can bring them back in between if you need me to."

"Believe me, lady, we've got plenty of tools. Most are pretty bunged up, but they still work. What did you have in mind?" He pulled the rag from his pocket and wiped his hand first, then his individual fingers.

"Something that would be standard in the pit, for maintenance during a race."

"That would be most everything. Standard tool box."

The name *Brett* was embroidered on his shirt. "You wouldn't happen to actually have a tool box you could loan me, too? That would be a great prop, Brett."

He squinted toward the cluttered corners of the shop, where an assortment of tool boxes and drawer units lined the walls. "Guess I can loan you mine. But I'll need to take an inventory before you take it. I want everything back."

"Whatever you need. And I'm happy to pay you a rental fee, too. I have a budget, and I'm saving a lot by getting this on a lease basis instead of purchase."

"I'd think most everybody has tools at home, but I guess you don't." Brett smirked.

"We recently moved here. The tools haven't been discovered yet. They're in the garage, someplace."

When he grinned, Brett showed very straight, white teeth. "I get that. My wife and I moved five years ago and we're still discovering things in boxes in the garage that we forgot we brought with us." He selected one of the smaller tool boxes and carried it over to a work table. When he opened the lid, an assortment of tire gauges, drill bits, nails and screws filled the upper tray. He lifted the tray and showed me wrenches, pliers and screwdrivers in the bottom of the tool box. "Let me get a piece of paper to make notes."

While he was gone to the office, I fingered the tools. The original red coating had worn off some. In the bottom of the tool box, there was an odd tool with a long handle and a double-pointed head that I could not identify. I picked it up, wondering about its use.

"That's a window hammer/seat belt cutter. In case you get trapped inside your car and have to break a window to get out."

"I saw something about that tool on TV."

"Haven't ever used one myself, but it sure could come in handy." He spread a sheet of paper on the bench and made a list of the items in the box. "You don't need all of these, but I don't have anywhere else to keep them if I loan you my tool box. They'll disappear for sure if I leave them on a shelf. Be sure I get it all back, okay?"

I promised the tools would be returned immediately after the fundraiser. When he'd finished taking inventory, I gave him my name and phone number. He carried the tool box to my car and put it on the floor of the backseat.

As I waited to turn onto Lake Road and drive back into town, a battered silver sedan drove past. A Native American man in the passenger seat grinned out of his open window and flashed the 'Peace' sign.

It could have been the man from the high school. What did Bosque look like?

I rubbed at the gooseflesh on my arm and pulled into traffic.

Another small group of fluttering monarchs winged their way down the street. A few blocks before the high school, I pulled into the parking lot of the Arboretum on Grand Avenue. Abundant late-season flowers made this a likely stop for the migrating insects. I wandered across the lawn to a sunlit bench where I could see the sky and watch for orange and black wings.

My phone dinged, notifying me of a new message. Vera had written: *Augie Doggie at the dog pound. Home with us now.*

Thank goodness.

I closed my eyes, lifted my face to the sun and thought about Trudy's injuries. Had she been my surrogate? Had someone wanted to beat me up?

During the past eight years, I'd encountered devious people willing to hurt or even kill others, either because of imagined wrongs or to cover up their own deceitful acts. Had one of those people reentered my life? Maybe. But everything happening right now could be related to Reba's death. Someone might want Sam to pay the price, guilty or not.

Cool air tingled on my skin. Clouds had floated across the sun, riding on the breeze blowing out of the east. In front of me, a Monarch battled the wind, his body turning sideways as he fought to fly forward. His tumbling wings failed; he fell to the ground, then crawled over the grass. I reached to let the insect creep onto my hand and then placed the butterfly near a gold chrysanthemum bush. His wings opened and flattened as he rested.

For a very short second, I envied that insect's peaceful existence. It was short, and he was programmed to fly and drink and breed for the few weeks he'd been given in the warm sun. He lived to pollinate plants and reproduce, without worry or concern.

Like most people, I often struggled with the idea of my own purpose, when I had time to considerate it. My daily purpose was obvious, with minute-by-minute goals. I wasn't sure about the big picture.

Today, someone intended to harm me, Sam and Trudy. Who?

I had to stop them.

Chapter 40

Raindrops hit the windshield as I drove home from school hours later. The dreary weather matched my spirits. I had no idea who was behind this vendetta against Sam and me. And I had no idea how to either find them or fight them. The afternoon had passed with me on autopilot, working with my students, leading them through experiments, answering their questions.

I tried not to dwell on the barely-disguised sneers and comments made behind lifted hands. I ignored the teachers' looks and half-smiles as they passed me in the hallways. I held my head up and got through the day. Whatever Sam was enduring in Oklahoma City at the court had to be so much worse.

The soothing aroma of baking bread enveloped me at home. I hung my raincoat on a peg in the mud room alcove and shivered away the damp chill that lingered on my skin. The hot oven had warmed the kitchen, and a trio of lit candles blazed on the island where Mother sat, a magazine in front of her.

"You're early," she observed, looking up briefly before returning to the magazine and flicking another page.

"Woof!" Queenie and Zeus lumbered across the kitchen to greet me. I squatted to pet both dogs. Their fur was warm, soft and thick as I ran my fingers through it. They wriggled, edging as close as they could, lifting their big heads, tongues lolling, ready to bathe my face in doggy saliva.

"How was your day?" Mother asked.

My answer was rote, surface talk, not at all what had been on my mind for most of the afternoon. "I went out to find props today. Now that the dinner theater is back on, I've got to get serious about finding the right things."

"And did you?"

As I talked, she got up to peek into the oven, and pulled pot holders and a cooling rack from the cabinets. When I stopped talking, she asked, "Is Sam coming home tonight?"

"No. The inquest is extended until tomorrow. He'll stay in Oklahoma City."

"What about that Indian, the one who said Sam hired him to kill Reba? Is he in Oklahoma City?"

"I don't know where he is, Mother. Why?" I filled a glass with water from the refrigerator spigot.

She slapped the pot holders down on the counter and crossed her arms. "Some Indian's been hanging around the neighborhood. Saw him drive by several times. And there's a white car I've been seeing a lot. Not to mention that dark blue sedan that followed us to Muskogee on Sunday."

"You've seen these three cars drive past the house today?" I wasn't convinced that Mother was seeing anything other than regular traffic on the busy street in front of our house. And it seemed to me she'd spent most of the day staring out the window.

"I don't keep a journal. But I saw all three of those cars this morning from my bedroom, this afternoon from the living room, and a few minutes ago when I went outside to water the hanging baskets on the front porch." She crossed her arms and leaned against the stove. "Any idea who they belong to?"

"Neighbors, I guess." I carried my satchel over to the dining room and tossed my purse on the short counter next to the house phone. She'd seen a Native American driving by, and I'd seen one at the school first thing this morning, and a few hours later, on Lake Road. He'd made the peace sign with his fingers. What were the chances the men were one and the same?

"What's going on with that murder investigation into the teacher? Your lover."

I glared. "Stop saying that. He was never my lover. I barely knew him. Those notes were planted in my coat." I ran my fingers through my hair and took a deep breath. "Sam and I agree that someone is trying to ruin our lives. We don't know who, and we don't know why. We are worried that there's been carryover to Trudy, and that other family members may be in danger, too."

"Hah. You think anyone would try to burst in here and hurt me with these two beasts on guard duty?" She glared at the dogs; they looked up with soulful eyes and wagged their tails.

"Arff," Zeus barked.

I wanted to smile, but one look at her face kept me from it. She was serious. "Maybe after the inquest, things will calm down."

Princess leapt onto the kitchen table and purred as she tiptoed over to me and sat, licking her paw coyly. I picked her up and lowered her on the floor. "Not on the table, Princess. You know better." She circled my legs, rubbing and purring and then scampered out of the room as if something was chasing her.

"I doubt that anything will calm down," Mother stated. "I've got a bad feeling that if whoever is doing this doesn't get what they want, the problems won't stop until Sam is in jail and you are unemployed and alone." The oven dinged, and Mother picked up the pot holders and pulled the loaf pan out of the oven, placing it on the cooling rack.

Outside, thunder growled.

Mother stood next to the stove, her body stiff and straight. I knew this posture well, she was worried. "You think that's all they want? Sam in jail?"

"Why else would they have told that story about him and the murder-for-hire plot?" Her face crumpled.

Mother was a complainer, mostly about things that affected her. I'd never known her to take an active interest in something that was happening to someone else. But, she and I hadn't lived together in more than twenty-five years. Most of our phone conversations centered around my siblings' problems, or her health. Now she was living here, part of our immediate family. She cared about us, and she needed to know what was happening. I went to her and hugged her. For once, she didn't pull away.

"Mother, I'm sorry for not telling you everything. I didn't want you to worry. I don't know why these things are happening right now, or who is behind it. Neither does Sam. I feel ... helpless." And I did. If I thought about any of it too much, panic would overcome me. Panic and hopelessness. And fear.

She sniffed. "Thank you for letting me live with you, Jamie," Mother breathed. "I want to be useful. And I want to help." She pulled out a bread knife and laid it on the counter. "I've been awful about it. And I'm sorry." She pulled in a ragged breath and wiped her eyes.

My own eyes filled with tears. My mother seemed like a different person, someone I'd wished she was for my entire life. I swallowed the lump in my throat. "I'm glad you're here. It's nice to have another person to talk to."

Princess dashed into the room again and jumped straight for my lap. I caught her and stroked her silky fur before lowering her to the floor.

The thunder rumbled, louder this time.

"I'll check the Weather Channel forecast," I said. "Black clouds were building as I drove home. I think we're in for a storm."

"I'm not so sure about that tornado shelter in the garage," Mother said, crossing the room to look outside. "Seems awfully tiny. What if we get in there and can't get out?" She chewed at her lip.

"It is tiny, but it's a safe place. Chances are we'll never have to use it." I wanted to reassure her, but I had a feeling we'd be seeing the inside of that shelter before Spring was over.

As I flipped on the television in the living room, the doorbell rang. When I peeked outside, Lucas Mazie stared in at me.

"I should have called first, but I was driving by," Lucas said as I pushed open the glass storm door. "Sam back from Oklahoma City?"

I shook my head. A steady rain was falling as the evening darkened. "He stayed in Oklahoma City because the inquest isn't finished. He'll probably call you tonight. How's your mom?"

"Her stomach has calmed down, but she's restless and worried. Have you heard from Trudy today? Is she back in Pawhuska at Vera's?"

"Yes. I don't want her–or anyone–going to that house alone. We need to go through it from top to bottom. Someone still has access. I'm worried."

"With good reason."

Mother came into the hallway from the kitchen. "Lucas, I thought I heard your voice. I baked some bread. Would you like a slice?"

"I stopped by to see if Sam was home, Mrs. Jamison. I should get back to Mom's. Our take-out supper is in the car."

Mother joined me at the door and peered around Lucas to where his dark gray Tacoma pickup was parked in the driveway. "I'm sorry you can't stay. I hope you'll come back over before you return to Missouri."

"I'd like to take you all out to supper before I go. I've heard The Rusty Barrel does a decent steak."

Mother looked at me and shrugged.

"That would be nice, Lucas," I said. "I hope Theresa will feel like joining us, too."

"We'll see. She's not much of a steak eater, but I'm sure they have other things on the menu. I'll talk with you later." Lucas ducked his head, jumped over the porch steps and dashed through the rain to his truck.

"He's a nice man," Mother observed. "He and Sam are both nice men." She marched down the hallway toward the kitchen.

A *nice* man. That was not the description of Lucas that I'd heard from others who had known him years ago, including Sam. It appeared that Lucas had changed, or he wanted us all to believe he had. I wanted to get to the bottom of the race car driver's death. I hoped that I'd have another chance to talk with him about it before he returned home.

Mother was a different person tonight. What had happened? Neither Sam nor I had said anything profound or provocative to her. We'd been very careful not to. But somehow, her attitude seemed different. Who was to say whether this was a new persona, or whether she would be back to her old sarcastic, worrying self in another few days.

Rain drips from the hood of the Watcher's slicker. Inside the house, lamps burn, filling the rooms with a soft glow.

Jamie and her mother. So domestic. Will the Mother leave when they are both dead? I suspect so. There will be a For Sale sign in the yard, and an estate sale to get rid of all the furniture, clothing and household stuff. I might even attend, might even buy something, might even offer my condolences to the people running the sale. It would be nice to have some mementos. I should have stolen them Sunday, when I had free range of the house and everything in it. My bad, as they say.

A wind gust whips around the tree, and a branch lashes the Watcher's face.

Nasty night. Perfect. It's happening at last. And if the rain continues ... *Laughter erupts.* Like I have always dreamed it would be.

The Watcher stares at the house for several more minutes, and then slinks away into the night.

Chapter 41

Thursday

I woke up Thursday with a sick feeling in the pit of my stomach. It couldn't have been anything I ate, more likely the fact that I didn't eat. After three slices of Mother's delicious sourdough bread, buttered and slathered with strawberry jam, I hadn't eaten a bite of the leftover stew she'd warmed up last night. But it wasn't hunger I was feeling. I hadn't had this feeling since grad school, on the morning of a critical semester exam. Anxiety coated with fear.

Rain poured from a gray sky, clouds thick as pudding. Saturated leaves littered the lawn and lay in the street where they lifted briefly as tires rolled over them and then hugged the cement again when the cars had passed.

Was it raining in Oklahoma City? What a dreary day for an inquest. What a dreary day for anything. The only good day, with this kind of weather, was one that featured a cabin in the woods, a roaring fire in the fireplace, and the person you loved most in the world. Sam and I had such a day in such a cabin during our honeymoon seven years ago at Osage Hills State Park.

The memories were sweet. One day, we had gone for a long hike in the woods while rain dripped from the trees, then we returned to the cabin and built a fire in the cabin's old stone fireplace. We cuddled in blankets on the sofa and fed each other brownies and champagne leftover from our wedding reception. Outside the cabin, raccoons had rummaged in the garbage, two of them bold enough to climb up on the picnic table and peer into the cabin through the picture window, watching us as we watched them.

I should have gone to the city to be with Sam. I'd thought it a thousand times the previous day, and I thought it again, now. It wasn't good enough to get a report on the telephone. His voice was too far away, and too emotionless. Sam was good at keeping his voice at an even tone. It was only when I looked in his eyes that I knew what he was really thinking, really feeling. I felt disconnected and empty without him.

My classroom smelled of the dampness, courtesy of old windows that didn't seal well. I moved along the row of windows, swabbing at the condensation and little pools of water that had accumulated during the all-night storm. The low clouds gave no sign of the sun high above them, and the weather report I'd heard during breakfast had called for more rain today and tomorrow.

Whispering voices drew my attention. Brooklyn and Zeke, two of the Drama Club students, peeked into my classroom.

"Mrs. Mazie?" Brooklyn asked. They looked at one another before crossing the room. Zeke stopped midway and turned to watch the door. "Zeke and I went to the hospital and saw Caleb last night."

"How is he? I had really hoped he'd be able to go home by now."

"Not yet." Emotions crossed her face. "He said something ... and we need to tell someone." She frowned.

"He's talking? Does he remember what happened?" I rubbed my arms, chilled both at the weather and at thoughts of what Caleb had endured at the hands of his kidnapper.

"Maybe. And it's not what people are saying. He didn't mention your name, and he ... well ... I'm pretty sure he was trying to tell us that it wasn't you who kidnapped him. It wasn't you who ... hurt him."

"Who was it? If you know, you need to tell the police."

Both students shook their heads. Zeke spoke up from across the room where he remained stationed at the door. "I'm not sure if he was trying to tell me she did it, but he kept saying, *Romy.* The drama teacher. Do you think she might have kidnapped Caleb?"

Romy? For a few seconds, I couldn't breathe.

"We have Drama Club after school today," Brooklyn said softly. "I don't think I can go. I don't want to see her. If she *was* the kidnapper, I can't hide what I know. She'll know we know." Brooklyn bowed her head.

These kids were worried that if Romy was the kidnapper, she would come after them to silence them. I had to admit, the drama teacher had acted odd yesterday at rehearsal. Was it possible she *was* the kidnapper? Anger sparked in my brain.

"Hey, you're in Drama Club, right? So, be an actor," I said. "You can convince her everything is fine. Play the part. Afterward, we'll go to the police."

261

"Won't it look bad for you to go to the police with us? We're helping you. Won't they think you made us go, that you're making us lie for you?" Zeke asked.

"Shhhh." Brooklyn jerked her head toward the door where some of my first period students were peering into the room.

"Come on in. Good morning," I called. I motioned for Zeke and Brooklyn to join me in the center of the room as students began to take their seats. "You two think about it and let me know," I whispered. "If you want, I'll go with you after school. Otherwise, go alone. It will help Caleb if you let the police know what he said." They nodded. "Thanks for coming to talk to me."

Brooklyn and Zeke wove their way around students who had gathered in the aisles as they left my class.

Caleb was awake and remembering. He could be implicating Romy in his kidnapping. It was a relief to know that the perpetrator might soon be caught, but until then, she could do more damage to someone. Even me.

The drama teacher was an accomplished actress. Even though she hadn't taught at the high school very long, the other faculty seemed to have absolute confidence in her abilities. I'd never heard a negative word about her in the faculty lounge, or anywhere. She'd picked an odd play as the fundraiser, but no one had questioned her selection. She had easily convinced them that the community would be interested in this play because of the history of the Ponca City Grand Prix.

The criminals I had encountered over the past eight years were sociopaths. They had no empathy for others, no concern that what they had done was wrong.

They were also very good actors. Did Romy fit all the characteristics of a sociopath? Did she lack empathy? I wasn't sure. I only knew that she had a problem with me; she was jealous.

Rain hammered at the windows of the classroom as students worked at the lab tables, conducting their experiment for the day, a procedure that pulled DNA from the leaf of a plant. I stared out the window panes, fascinated by the distortion caused by the water droplets, and the way the colors from outside blended and smeared into shapes unlike those on the other side of the glass. Were there people in my life right now who were like the distorted landscape, projecting one person on the surface while another shadowy reality lurked beneath?

"Mrs. Mazie? I have a question," a student called. I crossed the room to the lab table and listened to his question, then suggested he read the procedures before starting the experiment.

"Mrs. Mazie? This isn't working right," another student called. I maneuvered through the room to reach them. After the students explained what wasn't working, I suggested they not skip steps. They should begin the experiment again, this time, following the instructions in their workbook to the word, instead of trying to save time.

At my desk, on the other side of the room, my cell phone rang.

I hurried across the class. The Caller ID read, *Theresa*.

"Hello, Theresa. Is everything okay?"

"Jamie, have you heard from Sam?" Her weak voice shook.

"Not yet today. Have you talked to him?"

"No. Lucas is here waiting with me. If you hear from Sam, will you call me?"

"I will. If you'd like, I'll come by on my way home. I'd like to see you. Do you need anything?"

"I don't need anything, Jamie, but it would be nice to see you, too."

"I have a Drama Club meeting immediately after school, so it will be about 5. Is that okay?"

"Yes. With all this rain, the water is rising. The road may flood. Be careful. I am so fearful about what's happening at court today. Come before dark." Her words were slightly slurred. Was her medication affecting her speech? Could she have had a stroke? Surely Lucas would notice symptoms and get her to the hospital if that was the case.

"I'll see you a little later. Enjoy your time with Lucas. It's a treat to have him with you, isn't it?"

"Yes. It is a blessing." She sighed as she disconnected the phone.

Theresa's retirement village was near one of the tributaries that fed Lake Ponca. The lake had been low, with the caretaker's boat dock standing feet above the water, and the nearby boathouse practically on dry shore. The rain today was good, and if it continued all night, would go a long way toward alleviating the drought the area had been in all year. The pond at the retirement village would fill with water again, but I hoped that Theresa's fears were unfounded, and that there would be no road flooding.

The student members of the Drama Club had gathered in groups in Romy's classroom when I arrived after school, but Romy was absent. When I entered from the hallway into the back of the room, their voices dropped.

I waved at no one in particular. "Hi, everybody. Romy not here?"

The students exchanged looks. Finally, one of them said, "She left a note on her desk. She's running late. You're supposed to start the meeting."

I crossed the room toward her desk and the small stage, trying to recall the way these meetings usually went. Romy had thrown me into this cold, with no warning. Why? One part of me felt angry, the other part felt concerned. I'd never known Romy to be late, and she'd never yet missed a meeting or rehearsal. A thought jumped into my head. Was her absence related to Caleb, and his reappearance?

"Take a seat, everybody." I scanned the surface of her desk, looking for notes to me, or a folder labeled Drama Club, or anything that might give me an idea of what this meeting was supposed to accomplish. She'd left nothing other than the short note the student had mentioned.

I turned back to the class. "Okay. I think most of you were at the rehearsal Tuesday, so you know the play is back on, and you know what your job is. Maybe we should tackle questions first. I'll keep a list as we talk so that Romy can add her thoughts and comments when she gets here. Does anyone have a concern about the play, their role in the play, or the performance?"

A few hands shot up, and I called on the student in the back of the classroom first. "Caleb's back," he said. "Will he be working the curtain like he was assigned to?"

I dug in my memory. Romy had said something about this, hadn't she? "Caleb will not be in the production. I believe someone will be assigned to work the curtain. Is anyone interested in that job?" I jotted down the question and watched the classroom. Two students raised their hands. "Okay, Josh and Tim. I've got your names down. I'm sure Romy will get in touch with you about this. Next question?"

An hour later, we had covered questions and concerns and progressed to production details. I told them about the props I had collected, and about the way the play would be staged at Wentz Camp. The performance was a month away. Sometime soon, the cast and crew would meet at the Camp to see the staging and do a basic run through of the play. Without access to Romy's calendar, I couldn't set the date.

The students left the meeting in clusters, and I delayed. Should I call Romy to make sure she was okay? I wasn't comfortable with assuming that she'd dumped the meeting on me intentionally. She might be ill.

I eventually left the school, struggling over whether to call her even as I looked up at the heavy clouds. Water pooled on the sidewalk, and I stepped over and around as many puddles as I could, but by the time I reached the teacher's lot, my shoes were soaked. Then, the deluge began. Water fell as if giant buckets had been dumped out. I jumped over a big puddle and dashed toward my car, one of only three still parked in the lot. Needles of rain pelted my hooded rain jacket.

Once in the driver's seat, I buckled my seatbelt. My phone rang, but by the time I had dug it out of my purse, I'd missed the call. The Caller ID said *Theresa.*

In ten more minutes, I would be at her house. No need to call back. I started the car and drove onto the rain-slick street, my wipers on high speed.

Traffic moved slowly, except for one not-so-smart driver who weaved in and out, trying to get ahead of the slower traffic on Hartford, the town's four-lane major artery. That car's horn blew again and again, and its tires skidded. The vehicle hydroplaned briefly as it roared around a car ahead of me.

Rain slammed the roof of my car. I should have checked the weather report before I left the school. If I had, I would have delayed until this severe thunderstorm was over. I turned on my blinker and navigated into the righthand lane. In the heavy rain, most traffic had slowed to a crawl. I still had to drive several more miles before reaching Theresa's retirement village. Neighborhood streets, although slower, would be safer, and in the long run, probably faster.

I turned onto a side street. Wind shook the car, the dashboard vibrated. I navigated block after block, making my way through the neighborhood. Water raced along the curbs.

Finally, I turned the car north on the two-lane asphalt road. Beside it, on the other side of a bar ditch, the creek raged. Water splashed over the creek banks and crept across the narrow strip of grass to the bar ditch, filling the ditch and inching toward the street. If the rain lasted another hour, the street probably would flood.

I rounded a slight curve, peering through the heavy downpour as I passed a tow truck on the side of the road. Ahead, a white car was angled across the street, blocking both lanes. I slammed on the brakes.

My car skated across the road, hydroplaning on the thin skin of rainwater.

Frantically, I jerked the wheel, trying to keep from slamming into the vehicle on the road. At the last second, my car responded, and the tires pulled my SUV off the road to the right. My headlights reflected off the metal guard rail and the water in the bar ditch beside it.

I slammed into the guard rail. My airbags erupted.

The world went black.

Chapter 42

A bone-chilling shiver brought me back to consciousness. But I wasn't only cold. My entire body was submerged in freezing water up to my neck.

The SUV rested at an angle, nose down, in the water.

I remembered the car in the road and the tow truck I'd glimpsed. I remembered hydroplaning. And I remembered seeing the metal guard rail in the headlights. Had I gone through the guard rail? Was I in the bar ditch?

My teeth chattered. I reached down to my waist, seeking the seatbelt. When I found it, I pushed the button to disengage the lock. Nothing happened.

Peering into the dimness, I could barely make out the roof of the SUV and the frame of the windshield and windows in the blackness. Something glowed to one side of the vehicle, a circular beam. A flashlight? Was someone there, on the bank of the ditch?

"Help!" I screamed. "Help!" The light remained stationary. I wasn't sure if it was a streetlight, or a flashlight.

This didn't look right. I didn't remember the bar ditch beside the road being this deep, and I didn't remember the landscape looking like this at the place where I had skidded off the road. I must have blacked out.

I fumbled with the seat belt again, jabbing at the latch release. It didn't work. The icy water numbed my fingers.

An air bubble erupted on the surface of the water next to my head. Was the car sinking? I had to get out. Cold shivers crept up my body from my toes to my face. I peered through the rain-streaked windows. Where was I? I tried the door handle, but water pressed against the door, holding it closed.

"Help!" Outside the car, the light remained on. A dark shadow seemed to huddle nearby. Was there someone there, watching?

My heart raced, my teeth chattered. I gulped air, even though air was not the problem, yet. I had to get the seatbelt off and get out.

We kept a box knife in the glove box, but I would have to lower my head into the water to reach it. After sucking in a deep breath, I stretched toward the submerged glove box. The cold water closed over my mouth and the tip of my nose. I leaned as far as the seat belt would allow, but still could not reach the glove box button. I wriggled my body and stretched a few inches further. From what I could see through the dim light and the murky water, my shaking fingertips were still six inches away from the push button.

I sat up, gulped air and studied the darkness, searching for a landmark or something that would tell me where I was. Rain pelted the window, distorting anything beyond the glass.

Suddenly, something slammed into the rear of the SUV. The vehicle jerked and rolled another foot down the incline, deeper into the water. The water level rose to my chin.

"Help!" I yelled again, turning my body, trying to look behind me to see what had hit the car and made it lurch deeper into the water. I was more certain than ever that I was not where I had been when my car left the road. I had no clue how I had gotten here.

Suddenly, the torrents of rain eased and the circular beam of light to the side of the car illuminated a person behind my vehicle. I pounded the car horn.

Why weren't they helping me? I blinked, trying to see through the rain-smeared back window. The SUV shook again. Were they pushing me deeper into the water?

Where was I? This wasn't a ditch. And it wasn't a creek. Lake Ponca? The shape of a structure loomed to the right, and a line of trees beyond it.

I knew where I was: on the boat ramp next to the abandoned caretaker's house at Lake Ponca. How had I gotten here? I recalled the white tow truck.

My vehicle jerked and shifted again when another push came from behind. It shuddered but slipped no further into the lake. The front tires of my SUV must be stuck in the mud at the end of the boat ramp.

"Help me, please!" I yelled and pounded the horn, watching the figure behind the vehicle in the rearview mirror. They scrambled up the boat ramp and disappeared into the rain.

The mud had stopped the SUV from rolling farther into the lake. Still, I was not safe. I had to get out of the vehicle.

Rain slammed the roof and the front windows; the water was up to my chin. How long until the mud gave way and allowed the heavy SUV to sink deeper into the muck? Only two more inches and the water level would be over my nostrils.

I struggled with the seat belt again, but my efforts were futile. Blood pounded in my head.

I didn't want to die like this. Claustrophobia had always been my greatest fear, not drowning. But now, thinking about those two horrible ways to die, one seemed no worse than the other.

I thought of Sam, driving in from Oklahoma City with the results of the inquest. I thought of Mother, waiting for me at the house with supper on the table. I thought of my grown children in New Mexico, and my grandchildren, yet to be born, who would never meet their grandmother.

In quick succession, memories of the last eight years of my life passed through my mind. The mystery of my mother's first love, and the murder of her childhood companion at Osage Hills State Park. The resolution of the puzzle surrounding my husband Ben's death, and the deceit of someone close to me. The hidden history of my family, and the great-grandmother whose body I had found, and touched, as a child. Finally, my children's growing-up years, and my own. My mother and father, sister Ellen and brother Randy. Birthdays, vacations, Christmas.

Another bubble surfaced beside my face and burst; the water was up to my lips.

A new light flashed on, brightening the tiny slice of lake beyond the mostly submerged front windshield, and the interior top of the SUV. I jerked my head around. Headlights inched down the boat ramp behind me.

Fear exploded in my brain, and with the fear, a sudden recollection. In the tool box, on the floor of the backseat, was the very tool I needed to cut the seatbelt and smash the window to get out.

I reached my arm between the front seats and felt around for the tool box. I squirmed, angling my body so I could grasp the submerged box. I needed to access the flip latch on the front. My fingers curled around one corner, grasped tightly, and pulled. The box shifted. I stretched a little further.

The vehicle on the boat ramp bumped my SUV. My vehicle shook, rocked once, but didn't move.

I lifted my chin and sucked air in through my mouth, took one deep breath and then another and another, filling my lungs with air before reaching back, submerging my face to get a better grasp on the tool box. My fingers nudged the box, shifting it so I could reach the latch and flip the lid open.

Although I had seen the tool only once, I was sure of its shape. My fingers sought the handle of the tool tray. Once it was in my grasp, I pulled the tray up, shoved it to one side and stretched farther, reaching into the bottom of the box, searching for the double-headed pointed hammer.

When the other car bumped my vehicle again, the SUV shuddered and slipped in the mud. The water level reached my eyes. My fingers closed around the hammer.

Stretching to get my nose above the water line, I pulled in another deep breath.

The car on the boat ramp slammed into the back of my SUV again.

I pulled my arm through the gap between the seats and located the cutting edge in the hammer's handle with my other hand. Then, after situating the tool on the seat belt, I sawed, back and forth, back and forth. Eventually, the thick material of the belt parted, and finally, gave way.

Shoving my feet against the floorboards, I pushed myself up to the roof panel and turned my head to the side to reach the last pocket of air.

Bubbles rose around me. The saturated mud gave way beneath the weight of the car and sucked it deeper. Debris and algae rose up from the bottom of the lake and floated past the windshield in the brown water, flimsy edges of plants and trash waved, illuminated by the headlights of the car behind me on the boat ramp.

Now free of the seat belt, I tried the door once again, but it wouldn't budge. I lifted the tool and tried to tap the window beside me, but the hammer moved so slowly through the water that my strike had no effect on the glass. I pulled it back and tried again, swinging harder, but water resistance allowed for no momentum in my swing.

Grasping the tool tightly in my right hand, I pulled up my legs, maneuvered my body around and pulled myself between the split front bucket seats and into the back. The rear window was still mostly out of the water, leaving me room to swing the pointed hammer tool. I hoped there would be enough space to get the needed momentum.

First try, the hammer thudded, not even nicking the thick safety glass. Despair and fatigue darkened my world. It wasn't going to work. I was going to drown. A sob stuck in my throat. The water inched higher on my neck.

In the car, on the boat ramp, the Watcher laughs.
I never imagined it would be this much fun! Yippee! Bye, Jamie.

Chapter 43

I was not ready to die.

Shivering with cold and fear, I swung the hammer again. This time, it chipped the glass.

I swung the hammer again and again, each time a little faster, a little harder.

The SUV jolted and slipped deeper into the mud. Inside the vehicle, the water rose another two inches, reaching my chin and giving me even less space to swing the hammer.

I was running out of time.

The headlights on the ramp behind me went out. In my car, the only light came from the mercury vapor light on the old boathouse which cast a shimmering green light through the rain and into the vehicle where I was trapped.

This was not how I wanted to die. I wasn't ready. Sam needed my help and my support. So did my mother, and my son and my daughter. Even my brother, although he often didn't know who I was, needed my compassion and my love. My life couldn't end like this, here in this muddy lake. It couldn't.

Once more, I drew back the hammer. Using both hands, and all my strength, I slammed it as hard as I could against the glass. The blow landed on top of the chipped place. This time, the glass cracked. Another blow, and the window shattered.

Water rushed in through the broken rear window, washing the broken glass into car.

The SUV shuddered again, and the vehicle dropped another few inches.

I pushed against the back seat, forcing myself through the wave of water and out of the broken back window. I dove for the end of the concrete boat ramp. My vehicle shuddered again, and the muddy lake sucked it under the surface.

The water bubbled and gurgled behind me as I crouched in the pouring rain on the bottom of the boat ramp.

I peered through the rain, looking for the dark figure who had tried to kill me. Would the person return to see if the car had submerged and I was dead? I wouldn't wait to find out.

I slogged up the boat ramp and across the lawn toward the shadowy darkness of the trees on the other side of the boathouse. My wet clothes clung to me and my shoes squished as water oozed from them. I had to get away from the light, away from the possibility of detection.

The downpour continued, a constant barrage of rain drops. It was impossible to see more than a few yards ahead.

I shivered and shoved my sopping hair off my face and out of my eyes. Chills shook my body.

Before long, I would stop feeling cold as hypothermia took over my body. Finding shelter and warming myself were my biggest priorities. The boathouse was the nearest shelter. Would I be safe there? It almost didn't matter. I had to find shelter. I had to dry off and get warm.

After sloshing through the mud to the rear of the small structure, I tried the doorknob to the back door. It creaked open.

The old structure smelled of damp and mildew, of fish and stagnant water. Slowly, my eyes adjusted to the dim interior. I flipped the light switch next to the door and a bare light bulb above the door came on. Messy spider webs cast shadows from the ceiling across the walls. A pile of ropes filled one corner, and on one long wall, pegs held up a kayak and paddles as well as a pair of old, faded water skis. In the other corner, folded tarps had been laid on top of a small wooden table. On the floor nearby was a space heater and a tackle box. Someone had been fishing.

The opening to the lake, on the far end of the small boathouse, was covered by a sliding barn door, but because of the low lake level, a three-foot gap existed between the bottom of the door and the water. Other than the kayak, there was no boat in the boathouse.

A pile of rags covered part of the narrow decking to the side of the boat well. If the rags were clean, and thick enough, I could dry off and warm up. I cautiously eased my way around the decking to the rags and dug through the pile. Several old bath towels with frayed edges looked clean. Other rags were strips of clothing, but at the bottom of the pile I found a woman's sleeveless shirt and shorts, yellowed with age.

I shimmied out of my wet slacks and drenched blouse, and wrapped myself in the towels. I found an electric outlet, plugged in the cord to the space heater and turned the power switch. The heater coil glowed red.

After carrying the small table over to the space heater, I wrung out my wet clothes and draped them across the sides of the table. I squatted close to the heat, rubbing my arms and legs with another towel. My body began to warm.

Behind me, water lapped against the pylons of the boathouse. Rain pounded on the tin roof. I huddled on the deck of the boathouse, pulling heat into my shivering body. With the hypnotic sounds of lapping water and rain drumming on the roof, I slowly relaxed into a stupor.

In a dreamlike state, my mind took me to Trudy's house. The senseless destruction of so many of Elizabeth's things. The kitchen counter and the message. Broken pieces of delicate antique china scattered across the dining room floor. And Trudy, in the hospital bed, her face a mess of purple, red and yellow bruises, one eye swollen shut.

My imagination jumped in.

Reba, hanging from the rafters in a garage, an overturned chair beneath her. A shadow lurking in the corner.

My vehicle skidding off the road, knocking me unconscious. My car on the boat ramp, and the nightmarish figure pushing my SUV down the boat ramp into the lake. How did I get from the road to the boat ramp? Who did it? Why?

The door to the boathouse swung open, and an intense light beamed into my face. I pinched my eyes shut. My heart pounded in my throat.

I was defenseless.

"Oh, my. Jamie? Is that you?" Howard DeKalb asked.

I squinted. Shadows covered the man's face and the flashlight was so bright.

"What happened?" He flicked his light away from me.

My throat went dry. What was Howard doing here? He should have left work long ago. Had Howard pushed my car into the lake?

Shaking again, I grabbed my nearly-dry clothes off the table and stood. "I was run off the road," I finally said. He might already know that.

"Where's your car?"

I didn't hear a lie in his voice. He might be sincere. Or he might not.

I swallowed hard. "Somehow, I wound up here, in my car on the boat ramp. Someone tried to push it into the lake, with me trapped inside."

"Are you hurt?" He sounded concerned. He shone his light on me again. "Your clothes?" He moved his light to the space heater. The red coils glowed. He turned his back. "You need to get out of here. You should get dressed."

I slipped into my damp clothes. My mind raced. Why was Howard here?

"Did you see who ran you off the road?" He asked.

"They had on a hooded slicker. I couldn't tell if it was a man or a woman."

"And your car is ... where?"

"In the lake. You didn't notice it?"

"Never saw the car. We had a late conference call, and then I stayed to assemble my notes. I noticed the boathouse light on as I was leaving. We sometimes have to chase kids out of here. Matter of fact, I did so last week."

I zipped my slacks and slid my feet into my soggy shoes. I still wasn't convinced Howard was not the one who had pushed my SUV into the lake. But I was alone with him here, and I needed his help.

"Do you need to see a doctor?" His deep voice sounded concerned.

"Not really. But I should report what happened." I picked up the shirt and shorts I'd found beneath the rag pile. "Do you suppose whoever was here last week left these?"

Howard turned his flashlight on the clothes. He frowned. "I don't think so. They look old. Discolored."

The white and pink checked shirt buttoned down the front and had a tie that cinched at the waist. It had been a good decade since I'd seen a similar shirt. A label had been stitched inside at the back of the neck. *Handmade by Grandma Sally.*

"You want to call the police. My phone's in the car. And I bet your family is worried about you," Howard said.

"I was headed out to my mother-in-law's home before this happened." I thought about Theresa. How much time had passed since she called me? She, and my mother would both be sick with worry. "Maybe you should take me there. It's not very far from here. I can call the police from her house."

"If that's what you want. But you need to file a report." Howard opened the door to the pouring rain. He took off his jacket and offered it to me. I threw the jacket over my head and upper body. Together, we crossed the slippery lawn and climbed the slope to the driveway.

As we trudged, I studied the trees and buildings. Any one of them could be a hiding place for my assailant. I peered back at the boat ramp. The metallic top of my SUV was barely visible below the surface, and only noticeable because I knew it was there. In the morning, I'd return with a wrecker, to see if the vehicle could be salvaged.

For now, I was safe, with only the short drive to Theresa's between me and family.

"So sorry this happened to you, Jamie. Who would do such a thing?" Howard asked.

I wondered.

Chapter 44

"Does Mrs. Mazie live in an apartment, or a cottage?" Howard asked as he drove into the retirement complex.

"A cottage. I've only been here twice since she moved. I can't remember the number." I stared through the rain-smeared window at the complex of buildings, a three-story apartment tower surrounded by duplexes and single resident homes.

"I live here, too," he announced as he pulled into a parking space near the front door of the main building. "Don't think I've ever met your mother-in-law. Last name of Mazie, right?"

"I'm not sure how long she'll be able to stay in independent living. She hasn't been feeling well lately. A nurse has been making house calls. Hopefully, whatever she's got is a short-lived virus." A horrible thought occurred to me. If someone was after Sam and me, would their vendetta include Sam's mother? It had included Trudy. Theresa's illness had begun after our move here, about the same time Trudy's trouble with the ghosts started. And the same weekend Davis Harwell had been murdered.

We got out of the car. I pulled Howard's coat up over my head and dashed for the front entrance.

"Brent, the desk attendant, will look up her house number and call her from the desk phone," Howard said from behind me as we rushed through the automatic doors.

I ran my fingers through my hair. Disheveled and still wet, I no doubt looked like the proverbial cat drug in out of the rain. My cat Princess didn't *do* rain. No chance that she would ever be a wet cat if she could help it.

Howard introduced me to the employee at the welcome desk. "Brent, Jamie is Mrs. Mazie's daughter-in-law. Could you let her know that Jamie's here?" Howard turned to me, and whispered, "I expect you'll get someone to retrieve the car tomorrow. Let me know who's coming and when. I'll unlock the gates. Okay?"

I handed him his coat. "Thank you for rescuing me."

"Glad I was there to help. I don't like to think what could have happened to you. Make that police report, okay?"

Brent punched in Theresa's number, and handed me the phone. "I'm in the main lobby, Theresa. Could you send Lucas to get me?"

"Oh, my dear," Theresa moaned. "I've been so worried. Where have you been? Lucas will be right there."

"I'll explain. See you soon." Theresa had not sounded well.

"You'll need to borrow this. Looks like it's still raining." The desk clerk handed me an umbrella.

When I turned toward the front door, Howard stood waiting in the adjacent lobby.

"The rest of the evening will surely be better than the start. Certainly a rough one for you," he said sympathetically. "And then we have rehearsal tomorrow night. Are you pleased that the play is back on again?" Howard perched on the arm of a nearby wingback chair, his jacket folded in his lap.

"I'm not sure what I think about that play. It seems to be doomed, so many things have gone wrong." I straightened my pants and smoothed the fabric of my slightly-damp blouse.

The front doors swung open and Lucas burst into the lobby. He dashed over to me. "Jamie, I'm so sorry. We heard the news. None of us were expecting ..." He stopped and stared. "What happened to you?"

I can't imagine what I must have looked like, with my hair plastered to my head and my blouse and pants wrinkled and still partially wet. But my story could wait. Lucas had heard from Sam about the inquest. Bad news.

"What have you heard?"

Lucas's shoulders slumped. "The judge declared Reba's death to have been 'wrongful,' not suicide. Sam is being detained temporarily, until the next step is decided."

A shiver began deep inside my toes and sped up my skeleton to my head. Next step? Charge my husband with suspicion in the wrongful death of his first wife. A trial, and if convicted, prison.

"That can't be!" A tornado roared in my ears. The room spun. Lucas grabbed my arms as I pitched toward the floor.

"Let's get you to Mom's." He slipped his arm around me and pulled me erect.

"Let me get you a wheelchair," someone said. Howard?

Lucas muttered, "Thank you."

Howard pushed a wheelchair up next to us. "This will help. Can I be of assistance?"

"I think I can get her to my Mom's without help. Thanks for your offer."

"Certainly. I'm Howard DeKalb, by the way. I know Jamie from the play."

Lucas regarded Howard, frowning. "You're in the high school play?"

"Freshman Playhouse actor. Supporting the high school students." The man grinned crookedly.

Howard flipped down the foot rests of the wheelchair and helped me ease down into it.

"Nice to meet you," Lucas said. "I need to get Jamie to Mom's now. Thanks for your help."

I straightened and took deep breaths. *Sam was in jail.* I passed my hand over my eyes.

Lucas pushed me outside into the light rain. I opened the umbrella, and he held it above us as he rolled me down the sidewalk and around the building to an arc of small houses that curved away from the main structure.

"Lucas, what happened at the inquest?" I asked, full of guilt. I should have been there with Sam.

He wheeled me through a tiled courtyard with a tall ceramic fountain in the center. "Our phone call was short. He tried to call you but got your voice mail. Where's your car, and how did you get so wet?"

"I don't want your mother to hear this," I said, and then I blurted out my story. Theresa didn't need to know what had happened, or that I'd come close to drowning, trapped in my SUV. She had enough on her mind with this news about the inquest, and her own illness. Once again, I wondered if her illness had anything to do with what was happening to Sam.

"Jamie, you are lucky to have survived. You could have drowned," Lucas said as he pushed me up the driveway to the next duplex. "We'll call the police immediately."

"Tell me about Sam."

"The judge changed the ruling on Reba's death to 'suspicious,' not suicide. The police detained Sam and took him to the police station. The OSBI detective, Chase Longhorn, accompanied him."

Something pressed against my chest, preventing air from travelling into my lungs. It was as if I was in my SUV again, struggling to pull in a breath when most of my body was under water. But this time there was no water. I felt the doom–the danger–all the same. "I need to go to him."

"Try to call him first. But as far as going there ... not tonight, Jamie. The highways are slick and partially flooded after all this rain. I can take you first thing in the morning." Lucas pushed the wheelchair onto the porch of Theresa's cottage and helped me to my feet. "Let's not talk of this to Mom. She was doing better until Sam called. I'm worried about how she'll take more bad news."

I nodded in agreement. "Lucas, I need to file a police report. Will you go with me to the police station tonight?"

"After you've eaten something."

Theresa pulled the door open. Her already pale face blanched. "Jamie! What happened to you?"

Lucas and I hurried in, and after she'd fussed over me for a few minutes, Lucas helped his mother across the room to the recliner she favored.

"I'm all right, Theresa," I said. "I got caught out in the rain with car trouble, that's all." I perched on the end of the sofa near her chair. The initial shock over the results of the inquest had faded. Now, anger seethed inside me. Who was behind this?

"And poor Sam," she moaned. "Spending the night in jail."

I shook my head. I had no words with which to comfort her.

"You need some warm, dry clothes," she said, reaching out to touch the still-damp sleeve of my blouse. "Please, Lucas show her where my closet is. There are jeans, and flannel shirts for the night chill. Help her find something."

I placed the clothing I'd brought with me on the sofa. It seemed stupid to have brought the shorts and blouse from the boathouse. Even if I did find Grandma Sally, chances are she would have forgotten making the clothing, much less be concerned about getting it back to its owner.

"What's this?" Lucas glanced at the clothes on his way to show me Theresa's bedroom.

"Some clothing I found in the Wentz Camp boathouse. Handmade by someone named Grandma Sally."

He stared at the clothes. "Grandma Sally?"

"Does that name mean something to you?"

"I'm not sure." He led the way down the hall. "You found that clothing at Wentz Camp. That's crazy." He opened a door, motioned me inside, and then crossed the room to pull the closet door open.

"Why?" I looked through the hanging items, skipping over lighter weight clothes to find the long-sleeved flannels Theresa had spoken of. I selected a soft blue and cream flannel, and then chose a random pair of well-worn jeans.

"Grandma Sally put 'handmade by' tags in all of the clothes she made for her grandchildren, including Reba and Sharon."

I dropped the flannel shirt and jeans on the bed. My mind raced back to what Lucas had told me about the races on that last day. "When Sharon and Reba asked you to take them home, had one of them lost some clothes?"

Lucas nodded. "Reba came and got me at our racetrack pit. She was crying, said we had to go get her sister at Wentz Camp right then. Said someone had torn off Sharon's clothes. Sharon was only wearing her underwear and a beach towel when I picked her up."

"Someone assaulted her?"

"Sharon refused to tell me what had happened to her or her clothes. Reba seemed more upset than Sharon. I drove the girls home to Fairfax."

The clothes I'd found had not been torn. They were smelly and yellowed, but otherwise in perfect condition.

"I'll get supper dished up while you change your clothes. There's a hair drier in the bathroom, if you need it." Lucas left the room.

When I returned to the living room a few minutes later, Lucas was in the kitchen and Theresa was sitting in her chair watching the evening news. The old mantel clock read 6:15.

Supper. At home. Mother must be worried.

"May I use your phone? I need to call Mother, and I don't have my cell."

"Of course. In the kitchen." Theresa waved one hand toward the adjacent room, where Lucas was at work.

He'd arranged three place settings at the small corner dinette near a wide window. Outside, rain dripped from a yaupon holly tree. In the kitchen, he placed a dish in the microwave and set the timer.

Mother answered the phone on the first ring.

"Jamie, thank goodness," she blurted. "I've been worried sick. Where are you?"

"I'm at Theresa's. I was ... delayed after school."

"I'll hold supper for you, then. I was about to eat by myself."

On Theresa's table, a meal of brisket, beans and corn-on-the-cob waited. My mouth watered.

"Go ahead and eat without me, Mother. Theresa has supper ready, and Lucas will need to bring me home. My car is–well, it's off on the side of the road. I'll be there in an hour."

"You wrecked your car?" Her voice rose an octave.

"Not exactly. I'll explain later. Nothing to worry about."

"Doesn't sound like nothing." In the background, I heard the doorbell ring at my house. "Someone's here, Jamie. Expecting anyone?"

"Look out the window, Mother. Don't open the door to anyone you don't know. I'll be home soon."

Someone knocked at Theresa's door. "I've got to go, Mother."

"Jamie? I—"

"I'll be home soon."

Theresa struggled to get to her feet to answer the knock.

"Let me get that, Theresa," I said as I rushed into the room.

She dropped into her chair. "Might be the nurse. She came by a few minutes earlier to give me my evening medicine right after you called from the lobby. I asked her to come back by to check on me before she left for the evening."

I pulled the door open.

The woman at the door wore a nurse's uniform. Her eyes widened, and she took a step back. "Jamie? I ... um ... didn't expect to see you ... here," she stammered.

Belina carried a black valise. Free of facial makeup, she looked much older and much less like the vixen she was playing in the dinner theater.

"I didn't know you were a nurse," I sputtered. "Or that you worked here. You know my mother-in-law."

Lucas walked in from the kitchen.

"And this is my son, Lucas," Theresa said. "Lucas, this is my nurse, Belina."

Belina and Lucas stared at one another. Lucas frowned. "Belina? Sharon Belina Sanderson?"

Belina dropped the valise, backed toward the still-open door, and ran.

Chapter 45

Lucas darted after her.

Theresa's already pale face faded into milky white. She clasped her hands together. "The first time she came to give me my medicine, I thought she looked familiar. Why didn't she tell me who she was?"

When Belina and I had met at the theater, she didn't mention Reba, although she knew my last name. "She said her family was from Fairfax. And she's a cast member in the school fundraiser I'm helping with."

Outside, someone screamed. From the still-open door, I could see two figures struggling on the sidewalk. Lucas and Belina?

Across the living room, Theresa had closed her eyes; her body leaned left in the chair. "Theresa?" As I dashed over to her, her eyes rolled back in her head. Her chin dropped to her chest.

I ran to the kitchen and dialed 9-1-1, and described the emergency.

"Stay on the line until the police arrive," the operator instructed.

I laid the phone on the counter and ran back to door. Fifty yards away, Belina struck Lucas with her fists and shoved him.

"The police are coming," I yelled.

Lucas grabbed Belina's arms and she went limp. He pulled her along on the sidewalk, back to Theresa's house.

"I'm sorry, Lucas," she wailed. Sobs jerked her body. "Let me go."

Lucas shoved Belina through the doorway and into the house. "What did you do, Sharon?" he growled, shaking her shoulder; her head flopped.

A siren wailed in the distance.

Sharon's sobs transformed into guffaws. Face contorted, she doubled over with laughter.

"What did I do? To who? To your mom?" She laughed even harder.

Gooseflesh raised on the back of my neck. Another person had slipped into Belina's body.

"What–did–you–do?" Lucas glared. He shook her again.

Sharon tilted her head and studied Theresa, who sat, drooping, eyes closed, chin resting on her chest.

"It might not be too late for the antidote." Sharon laughed.

Lucas dropped Sharon's arm and hurried to his mother. He grabbed her wrist and felt for a pulse. "Call an ambulance!"

I lunged toward the kitchen, where I'd left the phone lying on the counter. "Are you there? Operator?"

"I'm here. The police are on their way. Only another minute."

"I need that ambulance. She's been poisoned. She's unconscious."

Sirens blared in the distance. Lucas patted his mother's cheeks, trying to rouse her.

"Stay on the line, ma'am. Are you in danger?" The operator asked.

In the living room, Sharon stood by the open door, arms crossed, a wide grin on her face. She stared at me.

"I don't think so. But my mother-in-law needs help." I laid the phone down again.

Sharon chuckled. "I would have liked to have been friends, Jamie. Really. But it wasn't meant to be. I'm sorry about your cousin Trudy."

"What about Trudy?" I stepped into the living room but kept my distance. I didn't know this woman. The Belina I had known had not been real.

"Oh, you know. All that ghost stuff. It was fun dressing up. 'Woooo–I'm Reba,'" she moaned and then laughed, hysterically. "Those notes to Sam really were from my sister, you know. She wrote them years ago. At the end, she was soooo scared of me! She'd do whatever I asked. Of course, I never delivered them to him."

"You're horrible. You frightened and hurt Trudy. You destroyed my aunt's house. Why?"

"It was fun! And you got the message, didn't you? The Mazies are part of your family. What they deserve, you deserve." She stopped laughing. "Oh, but I am truly sorry about your mother." Sharon's lower lip jutted out in an imitation pout. "Collateral damage?"

My stomach clenched. "My mother?" I'd talked to her only moments before. And I'd heard the doorbell ring in the background. "Sorry about what?"

Her face transformed again. Her eyes glittered. A deep-throated laugh bellowed from her. She doubled over, holding her stomach, shaking with laughter.

"My God," I breathed. "What have you done?"

Sharon lifted her head and stopped laughing. "Poof! Your house, and everything in it—including your mother and your lovely dogs and cat—will soon go up in smoke."

Chapter 46

I staggered back as if she'd struck me; the blood drained from my face.

An EMT appeared in the doorway, accompanied by a policewoman and two uniformed medics. "You called 9-1-1?" The EMT asked in a clipped tone.

"Here," Lucas called from across the room.

The crew of first responders pushed inside. Heart pounding, I grabbed the policewoman's arm. "My mother ... there may be a fire ... she's in danger ... and that woman–." I glanced at the spot where Sharon had been standing.

She was gone.

"What about a fire?" the policewoman asked. "Where?"

"My home. I don't have a car. Can someone take me there?"

Confusion reigned. Lucas's deep voice drowned out the cacophony. "She gave my mom poison," he bellowed. Lucas stood beside the empty gurney as the EMT's worked, his fingers combing through his long black hair.

The policewoman grabbed my arm. "Sir? Are you accusing this woman of poisoning your mother?"

"No! That's my sister-in-law. It's the other woman." Lucas's look darted around the room. "Where's Sharon?

I bolted into the kitchen, the two bedrooms and the bathroom. Sharon was not in the house.

"She was here when you arrived," I told the policewoman. "She said my home is on fire. We need to go there. Now."

The policewoman spoke into her shoulder radio.

"Did I hear you say someone poisoned Mrs. Mazie?" Howard asked from the doorway. He blinked as he stepped into the room, and stared at the EMT's working on Theresa.

I grabbed his arm. "Take me to my house." I pulled him back out the front door with me.

"Can't you drive any faster?" I sat forward in the seat, ignoring the dinging seat belt alarm. With one hand on the dashboard, I peered into the rainy night.

"The roads are slick, Jamie. We don't need another accident." Howard stared straight ahead.

"Do you hear sirens? Can you tell if there's a fire up ahead?"

"Impossible to know. Looks dark," Howard observed.

"But Belina said–"

"Belina?" he interrupted.

"She's the nurse at your retirement village. She said she poisoned Theresa, and that my house is on fire!"

"That girl. She does have a flare for the dramatic, doesn't she?" He sneered.

My heart pounded in my chest. Howard *knew* Belina, and not because of the drama club production.

Howard braked for a stop light. The car skidded, throwing me against the seatback. My heart hammered, and my tongue stuck in my throat when I tried to swallow.

He accelerated into the intersection when the light changed. The car lost traction again and threw me into the door when it lurched sideways. I latched my seatbelt.

Belina had said she didn't like Howard, that he was always flirting with her. At the time, I'd thought she meant he had flirted at play rehearsal, but I was wrong. He must have been flirting with her at the retirement village.

"You don't think she poisoned Theresa? And my house isn't on fire?"

A muscle twitched in his cheek. He kept his eyes on the rain-drenched road.

"That's not what I said. To repeat, Belina–or Sharon as you have discovered–has *always* had a flare for the dramatic. She did poison Theresa Mazie. And your house, with your mother in it, will soon be on fire, if it isn't already."

"Why is she doing this?" Panic stretched my voice thin. "And how can you be so calm?" My head hurt. Thoughts pounded. Belina/Sharon and Howard knew each other. Was Howard involved in Sharon's schemes?

He sighed. "You'll know soon enough." He turned the corner onto my street.

I peered into the darkness. No flames.

He pulled into my driveway.

I bolted from the car and ran for the house. There was no fire.

I leapt onto the front porch. The door was locked.

"Mother, it's me. Let me in." I pounded on the door and punched the doorbell. The melodic notes echoed inside the house.

No dogs barked. No lights brightened the dark night.

Chapter 47

I pounded on the door and shouted again. Sam and I had not yet hidden a key outside the house in case one of us, or Mother, got locked out. Without my key–which was in my purse in the lake–I couldn't open any door to the house. But I could get into the garage.

I rushed to the keypad beside the garage and punched in the numbers; the pad didn't light up. The electricity was off. I glanced back at Howard's car in the driveway. It was empty.

"Howard?" I shouted into the dripping rain before racing around the side of the house to the backyard. I hoped Mother had left the back door unlocked. But, like the front door, it was secure. In despair, I ran to the rear door that led into the garage.

It was not locked. In the garage, I flicked the light switch, but nothing happened. I stared into the darkness, waiting for my eyes to adjust. A tiny bit of light from the streetlight two houses down came through the narrow windows on the big garage door.

The remaining boxes had been shoved into two rows on one side of the garage. An open space wide enough for my SUV remained and gave access to the safe room/tornado shelter built in the corner, next to the hot water heater.

A muffled bark sounded. Queenie?

I tried the backdoor. The knob turned, and the door swung open.

Inside, the house was dark. I flicked the light switch but nothing happened.

"Mother? Are you here?" I ventured further into the house, touching the wall as I shuffled past the laundry room and into the kitchen. "Mother? Where are you? Queenie? Zeus?"

Something rubbed against my leg and I jumped, but a soft purr gave Princess away. I reached down and lifted the cat, cradling her in my arms and rubbing my cheek against her silky fur. Her purr rumbled against me, but then the cat thrashed and dove away, yowling. She vanished into the dark.

I reached for the wall, laid my hand against it, and listened. Another muffled bark sounded faintly somewhere behind me. The garage had been empty. Unless ... Were they in the tornado shelter? Had Mother panicked and locked them in?

I returned to the backdoor and stepped down into the garage. A bright light flashed in my face and then, the beam of light dropped to the ground. "It's me. Howard. Power must be off. I had this flashlight in the car. I saw someone go around the corner of your house as you went up on the porch. A blonde. Maybe Belina?"

"I didn't see her. And I haven't found Mother. I thought I heard one of the dogs. Out here. In the shelter?" I gestured toward the door in the corner of the garage. Built to appear to be a closet, the steel-walled room was equipped with two benches and shelving stocked with emergency supplies, including water, canned foods and a weather radio.

I hurried over to the corner room. Howard followed close behind, lighting the way with his flashlight.

"Mother? Are you in there?" I pounded on the heavy door. "It's safe to come out. Open the door."

Muffled barks sounded inside the room. Howard focused the light on the latch.

"Mother, open the door," I yelled.

The lock clicked, and the door swung slowly outward. Behind me, Howard's light clattered to the floor and went out, leaving me in impenetrable darkness.

"Mother?" I reached toward the dark room. "Howard? Give me your light." Blackness loomed in front of me and behind me. A dog–Queenie?–whimpered in the shelter.

I took a step into the darkness and stumbled. Something heavy slammed into my head.

Chapter 48

I gulped for air and opened my eyes to total darkness, unable to see the wet tongue that licked my face. Another tongue worked at my ear, cleaning it with ferocity. I threw my arms around the dogs, wincing at the stabbing pain in my head.

"Queenie. Zeus," I murmured. Pain increased with movement. The dogs crawled over me, licking and whining. I groaned and sat up.

The disorienting dark was absolute.

"Hello?" My voice didn't echo like it did in the double garage. This was a smaller space, but when I reached out in any direction, I touched only air. I lifted myself to my knees, and scooted, first one direction, and then another. I encountered walls, shelving, and benches.

I was in the tornado shelter.

Pushing the dogs away, on hands and knees, I felt for the door. Once I found it, I stood. I twisted the door lever, but the door didn't budge.

I'd been in this room briefly after we moved in to dust off the shelves and store a few supplies. Stocking the shelter completely had been low on my 'immediate

Mary Coley

attention' list, but I knew what was–and was not–in the room. I stepped back, encountered a bench, and sat.

Both dogs attempted to climb onto my lap. They licked my face and nudged me with their noses.

Something moved somewhere in the room. Queenie whined and hopped off the bench.

"No, dog. Go away," a voice whispered.

"Mother?"

The scratch of movement came from under the bench. Someone touched my knee.

"Jamie?" Mother asked in a low voice.

I grabbed her hands and pulled her up, hugging her shivering body close. "What are you doing in here, on the floor?" I had a pretty good idea that it wasn't anything _she_ had done, but something that had been done to her.

"I'm … not … sure." Her voice quivered.

"We were on the phone. The doorbell rang. What happened?"

"I remember going to the door. You told me not to answer it, but a sopping wet woman was standing on our porch. I thought it might be a neighbor, or a friend of yours from school." Her body shivered against me.

"Who was it?"

"I'm trying to tell you. I'm foggy about it." She pulled in a few ragged breaths. "I opened the door. The woman smiled. It was your friend. She came by earlier today, looking for you."

"What did she look like? And where were the dogs?" If the dogs had been inside they would have barked when someone came to the door, and Mother never would have let this person in the house.

"They'd been outside this afternoon. When the rain began, they laid down on the porch. Seemed happy enough. Then, you called. And the doorbell rang." She shivered again. "They were still on the back porch."

"Describe the woman."

She shook her head. "No need. I recognized her from her earlier visit. It was your friend from the play."

Belina?

"She came into the house. I was walking into the living room, when she shoved me." Mother swallowed and pulled in a quick breath. "I lost my balance and fell. I tried to get up. She must have hit me with something."

"Did she hurt you?" I ran my hand along her arm and up to her face, felt her jaw bone and her hair. My fingers touched something sticky on her face. "You're hurt!"

"It's nothing. I bumped the wall. It bled a little. I'm all right, Jamie."

"Are you sure? Belina hurt you."

"Belina? The actress? No, it was that drama teacher I let into the house. Romy. Isn't that her name?"

Chapter 49

"Romy?!" My thoughts ricocheted like balls on a billiard table. This didn't make sense. Sharon had admitted to playing 'ghost,' she had poisoned Theresa, and I was certain she had tried to push my car into the lake. And it was Sharon who had said my house was burning down.

Why had Romy come here and hurt my mother?

"I need to get out of here, Jamie. It's so hot." Mother groaned.

Mother's shivering had stopped, and now she felt feverish to the touch.

I wasn't sure if it was hot in the room, or the power of suggestion, but my throat tightened, beads of sweat popped out on my face and I was having trouble pulling in air to breathe. The blackness pressed against me.

No errant light could seep in around the safe room door, by design. I reached in front of me and stepped around the small room, recalling the layout of the benches and the shelving, and the placement of the door.

One of the dogs panted at my feet, an even huffing. The dog was either hot or nervous, maybe both.

Mother sighed. "Oh, dear."

I pulled in deep breaths, counted the seconds of my inhales and exhales, and tried not to panic. I'd been closed in, trapped in the darkness, before. I had hoped never to find myself in this position again. Unlike that other time, I knew where I was, and I had a reasonable hope of getting out.

The vent in the ceiling, and the fan within it, pulled air into the safe room from the house's heating and cooling system. But I couldn't remember if it had a separate switch that opened a vent for fresh air. I ran my hands over the panel of switches by the door. One by one, I flipped them either up or down. None of them did anything. No lights. No fan.

I fiddled with the door lever, pushed and pulled at the door. The dead bolt had been engaged and was not releasing. "It has to release from the inside. Otherwise, why have a lock on the door?" I mumbled into the darkness. "It's jammed."

"Don't you have a lantern in here? In case of emergencies?" Mother asked. Her weak, breathy voice had an edge to it.

"Yes. We do." Earlier this week, I had set the lantern on the shelf in the corner after replacing the big 9-volt battery. I reached for the shelving, ran my hands along the shelf and found the lantern. After I pressed the *on* button, the small room flooded with welcome light.

Mother looked horrible, her face a pasty white with blood smeared on her forehead and cheeks. She swayed on the bench where she sat, eyes half-open.

"The door must be jammed. Maybe if I had the key I could get it to release," I muttered. We'd purposely had the lock on the safe room made to match the doors of the house.

"You don't have your keys?" Mother's voice was low and strained; her eyes looked sunken.

"I don't have my purse." I tried the lock release again. It didn't budge. I needed to get us out of here. My head pounded.

She pushed something into my palm. "Here's my key. I always keep it in my pocket, in case I accidentally lock the door when I go out with the dogs."

I inserted the key into the slot and turned it. I shoved the door and then pulled it toward me. Finally, the bolt clicked.

Both dogs bolted past me. Mother and I stepped into the garage together. With the safe room's lantern, the garage was light enough to see the piles of boxes on the opposite side.

"Woof!" Zeus stood on point in the center of the unoccupied garage bay, next to a body.

I shuffled toward the figure, and knelt to touch the man, His rain coat was still damp from the rain.

"Howard?" I felt for a pulse. Weak, but there. And he was breathing evenly. He'd been holding the flashlight. Had he hit me over the head or had someone hit him?

The flashlight lay on the floor a few inches away. I flicked it on and shined it around the garage. The beam caught the bright eyes of the dogs, and Mother's face.

The back door swung open and the dogs growled. Romy sauntered into the garage, her hands tucked into the pockets of a slicker. "Hmmm. You managed to get out. Guess that chewing-gum-in-the-lock trick didn't work so well. Would have been easier if you'd stayed in there."

Her dark eyes perused the garage, taking in Howard on the floor, Mother, and the dogs at my feet. Her look settled on me. She grinned.

A chill raced down my back. Queenie growled. How could it be that I had only recently seen this crazy side of Romy?

She pulled one hand out of her pocket. The barrel of the revolver shimmered. "Don't try anything, Jamie. It's time to end this. You married into a hell of a family. And that's too bad. I like you."

"End what? I have no idea what you're talking about." I frowned. She reminded me of someone. Who? "There's nothing wrong with the Mazie family. I'm proud to be Sam's wife."

"You don't know the truth about how your husband destroyed my daughter, Reba. Or how his brother ruined my daughter Sharon's life," she growled. "Poor Reba. Sam drove her crazy, so crazy she killed herself. And Lucas took advantage of Sharon, brought her home half-naked after that stupid race. Sharon never was the same after that."

Her words echoed in the garage.

"Sam said you'd disappeared," I said, shaking my throbbing head. Romy was Reba's mother? "He thought maybe you were dead."

"Humph," she grimaced. "He's gonna wish *HE* was dead when he finds out what happened to you and your mother, your dogs and your house."

Mother coughed. "What are you going to do?"

Romy was deranged, and she wasn't going to do anything if I could prevent it. I surveyed the garage, looking for Sam's tool box or something to use in self-defense.

My mind replayed Romy's words. "You said Reba killed herself. You know there's been an inquest into Reba's death to consider if someone staged the suicide after killing her. A man named Bosque confessed to it. Said someone paid him to do it."

Romy's face blanched. "They've reopened the investigation? Did they dig my baby out of the ground?" Her eyes widened.

"Yes. Last week. You knew, I'm assuming, that she didn't ever have a baby. She wasn't even pregnant. She deceived Sam."

Romy staggered back against the wall. "But, Sharon went to the doctor with her for the ultrasound." Confusion crossed her face but then disappeared. "You're lying. My poor Sharon was the one who found her. Sharon did CPR, but it was too late." She wiped her mouth with one hand.

Why would both Sharon and Reba lie to their mother about the baby? Sam had never mentioned that Sharon found Reba after she died. Had she been *with* her when she died?

"No," Romy insisted. "Reba's baby was born dead. And Sam didn't care. Reba was inconsolable. She went to live with Sharon."

I nodded as if I agreed, but her version of history was wrong.

Romy shook her head. "My girls had a falling out after that race. Had to do with those Mazie boys. Sam and Lucas. But the girls reconciled. I had such hopes for them before Reba died. I still don't understand why she committed suicide."

My thoughts raced to find a logical explanation that tied the events of the past week together. Too many things had happened for this to be only about Sam and Lucas. "If this is all about the Mazie boys, why did you kill Davis and Rusty? And why did you kidnap Caleb?"

Romy blinked. "Wha-at? I didn't kill those men or kidnap that kid. Why would I?" She stiffened as Princess darted past her and ran to me. "Darn cat." The gun barrel shook. She gaped at the weapon, peeled her hands off the gun grip and repositioned them.

The cat twined around my legs. If Romy didn't kill the two men and kidnap Caleb, that left only Sharon. Was it possible Romy didn't know what her own daughter had done?

Romy glanced at the open door behind her. A figure appeared at the edge of the shadows. She shifted her weight. "Get out here, Sharon. We've got to do this together. Now."

Chapter 50

Sharon stepped into the dim light of the garage. When I flicked my light on her face, she shielded her eyes from the beam. Both dogs growled.

"What are you doing, Mother?" Sharon sneered. "Take care of them."

She lowered a red gasoline can to the floor. Gas fumes floated to where I stood.

"Mm mother and I haven't done anything to you," I pleaded. "Leave us out of it."

"I can't leave you out of it," Sharon said. "You know too much, but not everything."

Someone rested their hand on my shoulder.

"No, not quite everything," a deep voice said in my ear. Howard grinned and shrugged. "Quite a little scenario here. And finally, you're getting to hear the truth."

"Romy doesn't know the truth about you and Sharon. You've been sabotaging the play. Did the two of you kill Davis and Rusty?" I didn't want to believe it. I wanted to like Howard. Earlier tonight, he'd seemed genuinely concerned about me. He'd helped me.

"You've got that wrong. Sharon's the mastermind," Howard said. "Yes, the race car driver ran off the road, and yes, someone distracted him. That playwright thought Lucas Mazie was behind it, but he was wrong. Sharon, it was all you, wasn't it?"

Sharon grinned. "I'd do it again to watch him die. My sister never got over it, though. She felt responsible, even though I was the one who distracted the driver. She wanted to go to the police, even years later. I had to convince her not to. Got some pills for her to pop. And then I helped her end her miserable life."

"Sharon!" Romy cried. "You ... you killed your sister?"

"Mother, you're stupid. All these years, and you never figured it out."

Howard snickered. "Oh, Sharon. What a creature you are. No wonder you distracted that driver. If I was a few years younger, I'm sure you would have distracted me from my purpose now. But I'm not a young man anymore."

"What are you talking about Howard? You're supposed to be helping me now. We're going to make sure that the Mazie family pays," Sharon scoffed. "The old Mazie woman's probably dead by now. I may not have gotten Lucas, but he'll feel the guilt. Sam will lose most of his family and spend the rest of his life in jail. Bosque's testimony will make sure of that. Best investment I ever made."

"Sharon? What about the race car driver? And your sister. Tell me the truth." Romy's voice cracked.

"Oh, Mother. Shut up. Aren't you feeling light-headed yet? I thought those pills would be kicking in by now." Sharon scowled.

"Don't talk to me like that," Romy shrieked. "I've done everything I could for you, and it was never enough." The gun jiggled up and down, shaking along with her hands. "When you waltzed back into my life last year, I shouldn't have taken you in." Her knees buckled but she grabbed the wall and steadied herself. "I've made a good life here, teaching. That's all over now, because of you. Tell me the truth. Did you kill your sister?" Her shrill voice echoed in the garage.

The dogs got to their feet, their hair bristling and low growls rumbling in their throats. They sensed my fear. Their instinct to protect me was strong.

Sharon doubled over with laughter. "This is priceless. You haven't a clue about me, do you? You thought I'd finally gone straight, went to nursing school and became an upstanding citizen. Really?" She cackled. "Do you know how many old people don't have anyone to leave their money to when they die? So easy to convince them I'm like a long-lost daughter. So easy to hurry along their date with Death." She looked slyly at Howard.

"You've been killing old people?" Romy's mouth dropped open.

Sharon laughed again and bent to grab the gas can. She sloshed liquid onto the garage floor. "Mother, that's what I do. That race car driver was the beginning of my life's work."

"The beginning," Howard repeated, thoughtfully. "But you know, sweet Sharon, that the person you kill is not the only victim. Everyone who loved that person is a victim. You – ruin – lives."

"What do you care, old man? You're the one that introduced me to Theresa Mazie. You're the one that suggested this final part of the plan." She splashed more gasoline on the floor.

The growls of the dogs grew louder.

"That driver you killed was engaged to my daughter," Howard stated. "Two months after we buried him, we buried her. She overdosed one night because she couldn't live without him." Howard choked. His eyes filled with tears. He clenched his fists.

"You thought I was helping you," he hissed. "I'm not. I wanted to be here to see you die. Are you ready?" He pulled a silver cigarette lighter out of his pocket and flipped the lid back. Howard stepped toward Sharon, his arm extended.

"Queenie! Zeus!" I shouted.

A dark blur vaulted from the floor at my feet. Queenie, all solid sixty pounds of hound, clamped her teeth on Howard's hand. He fell, and the dog went with him, landing on top of him, growling, her jaws grasping his wrist.

At the same instant, Zeus charged Romy and knocked the gun from her hand. She staggered and lost her balance. The dog went down with her, her arm secured in his mouth.

Sharon reached for the gas can. I threw the flashlight. The heavy metal cylinder crashed into her face.

Chapter 51

I snatched Romy's gun. "Mother, can you go next door to the neighbor's and call the police?"

She pulled herself up off the floor where she had crouched and moved unsteadily past Romy and into the house. I clutched the gun with both hands, and shifted my aim between Romy, Sharon and Howard.

The dogs' jaws were clamped onto Romy and Howard. They growled and tugged, trying to shake their prey like stuffed toys. Sharon lay still on the floor.

My brief high school career in slow-pitch softball had paid off once again.

"Get this dog off me! He's tearing my hand off," Howard begged. "I'm on your side, Jamie."

"Jamie, please!" Romy sobbed. "I can't feel my arm."

"Not until the police get here." I held the gun steady with both hands and stood to one side where I could see all three of them clearly.

"I'll help you, Jamie," Howard offered. "All I wanted was to take care of this ... witch. I've waited my whole life to make her suffer for what she did to my little girl. You want her to suffer too, don't you?" Howard had curled into a fetal position on the floor, but Queenie continued to shake his arm.

I watched Sharon for any sign that she was regaining consciousness. I'd have a fight on my hands if she made a surprise attempt to get the gun back. If she came at me, both dogs might release their vicious holds and come to my aid. Sharon and Romy, with the gun on their side, could make quick work of me and two dogs. And probably Howard, too.

"Jamie, please let me go. I promise I'll disappear," Romy pleaded. "I swear I didn't know Sharon's real purpose in all of this. I didn't know she was a–monster."

Sirens screamed on the street, and tires squealed in my driveway. My arm muscles trembled.

As if in slow motion, Sharon tucked her outstretched legs and rolled over on her back, knees bent. Her eyes focused on me.

"Don't try anything, Sharon," I warned. "I *will* shoot."

She pushed off the floor and charged. I sidestepped, and she flew into a pile of boxes. As the boxes crashed to the floor, she got up and charged again, hands curled into fists.

"You're dead," she snarled and charged again.

I squeezed the trigger.

The gun's recoil knocked me backward into the door frame.

Sharon fell.

"Put down your weapon! Police," a deep voice yelled behind me.

I laid the gun on the ground, then raised my hands.

Bright lights swept the garage, and policemen moved past me, guns ready.

"Shoot this vicious animal," Romy pled. "I didn't do anything, Officer. It's all a misunderstanding."

"Queenie. Zeus. Drop it," I ordered. "Come." The dogs released Howard and Romy and trotted to me, low growls still rumbling in their throats.

Chapter 52

"Now let me get this straight," Detective Roland Blaise said gruffly. "You say that Belina Sanderson is Sharon, the sister of your husband's deceased wife, Reba, and that Sharon, not your husband, had Reba killed because Reba was going to squeal to someone that Sharon had caused the death of a race car driver at the last Lake Ponca Grand Prix race?" He shook his head.

I squirmed on the thin plastic cushion of the chair in the interrogation room at the Ponca City police department. "Yes," I confirmed. "And she also killed Davis Harwell and Rusty Clement, kidnapped Caleb, and tried to kill me at Lake Ponca. Not to mention that she trashed my cousin Trudy's Pawhuska home and physically assaulted her while dressed as Reba Mazie's ghost. Oh, and she poisoned Sam's mother."

"Do you have any solid proof that she did these things?"

"She bragged about it while her mother held us hostage in my garage. My mother heard her, and so did Romy Vaughn and Howard DeKalb. Are the sworn statements of four people enough proof for you?"

"Is there any other evidence to substantiate your claims? Ms. Sanderson denies her involvement in any of this. Her mother is in the hospital, and DeKalb is uncooperative."

Frustration pounded in my head. "Isn't it your job to investigate? Shouldn't you search her home? Look for evidence?"

"I have to have something to use to get the judge to approve a search warrant. I can't go on hearsay."

"But–"

Someone shouted in the hallway. The door opened, and a police officer stuck her head inside. "There's a Lucas Mazie here, Mrs. Mazie's brother-in-law. He insists that he see her."

Blaise pushed his chair back and stood. "All right. Might as well. I'm not getting very far here."

Lucas rushed into the sterile room. "Did he take your statement about your near-drowning? And did you tell him what Sharon did to Mom?"

"Detective Blaise insists he doesn't have probable cause to hold Sharon for anything. Maybe you should tell your side of things. How is Theresa?"

"She's in ICU." Lucas addressed the detective. "Sharon Sanderson posed as a nurse and poisoned my mother. Mom was transported by ambulance to the Ponca City hospital, where they pumped her stomach and sedated her. Right now, she's in stable condition."

Blaise motioned for Lucas to sit at the table. "How do you know Sharon Sanderson poisoned your mother?" Blaise asked.

"She told us she did. Jamie called 9-1-1. You can confirm with the policewoman or the EMTs with the ambulance that my mother was very ill. She was transported to the hospital."

"Did you see Ms. Sanderson administer the poison?"

"No. But she said she did."

"Right now, she's under guard at the hospital and receiving care for a gunshot wound. Plus, she has a nasty bruise on her forehead, where she says you struck her with a flashlight." The detective looked at me.

"She was pouring gasoline on my garage floor and threatening to light it on fire."

"She says that the man who was with you, Harold DeKalb, intended to light the gasoline and kill all of you," Blaise fired back.

Of course, Sharon had twisted the story. "That's not exactly the way it happened," I said.

Someone knocked at the door, and once again, the policewoman stuck her head inside the room. "Mrs. Mazie's husband is here. And OSBI Agent Chase Longhorn is with him."

Blaise sighed loudly, ran his hands over his head and stood up as Sam and Longhorn stepped into the room. Sam rushed to me.

As he held me, Longhorn spoke in a low voice to Detective Blaise. The Ponca City Detective stalked from the room.

"Lucas said you'd been arrested," I blubbered to Sam. "But you're here."

Sam nodded at Chase Longhorn. "I was retained, not arrested. It turns out that for the past two weeks, Longhorn's been tailing Bosque. He's reviewed his bank documents and phone records and studied traffic video.

He found Bosque present in the areas of both murders, as well as Caleb's kidnapping."

"That's the proof they need," Lucas said.

"And he's had consistent interaction for the past ten years with a woman who calls herself Belina Sanderson," Sam continued. "This afternoon, they conducted a search of her residence, the home of Mrs. Romy Vaughn, a.k.a. Romy Sanderson. Reba's mother."

"We found what we needed to link Belina to money deposited in Mr. Bosque's bank accounts," Longhorn said, "both recently and at the time of Reba Mazie's death. The D.A. believes it's enough to legally prove a connection. Mr. Mazie is not in custody."

"Oh, my God, Sam." I threw my arms around his neck.

"We found DNA and other evidence indicating that Caleb was held captive in the Sanderson's basement." Longhorn stood stiffly by the door, his eyes on the floor.

"I don't think her motive for Caleb's kidnapping was anything other than causing trouble for me. Caleb was a smart kid, and he was in the play. Maybe that was all the reason she needed," I speculated. "But what was her motive in terrorizing Trudy, and trashing her house? And what was her motive to kill me?"

"She wanted to hurt me any way she could," Sam said. "She wanted me to pay for what she did to her sister. She had Bosque kill Reba and then paid him again to throw suspicion on me. It worked," Sam said drily, looking at Longhorn.

"It did throw suspicion on you. When someone points a finger, it's always possible it's pointing in the right direction." Longhorn stroked his eyebrow. "I could say I'm sorry, but that's not how it's done in law enforcement. We caught the perpetrators, now we have to be sure we have an airtight case, so they can be punished according to the law."

Sam and I looked at one another. Underneath the joy that both of us felt at Sam's release and Sharon's arrest lingered sadness. It was unspoken, but clear. Sharon had terrorized Reba, drugged her so that her sweet personality, the persona Sam had fallen in love with, disappeared.

Would Sam's marriage have lasted if Sharon had not been Reba's sister? Would they have had children? Would they have been happy? Would I have ever met and married Sam?

"We've got a phone call to make, honey," Sam said. "Trudy needs to know that it's safe to go home. We need to tell her that she doesn't have to worry about Reba's ghost–or any ghost–anymore."

Sam pulled out his cell phone and punched in her number.

Epilogue

Sam and I drove to the cemetery for Reba's reburial. The cloudless azure sky and a south wind pushed aside any thoughts of winter. It was glorious fall.

Earlier, he and I created a bouquet of goldenrod, asters, prairie onion, and boneset. We added a cut stem from the purple butterfly bush in Trudy's garden and placed the bouquets of wildflowers on the mounded brown soil of her grave.

Standing together at graveside, Sam's face relaxed in peace. The haunted look I so often saw in his eyes had disappeared.

A monarch butterfly slipped past us, riding the air currents, then turned and dropped onto the purple bloom.

Sam kissed my cheek. "As horrible as this has been, it's a relief to know what really happened. The truth vindicates her. She didn't choose to die."

"And the truth vindicates you. None of it was your fault, either. You are free to fly, Sam. No more chrysalis of sadness."

A wide smile spread across his face as the monarch lifted on the breeze and fluttered away.

About the Ponca City Grand Prix Races

An official road race, sanctioned by the Sports Car Club of America (SCCA) and sponsored by the Ponca City American Business Club (AMBUCS), the one-and-a-half-mile track was a roughly oblong section of the asphalt road through Lake Ponca Park, east of Ponca City, Oklahoma. Shaped like the head of a golf club 'driver,' the race track featured six turns in its short length, providing a challenging track for participating racers. Over twenty categories were open to cars ranging from street stock to formula race cars.

The first race was held over the weekend closest to July 4th, 1962, and races were held every year through 1981. In 1976, the race was officially designated a Bicentennial Event. The event was held sporadically after 1981. In 1992, the final races were heralded as the 25th annual event.

The three-day event featured concessions and a spectator area and required more than 300 volunteers to set up and maintain the race area. In a record year, 10,000 spectators attended.

Source: McCarville, Mike. "The Ponca City Grand Prix," Oklahoma Today, Summer 1977, Vol. 27, Number 3. P. 4-9.

About Wentz Camp

Wentz Camp was built between 1928 and 1935 in the Romanesque Revival style, using native limestone, on 33.5 acres of land north and east of Lake Ponca. The facility was funded by Oilman Lew Wentz.

Visitors pass through the dressing rooms of the pool house to access the swimming pool's hillside viewing pavilion. Designed to seat 500 spectators, the area consists of 23 deep stairs, each covered with small mosaic tiles. Below the stairs, a tiled pool deck surrounds the 150-foot by 40-foot pool.

Wentz was highly successful in the Oklahoma oil fields in the 1920s. He sold his fields and oil interests in 1928, thus his fortune survived the Crash of 1929. He continued to live in Ponca City, where he invested in business enterprises, and contributed philanthropically both to the community and to statewide programs for the arts and for the betterment of young men. Wentz set up student loan foundations at both Oklahoma University and Oklahoma State University. He was politically active and held the office of Republican National Committeeman from Oklahoma from 1940 until his death in 1949.

Upon his death, Wentz Camp was donated to the City of Ponca City.

From the Author

Writing has provided an outlet for my busy imagination ever since I learned to write in the second grade in Enid, OK. Although I have always worked professionally in jobs requiring extensive writing ability, it is writing fiction that makes my muse dance.

While working as a historic park planner and naturalist for the Oklahoma Tourism and Recreation Department, the paring of history and mystery solidified in my writing. Then, as a special feature writer for the Ponca City News in the late 1980s, my love of little known places and ordinary people expanded.

Everyone has a story, and every place has a life of its own. The writer's job is to ferret out that story and that life and make it real for the reader.

–Mary Coley

About the Author

Mary Coley splits her life between Tulsa, Oklahoma and north central New Mexico. A certified interpretive guide, naturalist and environmental educator as well as a writer, Mary blogs about writing and nature at http://marycoley.me. She is a recognized professional both in the environmental education field and as an author. Her book, *Environmentalism: How You can Make a Difference,* published through Capstone Press, received a first-place award for Best Juvenile Book from the Oklahoma Writers Federation, Inc. A frequent winner in annual OWFI contests, Coley has also published two volumes of short stories, including several stories previously published in anthologies.

She is a member of The Tulsa Nightwriters, The Oklahoma Writer's Federation, Mystery Writers of America, Sisters in Crime, and the Society of Children's Book Writers and Illustrators, and is a frequent participant in the Around the Block Writer's Collaborative workshops.

Chrysalis is the fourth book in the Family Secret Series, featuring amateur sleuth/science teacher Jamie Aldrich. Coley has also written stand-alone novels, and is currently at work on a middle grade mystery set in southeastern Oklahoma.

Visit her website at www.marycoley.com, or her blog at www.marycoley.me.

27520358R00209

Made in the USA
Lexington, KY
04 January 2019